1I0672384

DISCARD

JAN   2018

Chicago Public Library
Canaryville Branch
642 - 46 W. 43 St.
Chicago, Illinois 60609

Animal Jam®

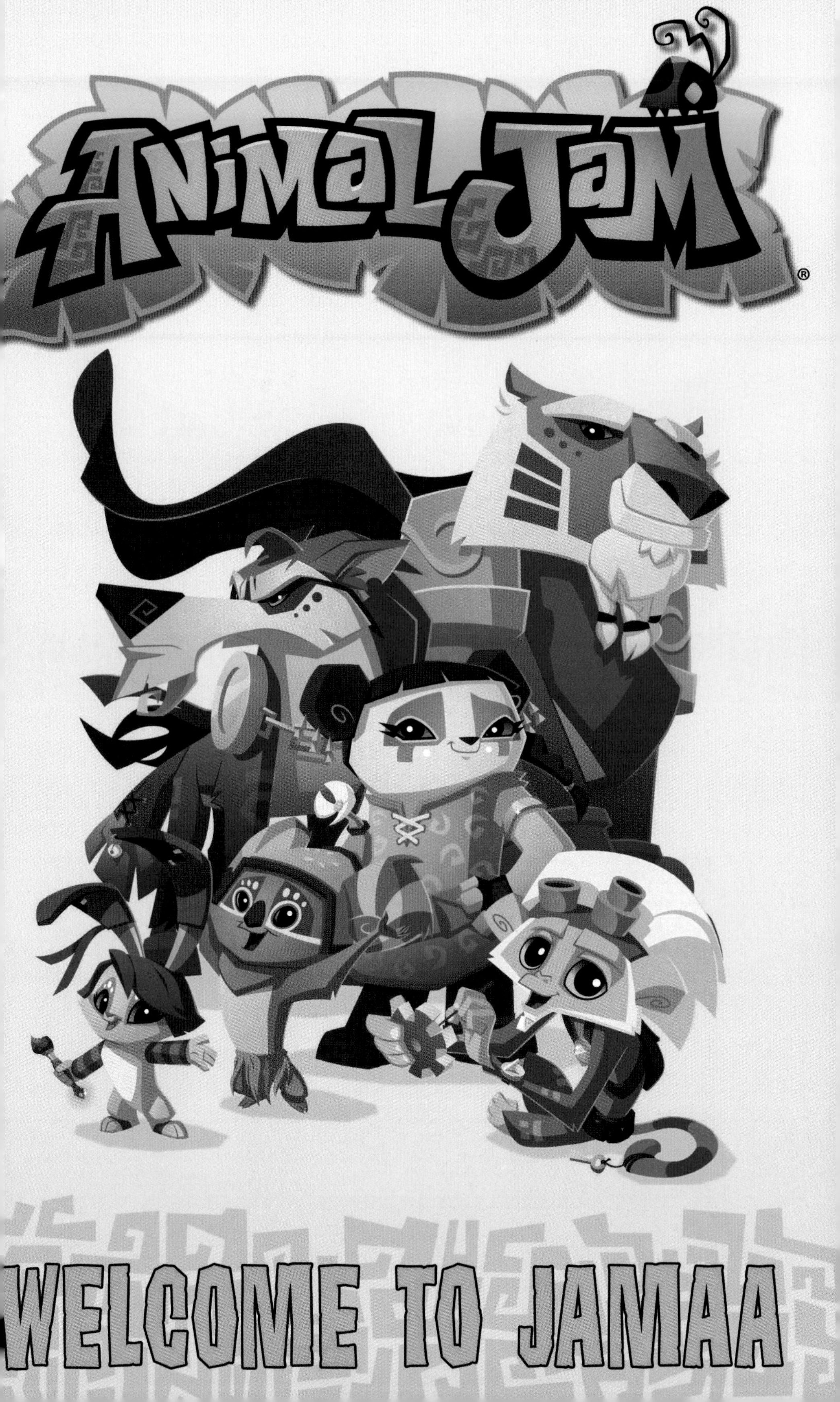

WELCOME TO JAMAA

WELCOME TO JAMAA!

Written by FERNANDO RUIZ
Art by FERNANDO RUIZ
Color by PETE PANTAZIS
Letters by TOM NAPOLITANO

THE TROJAN ELEPHANT

Written by FERNANDO RUIZ
Art by FERNANDO RUIZ
Color by PETE PANTAZIS
Letters by TOM NAPOLITANO

KIMBARA OUTBACK

Written by ERIC M. ESQUIVEL
Art by FERNANDO RUIZ
Color by PETE PANTAZIS
Letters by TOM NAPOLITANO

MINE! ALL MINE!

Written by FERNANDO RUIZ
Art by FERNANDO RUIZ
Color by MOHAN
Letters by TOM NAPOLITANO

JUNGLES OF JAMAA

Written by ERIC M. ESQUIVEL
Art by FERNANDO RUIZ
Color by MOHAN
Letters by TOM NAPOLITANO

SNOWBALL FRIGHT

Written by FERNANDO RUIZ
Art by FERNANDO RUIZ
Color by MOHAN
Letters by TOM NAPOLITANO

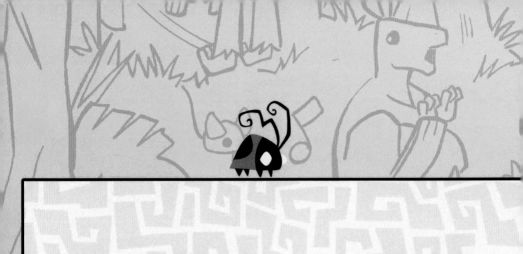

GRAHAM'S WORKSHOP

Written by ERIC M. ESQUIVEL
Art by TONY FLEECS
Color by MOHAN
Letters by TOM NAPOLITANO

Issue Covers By
FERNANDO RUIZ & PETE PANTAZIS
TONY FLEECS

Edited by
ANTHONY MARQUES

Collection cover by
WILDWORKS, INC.

Collection design by
CATHLEEN HEARD

DYNAMITE®

k Barrucci, CEO / Publisher
n Collado, President / COO

Rybandt, Executive Editor
t Idelson, Senior Editor
hony Marques, Associate Editor
n Ketner, Assistant Editor

on Ullmeyer, Art Director
ff Harkins, Senior Graphic Designer
leen Heard, Graphic Designer
is Persson, Graphic Designer

s Caniano, Digital Associate
el Kilbury, Digital Assistant

ndon Dante Primavera, V.P. of IT and Operations
Young, Director of Business Development
Payne, V.P. of Sales and Marketing
e MacKenzie, Marketing Coordinator
O'Connell, Sales Manager

Online at www.DYNAMITE.com
On Facebook /Dynamitecomics
On Instagram /Dynamitecomics
On Tumblr dynamitecomics.tumblr.com
On Twitter @dynamitecomics
On YouTube /Dynamitecomics

WILDWORKS

Hardcover Edition:
ISBN-13: 978-1-5241-0386-6

Scholastic Paperback:
ISBN-13: 978-1-5241-0387-3

First Printing
10 9 8 7 6 5 4 3 2 1

ANIMAL JAM™: WELCOME TO JAMAA. First printing. Contains materials originally published in magazine form as ANIMAL JAM™, Volume 1: Issues 0-3. Published by Dynamite Entertainment, 113 Gaither Dr., STE 205, Mt. Laurel, NJ 08054. © 2017 WildWorks, Inc. All rights reserved. Dynamite, Dynamite Entertainment and its logo are ® & © 2017 Dynamite. All rights reserved. All names, characters, events, and locales in this publication are entirely fictional. Any resemblance to actual persons (living or dead), events or places, without satiric intent, is coincidental. No portion of this book may be reproduced by any means (digital or print) without the written permission of Dynamite Entertainment except for review purposes. Printed in Canada.

For information regarding press, media rights, foreign rights, licensing, promotions, and advertising e-mail: marketing@dynamite.com

PEFC Certified
Printed on paper from
sustainably managed
forests and controlled
sources
PEFC/01-31-106   www.pefc.org

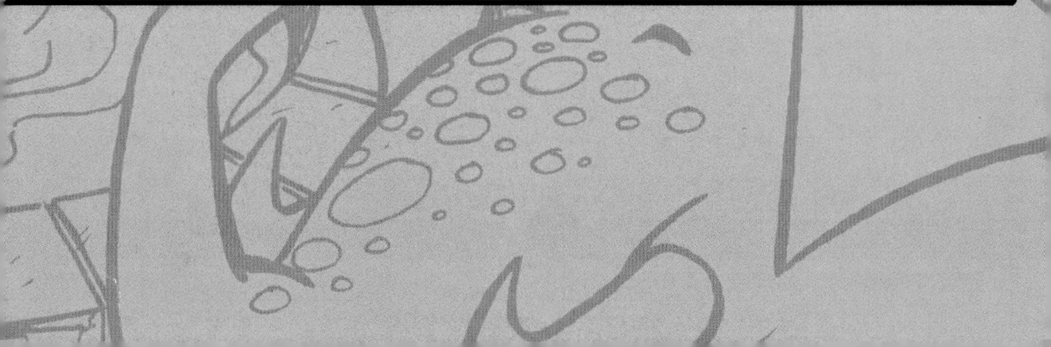

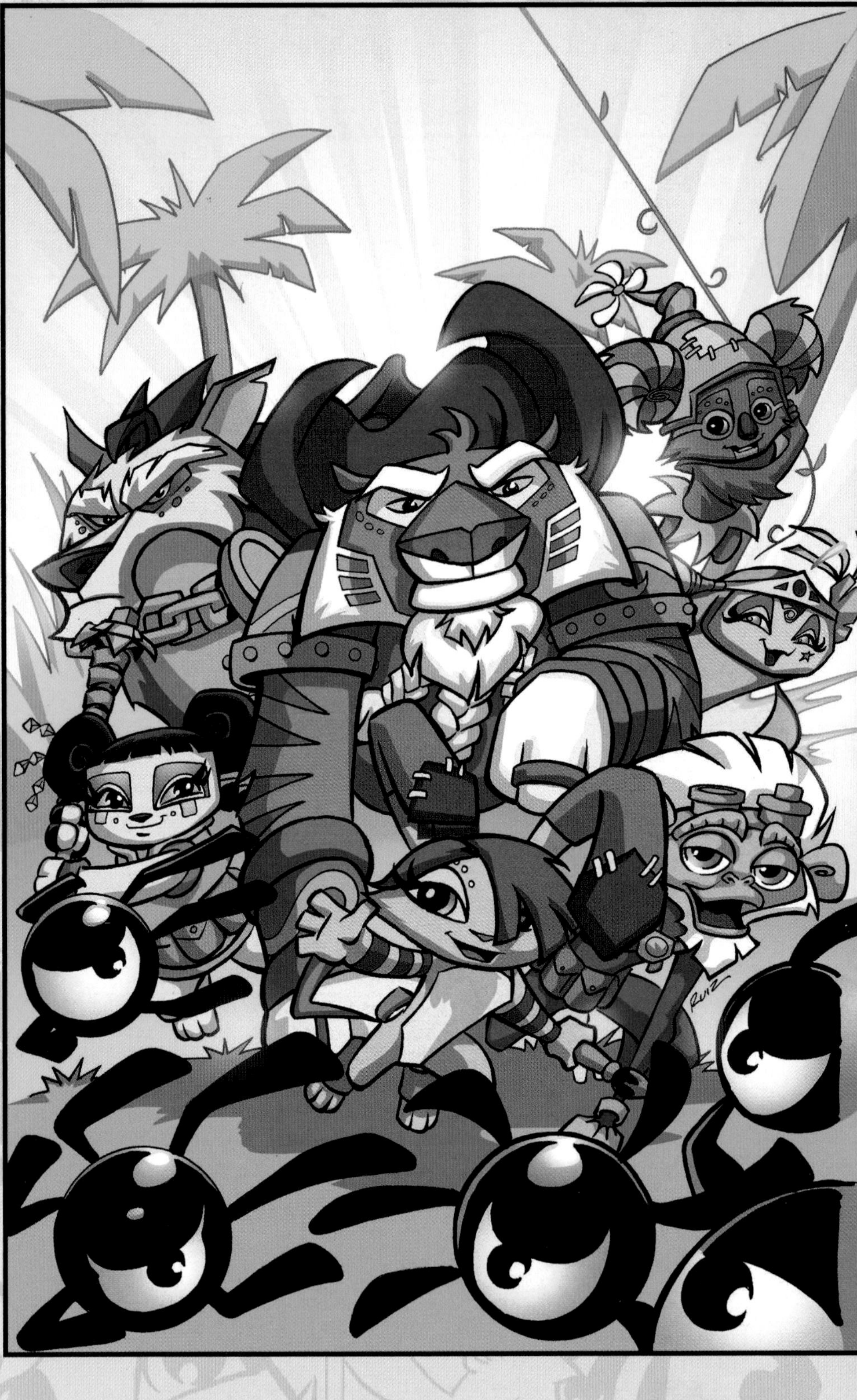
RUIZ

Issue #0: Cover Art by **FERNANDO RUIZ & PETE PANTAZIS**

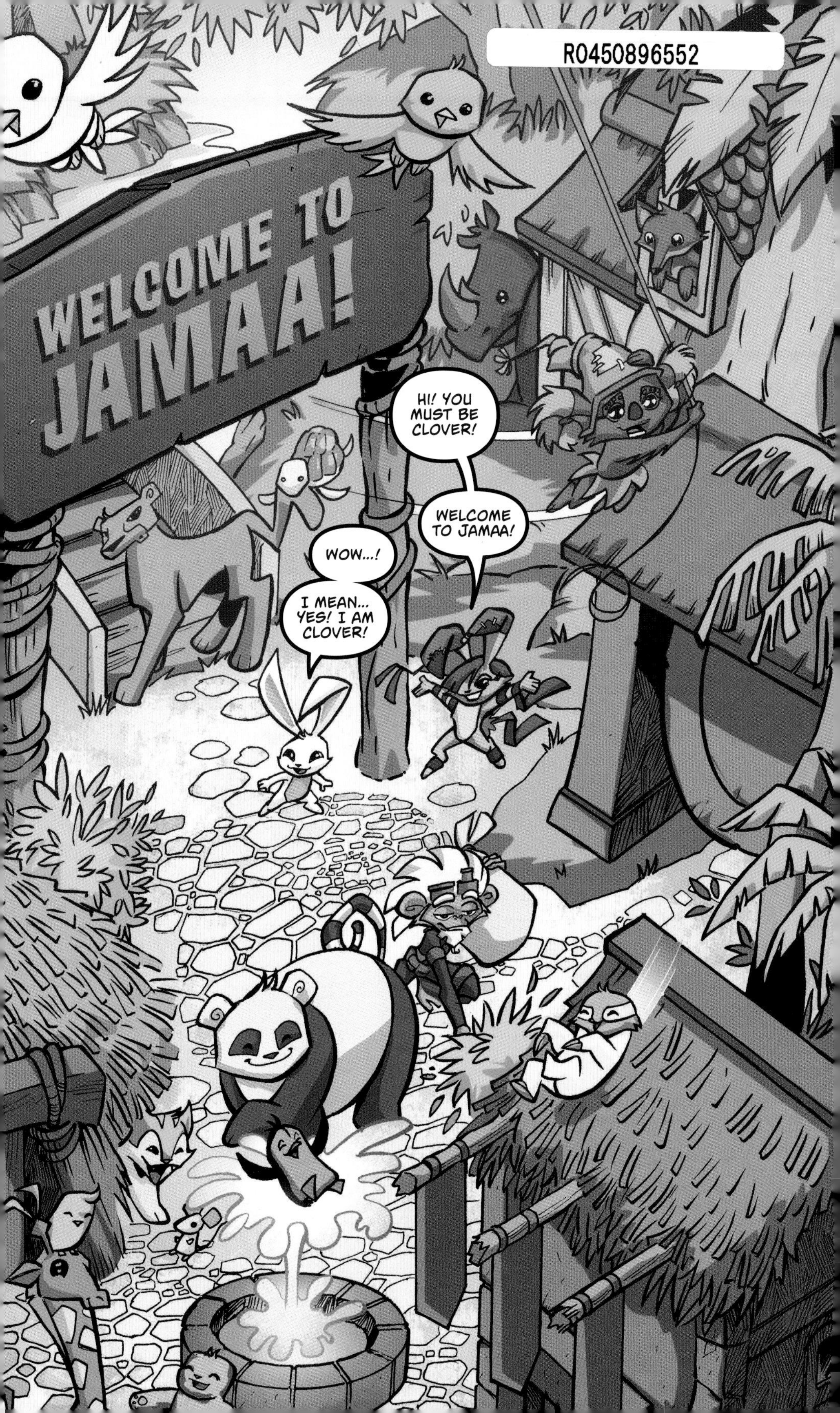
WELCOME TO JAMAA!
HI! YOU MUST BE CLOVER!
WELCOME TO JAMAA!
WOW...!
I MEAN... YES! I AM CLOVER!

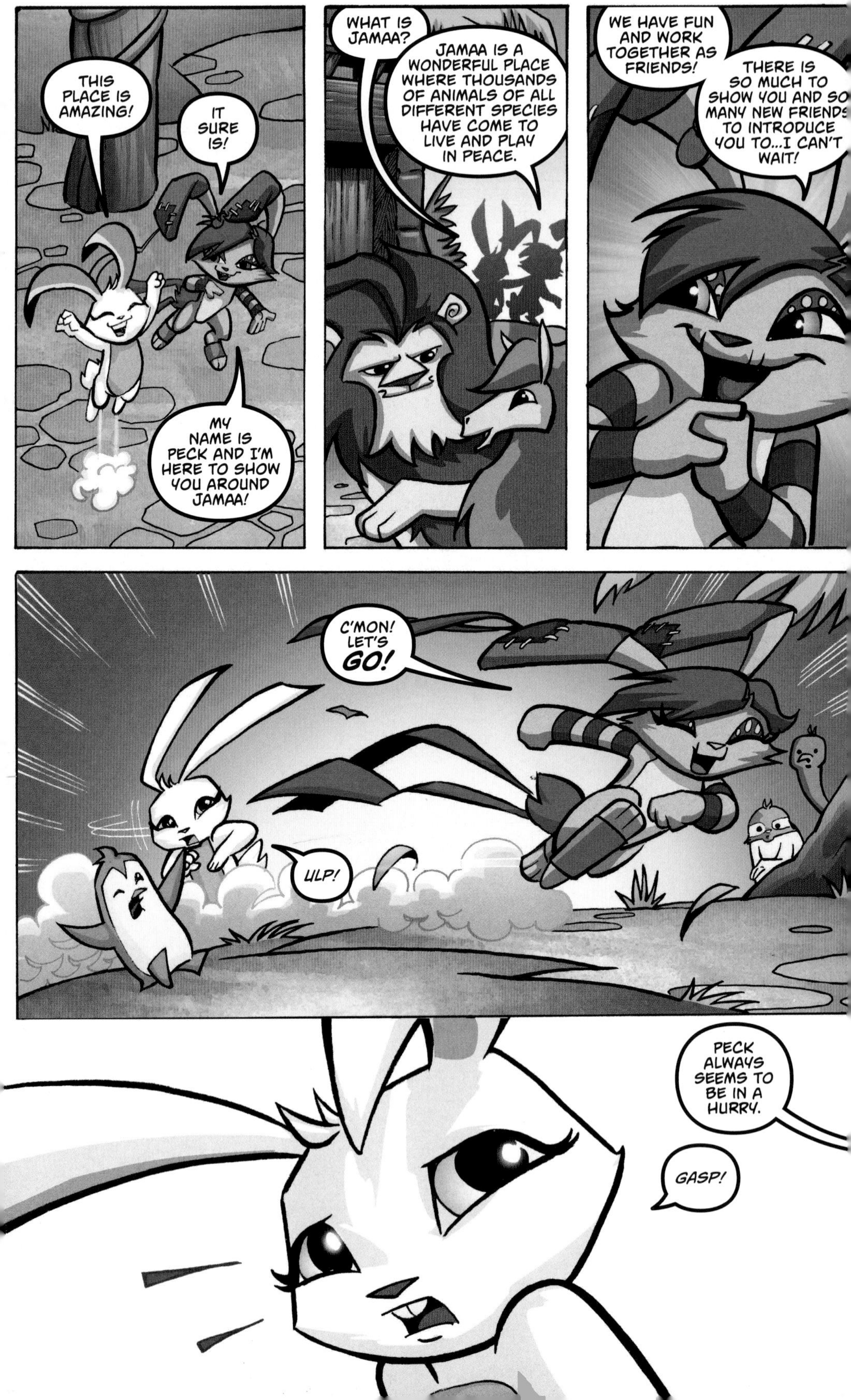
THIS PLACE IS AMAZING!
IT SURE IS!
MY NAME IS PECK AND I'M HERE TO SHOW YOU AROUND JAMAA!
WHAT IS JAMAA?
JAMAA IS A WONDERFUL PLACE WHERE THOUSANDS OF ANIMALS OF ALL DIFFERENT SPECIES HAVE COME TO LIVE AND PLAY IN PEACE.
WE HAVE FUN AND WORK TOGETHER AS FRIENDS!
THERE IS SO MUCH TO SHOW YOU AND SO MANY NEW FRIENDS TO INTRODUCE YOU TO...I CAN'T WAIT!
C'MON! LET'S GO!
ULP!
PECK ALWAYS SEEMS TO BE IN A HURRY.
GASP!

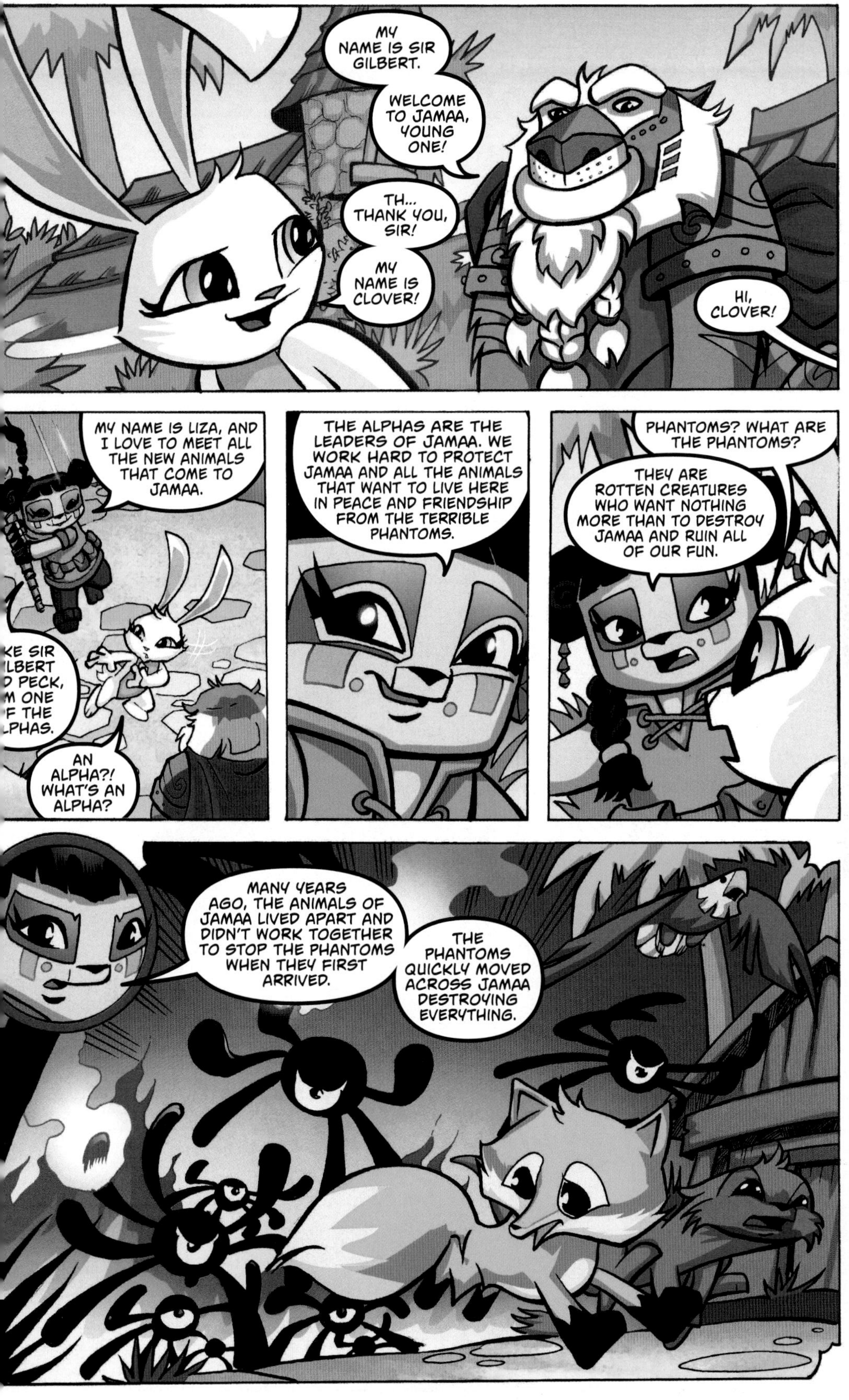
MY NAME IS SIR GILBERT.
WELCOME TO JAMAA, YOUNG ONE!
TH... THANK YOU, SIR!
MY NAME IS CLOVER!
HI, CLOVER!
MY NAME IS LIZA, AND I LOVE TO MEET ALL THE NEW ANIMALS THAT COME TO JAMAA.
KE SIR ILBERT D PECK, M ONE F THE LPHAS.
AN ALPHA?! WHAT'S AN ALPHA?
THE ALPHAS ARE THE LEADERS OF JAMAA. WE WORK HARD TO PROTECT JAMAA AND ALL THE ANIMALS THAT WANT TO LIVE HERE IN PEACE AND FRIENDSHIP FROM THE TERRIBLE PHANTOMS.
PHANTOMS? WHAT ARE THE PHANTOMS?
THEY ARE ROTTEN CREATURES WHO WANT NOTHING MORE THAN TO DESTROY JAMAA AND RUIN ALL OF OUR FUN.
MANY YEARS AGO, THE ANIMALS OF JAMAA LIVED APART AND DIDN'T WORK TOGETHER TO STOP THE PHANTOMS WHEN THEY FIRST ARRIVED.
THE PHANTOMS QUICKLY MOVED ACROSS JAMAA DESTROYING EVERYTHING.

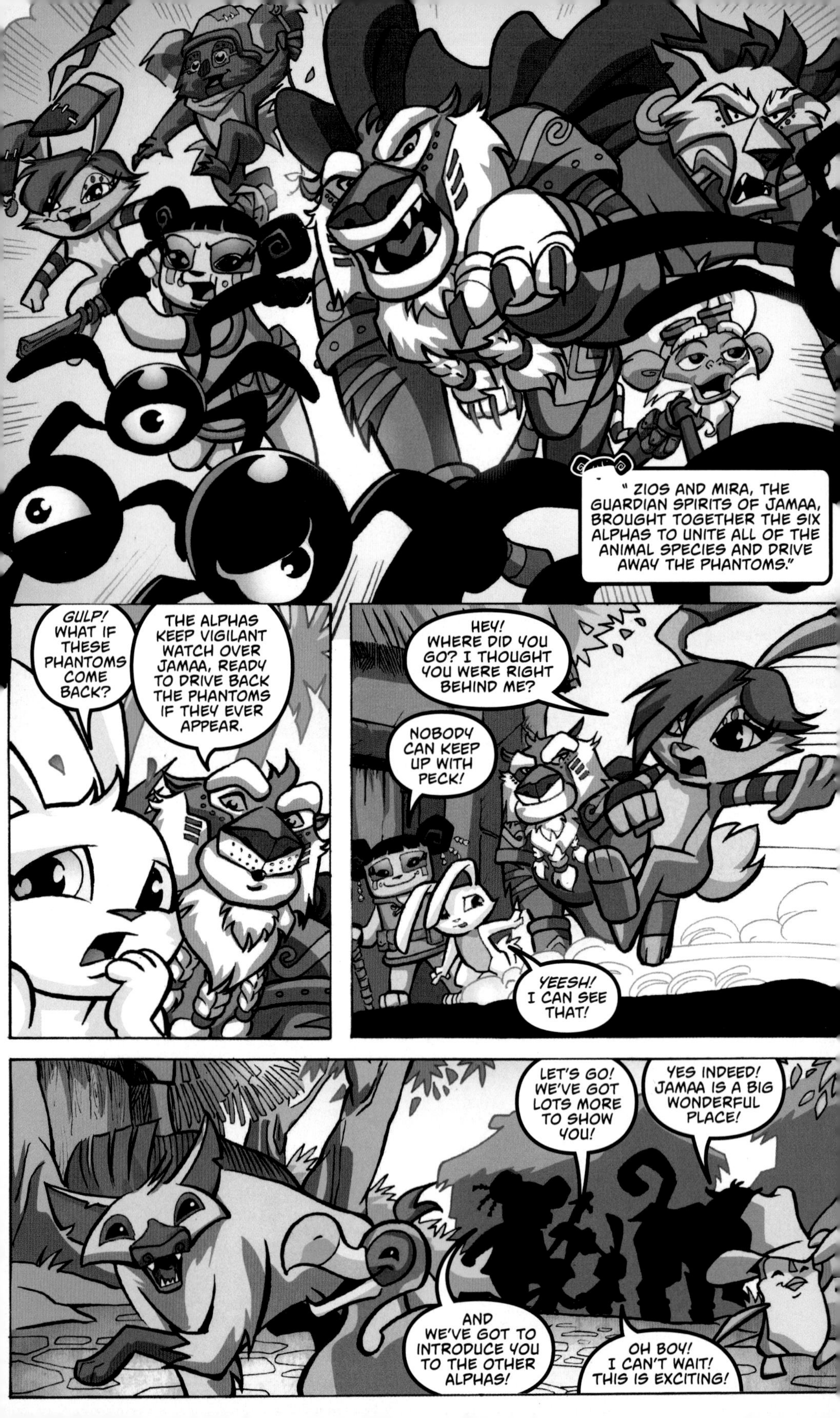

" ZIOS AND MIRA, THE GUARDIAN SPIRITS OF JAMAA, BROUGHT TOGETHER THE SIX ALPHAS TO UNITE ALL OF THE ANIMAL SPECIES AND DRIVE AWAY THE PHANTOMS."
GULP! WHAT IF THESE PHANTOMS COME BACK?
THE ALPHAS KEEP VIGILANT WATCH OVER JAMAA, READY TO DRIVE BACK THE PHANTOMS IF THEY EVER APPEAR.
HEY! WHERE DID YOU GO? I THOUGHT YOU WERE RIGHT BEHIND ME?
NOBODY CAN KEEP UP WITH PECK!
YEESH! I CAN SEE THAT!
LET'S GO! WE'VE GOT LOTS MORE TO SHOW YOU!
YES INDEED! JAMAA IS A BIG WONDERFUL PLACE!
AND WE'VE GOT TO INTRODUCE YOU TO THE OTHER ALPHAS!
OH BOY! I CAN'T WAIT! THIS IS EXCITING!

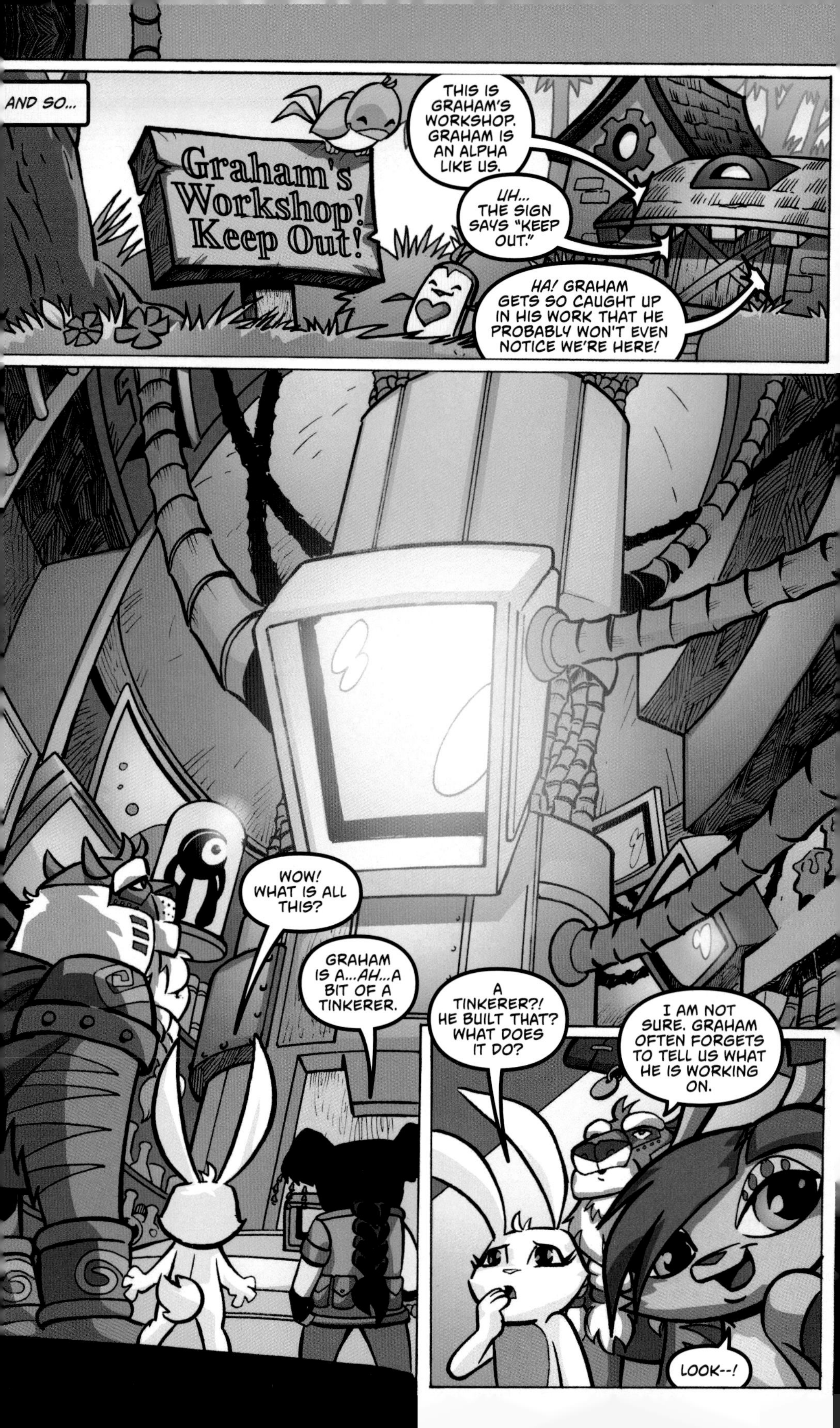
AND SO...
Graham's Workshop! Keep Out!
THIS IS GRAHAM'S WORKSHOP. GRAHAM IS AN ALPHA LIKE US.
UH... THE SIGN SAYS "KEEP OUT."
HA! GRAHAM GETS SO CAUGHT UP IN HIS WORK THAT HE PROBABLY WON'T EVEN NOTICE WE'RE HERE!
WOW! WHAT IS ALL THIS?
GRAHAM IS A...AH...A BIT OF A TINKERER.
A TINKERER?! HE BUILT THAT? WHAT DOES IT DO?
I AM NOT SURE. GRAHAM OFTEN FORGETS TO TELL US WHAT HE IS WORKING ON.
LOOK--!

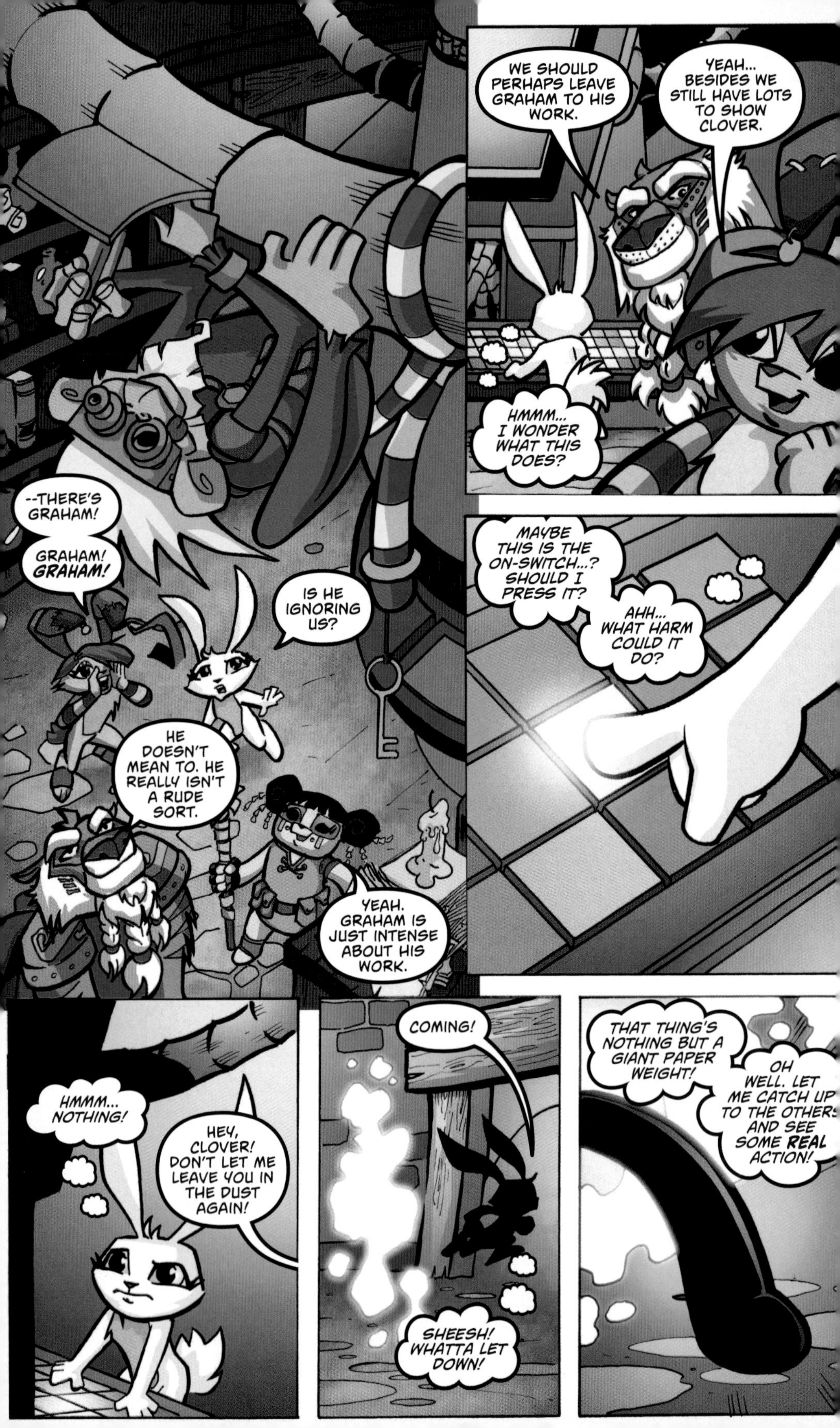
--THERE'S GRAHAM!
GRAHAM! *GRAHAM!*
IS HE IGNORING US?
HE DOESN'T MEAN TO. HE REALLY ISN'T A RUDE SORT.
YEAH. GRAHAM IS JUST INTENSE ABOUT HIS WORK.
WE SHOULD PERHAPS LEAVE GRAHAM TO HIS WORK.
YEAH... BESIDES WE STILL HAVE LOTS TO SHOW CLOVER.
HMMM... I WONDER WHAT THIS DOES?
MAYBE THIS IS THE ON-SWITCH...? SHOULD I PRESS IT?
AHH... WHAT HARM COULD IT DO?
HMMM... NOTHING!
HEY, CLOVER! DON'T LET ME LEAVE YOU IN THE DUST AGAIN!
COMING!
SHEESH! WHATTA LET DOWN!
THAT THING'S NOTHING BUT A GIANT PAPER WEIGHT!
OH WELL. LET ME CATCH UP TO THE OTHERS AND SEE SOME **REAL** ACTION!

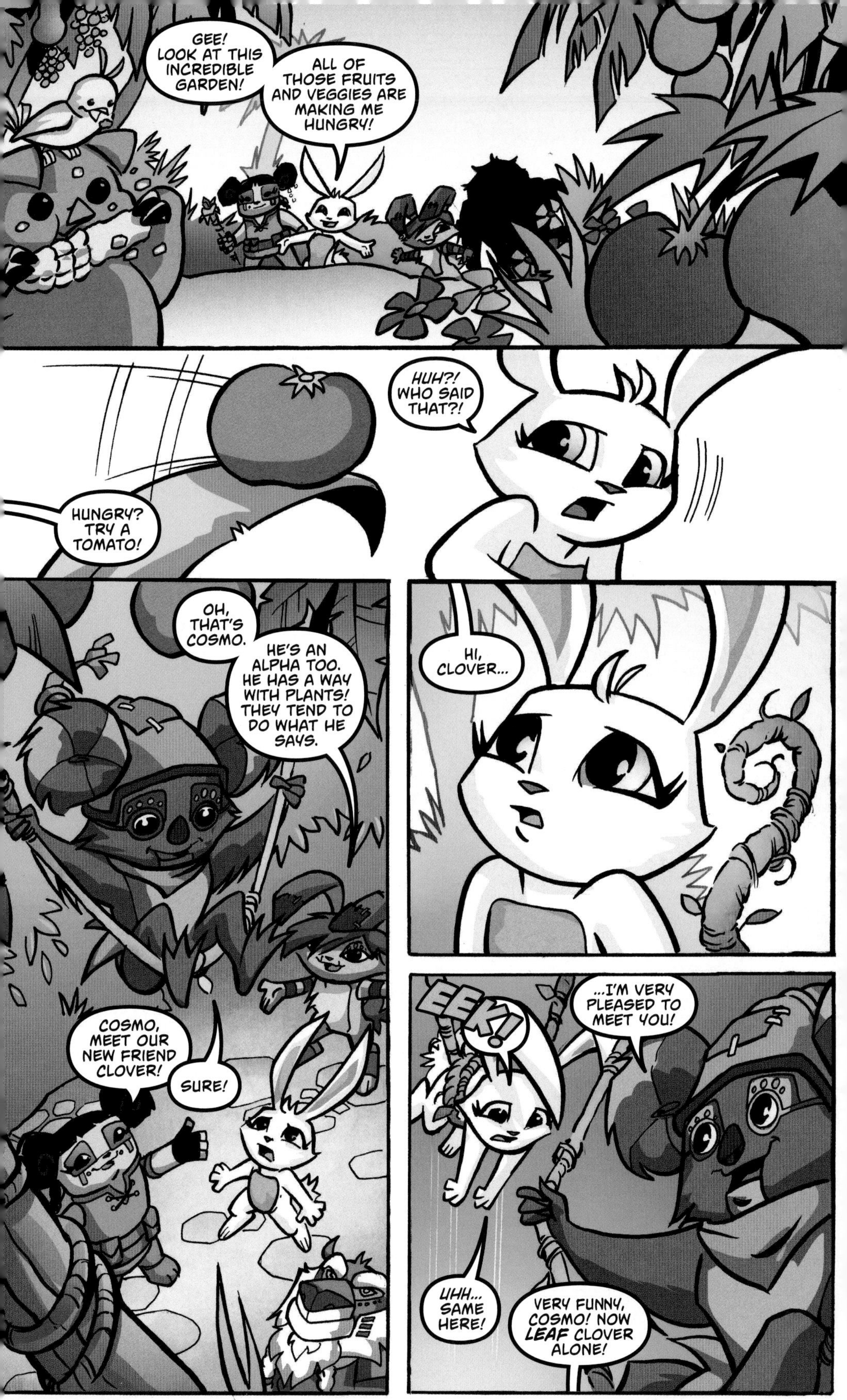
GEE! LOOK AT THIS INCREDIBLE GARDEN!
ALL OF THOSE FRUITS AND VEGGIES ARE MAKING ME HUNGRY!
HUNGRY? TRY A TOMATO!
HUH?! WHO SAID THAT?!
OH, THAT'S COSMO.
HE'S AN ALPHA TOO. HE HAS A WAY WITH PLANTS! THEY TEND TO DO WHAT HE SAYS.
HI, CLOVER...
COSMO, MEET OUR NEW FRIEND CLOVER!
SURE!
EEK!
...I'M VERY PLEASED TO MEET YOU!
UHH... SAME HERE!
VERY FUNNY, COSMO! NOW LEAF CLOVER ALONE!

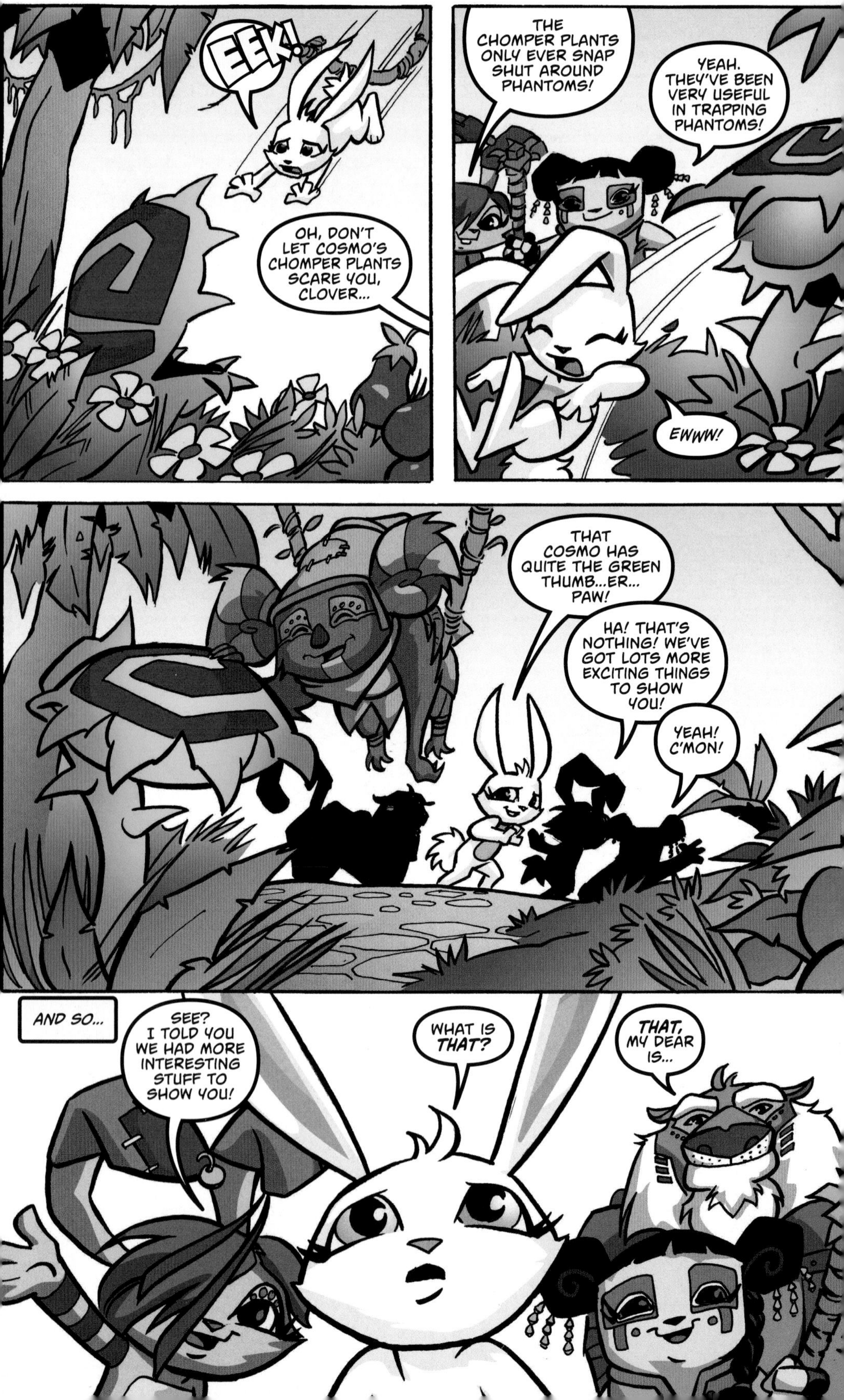
EEK!
OH, DON'T LET COSMO'S CHOMPER PLANTS SCARE YOU, CLOVER...
THE CHOMPER PLANTS ONLY EVER SNAP SHUT AROUND PHANTOMS!
YEAH. THEY'VE BEEN VERY USEFUL IN TRAPPING PHANTOMS!
EWWW!
THAT COSMO HAS QUITE THE GREEN THUMB...ER... PAW!
HA! THAT'S NOTHING! WE'VE GOT LOTS MORE EXCITING THINGS TO SHOW YOU!
YEAH! C'MON!
AND SO...
SEE? I TOLD YOU WE HAD MORE INTERESTING STUFF TO SHOW YOU!
WHAT IS *THAT*?
THAT, MY DEAR IS...

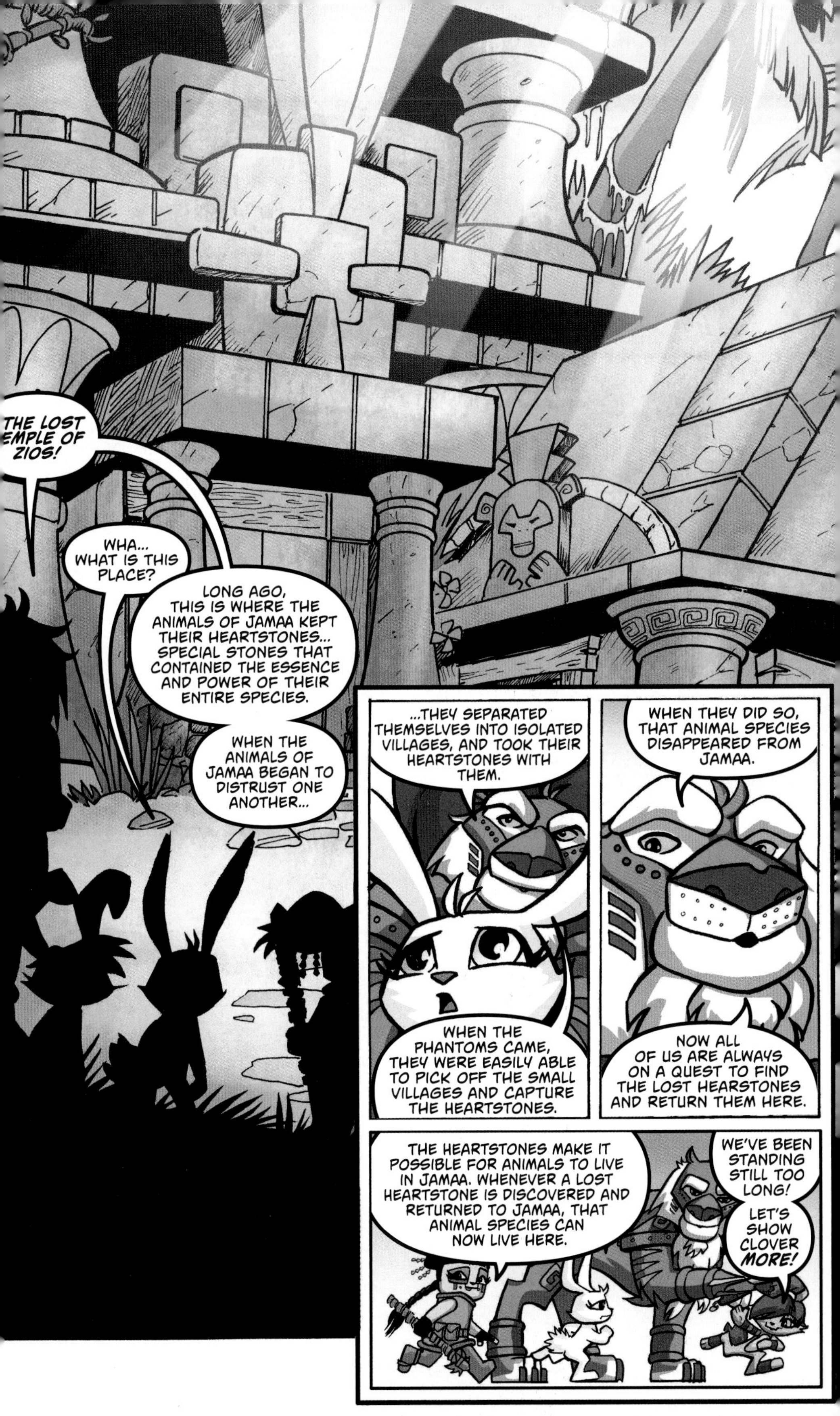
THE LOST EMPLE OF ZIOS!
WHA... WHAT IS THIS PLACE?
LONG AGO, THIS IS WHERE THE ANIMALS OF JAMAA KEPT THEIR HEARTSTONES... SPECIAL STONES THAT CONTAINED THE ESSENCE AND POWER OF THEIR ENTIRE SPECIES.
WHEN THE ANIMALS OF JAMAA BEGAN TO DISTRUST ONE ANOTHER...
...THEY SEPARATED THEMSELVES INTO ISOLATED VILLAGES, AND TOOK THEIR HEARTSTONES WITH THEM.
WHEN THE PHANTOMS CAME, THEY WERE EASILY ABLE TO PICK OFF THE SMALL VILLAGES AND CAPTURE THE HEARTSTONES.
WHEN THEY DID SO, THAT ANIMAL SPECIES DISAPPEARED FROM JAMAA.
NOW ALL OF US ARE ALWAYS ON A QUEST TO FIND THE LOST HEARSTONES AND RETURN THEM HERE.
THE HEARTSTONES MAKE IT POSSIBLE FOR ANIMALS TO LIVE IN JAMAA. WHENEVER A LOST HEARTSTONE IS DISCOVERED AND RETURNED TO JAMAA, THAT ANIMAL SPECIES CAN NOW LIVE HERE.
WE'VE BEEN STANDING STILL TOO LONG!
LET'S SHOW CLOVER MORE!

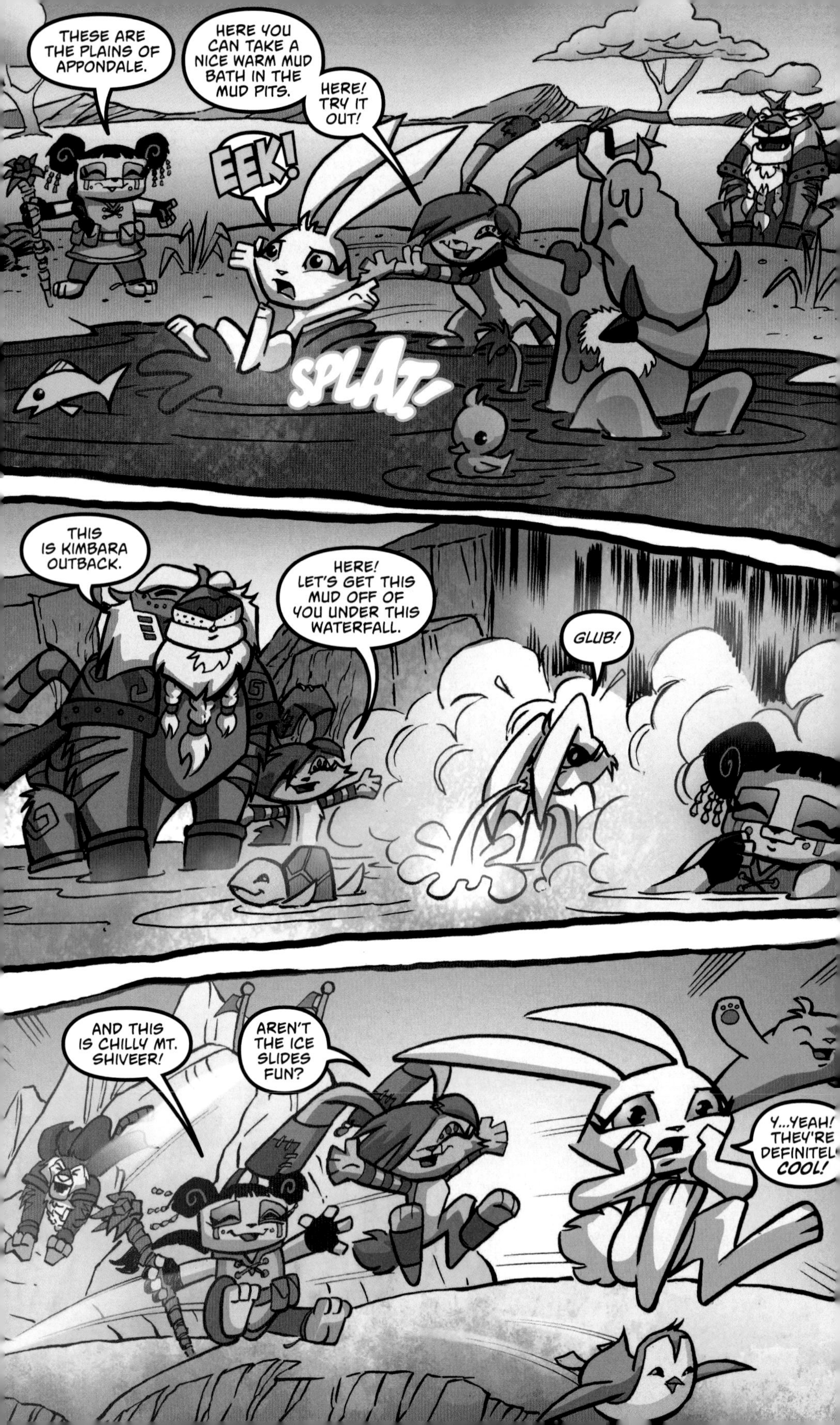

THESE ARE THE PLAINS OF APPONDALE.
HERE YOU CAN TAKE A NICE WARM MUD BATH IN THE MUD PITS.
HERE! TRY IT OUT!
EEK!
SPLAT!
THIS IS KIMBARA OUTBACK.
HERE! LET'S GET THIS MUD OFF OF YOU UNDER THIS WATERFALL.
GLUB!
AND THIS IS CHILLY MT. SHIVEER!
AREN'T THE ICE SLIDES FUN?
Y...YEAH! THEY'RE DEFINITEL COOL!

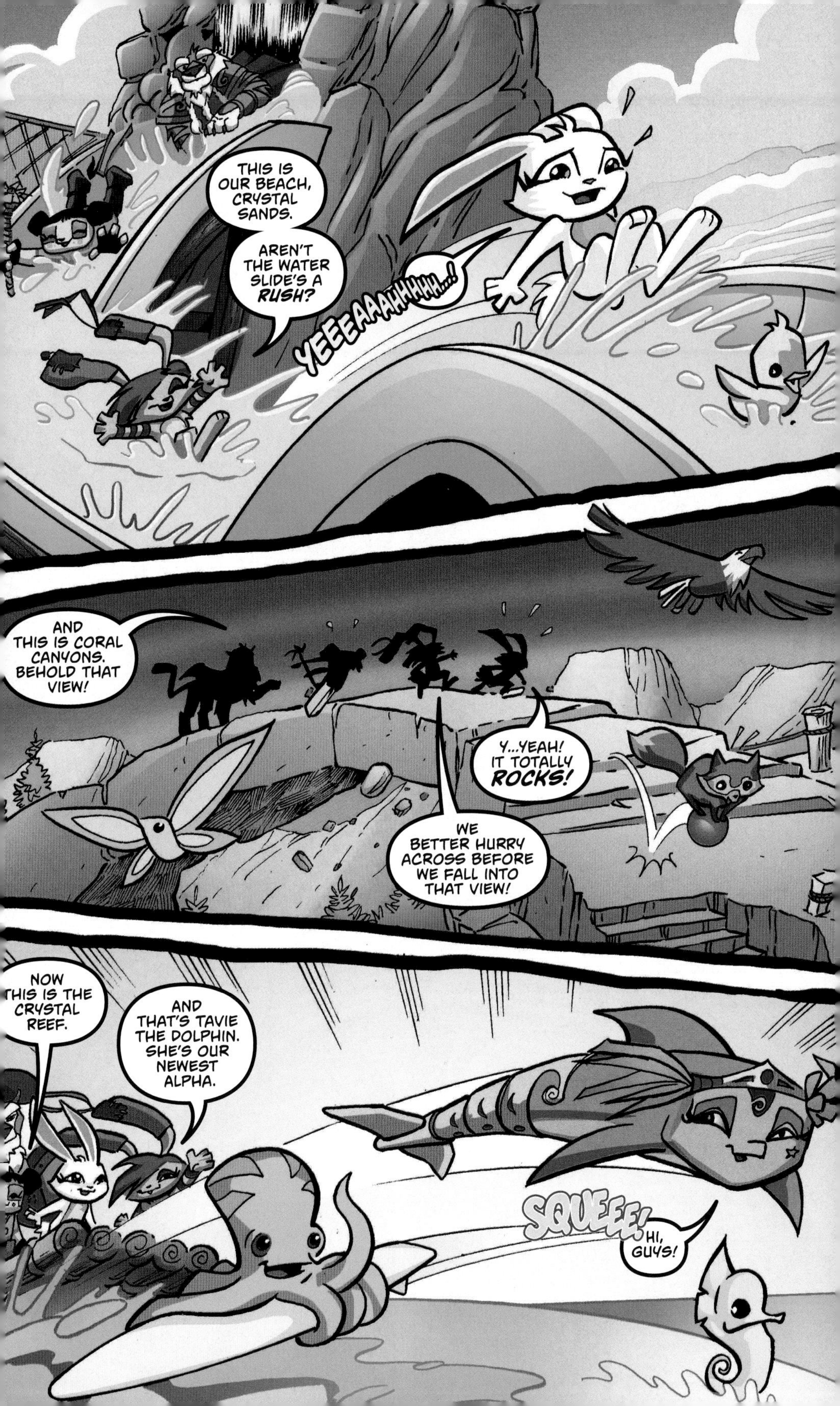
THIS IS OUR BEACH, CRYSTAL SANDS.
AREN'T THE WATER SLIDE'S A RUSH?
YEEEAAAHHHHH...!
AND THIS IS CORAL CANYONS. BEHOLD THAT VIEW!
Y...YEAH! IT TOTALLY ROCKS!
WE BETTER HURRY ACROSS BEFORE WE FALL INTO THAT VIEW!
NOW THIS IS THE CRYSTAL REEF.
AND THAT'S TAVIE THE DOLPHIN. SHE'S OUR NEWEST ALPHA.
SQUEEE!
HI, GUYS!

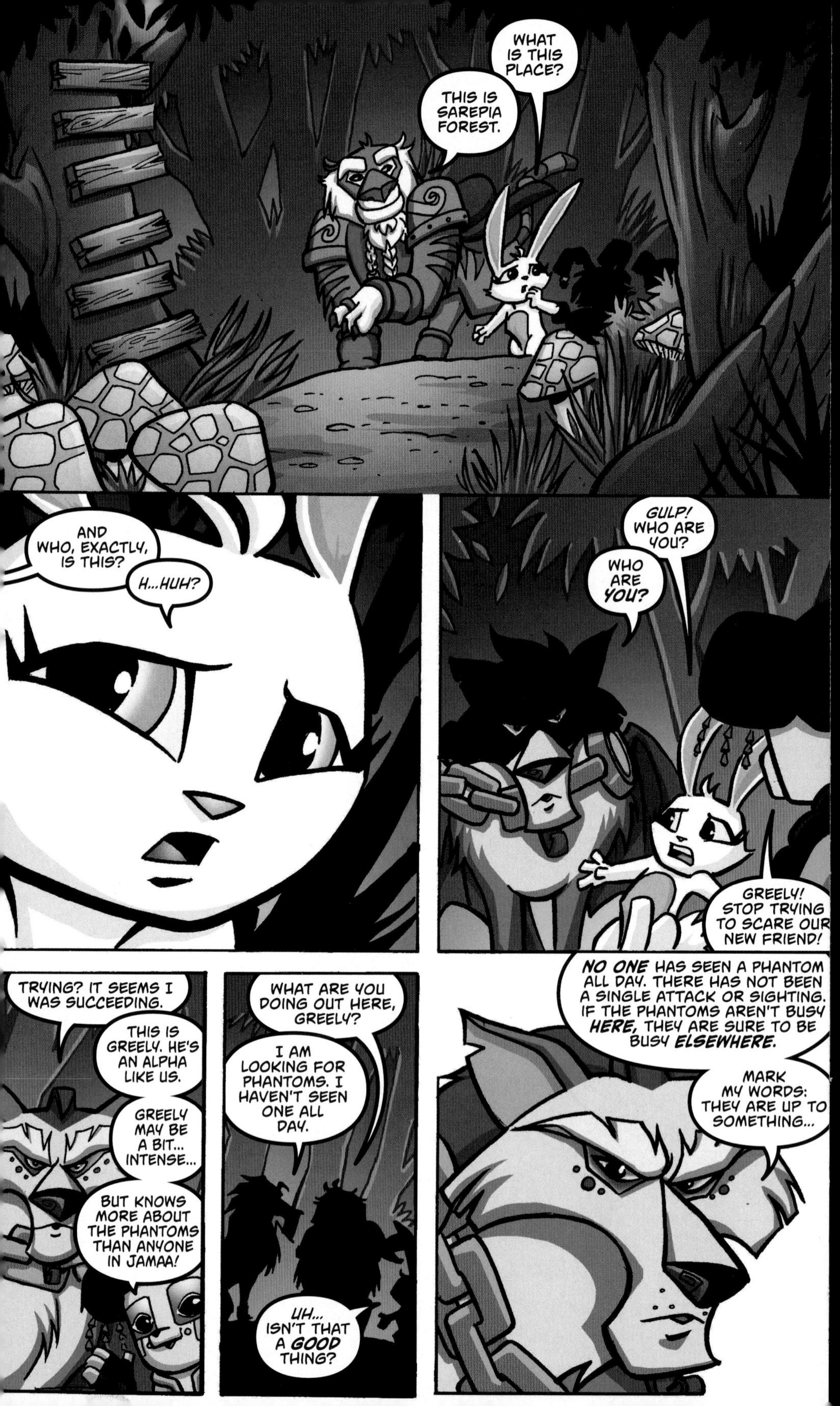

WHAT IS THIS PLACE?
THIS IS SAREPIA FOREST.
AND WHO, EXACTLY, IS THIS?
H...HUH?
GULP! WHO ARE YOU?
WHO ARE *YOU?*
GREELY! STOP TRYING TO SCARE OUR NEW FRIEND!
TRYING? IT SEEMS I WAS SUCCEEDING.
THIS IS GREELY. HE'S AN ALPHA LIKE US.
GREELY MAY BE A BIT... INTENSE...
BUT KNOWS MORE ABOUT THE PHANTOMS THAN ANYONE IN JAMAA!
WHAT ARE YOU DOING OUT HERE, GREELY?
I AM LOOKING FOR PHANTOMS. I HAVEN'T SEEN ONE ALL DAY.
UH... ISN'T THAT A *GOOD* THING?
NO ONE HAS SEEN A PHANTOM ALL DAY. THERE HAS NOT BEEN A SINGLE ATTACK OR SIGHTING. IF THE PHANTOMS AREN'T BUSY ***HERE,*** THEY ARE SURE TO BE BUSY ***ELSEWHERE.***
MARK MY WORDS: THEY ARE UP TO SOMETHING...

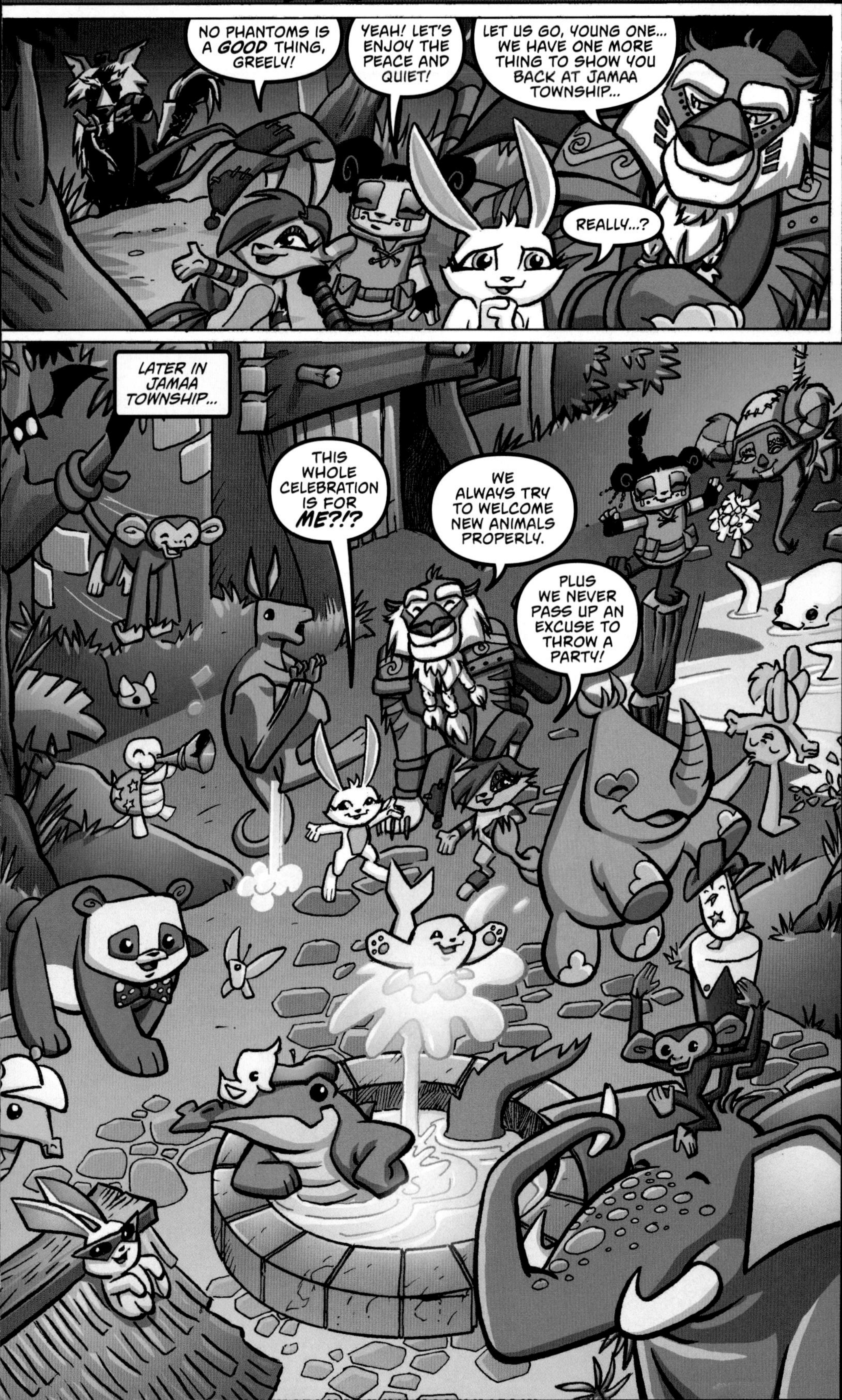
NO PHANTOMS IS A GOOD THING, GREELY!
YEAH! LET'S ENJOY THE PEACE AND QUIET!
LET US GO, YOUNG ONE... WE HAVE ONE MORE THING TO SHOW YOU BACK AT JAMAA TOWNSHIP...
REALLY...?
LATER IN JAMAA TOWNSHIP...
THIS WHOLE CELEBRATION IS FOR ME?!?
WE ALWAYS TRY TO WELCOME NEW ANIMALS PROPERLY.
PLUS WE NEVER PASS UP AN EXCUSE TO THROW A PARTY!

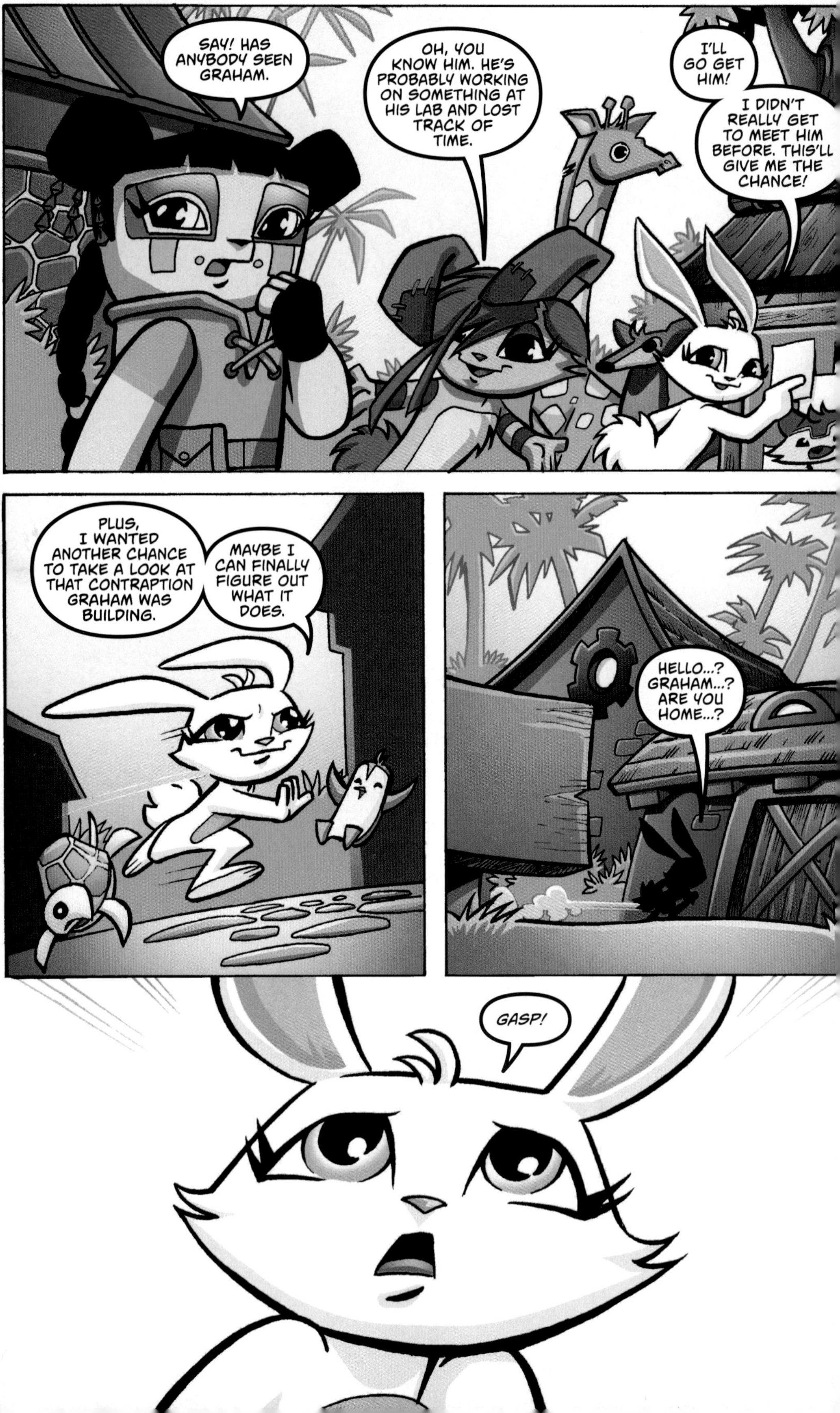
SAY! HAS ANYBODY SEEN GRAHAM.
OH, YOU KNOW HIM. HE'S PROBABLY WORKING ON SOMETHING AT HIS LAB AND LOST TRACK OF TIME.
I'LL GO GET HIM!
I DIDN'T REALLY GET TO MEET HIM BEFORE. THIS'LL GIVE ME THE CHANCE!
PLUS, I WANTED ANOTHER CHANCE TO TAKE A LOOK AT THAT CONTRAPTION GRAHAM WAS BUILDING.
MAYBE I CAN FINALLY FIGURE OUT WHAT IT DOES.
HELLO...? GRAHAM...? ARE YOU HOME...?
GASP!

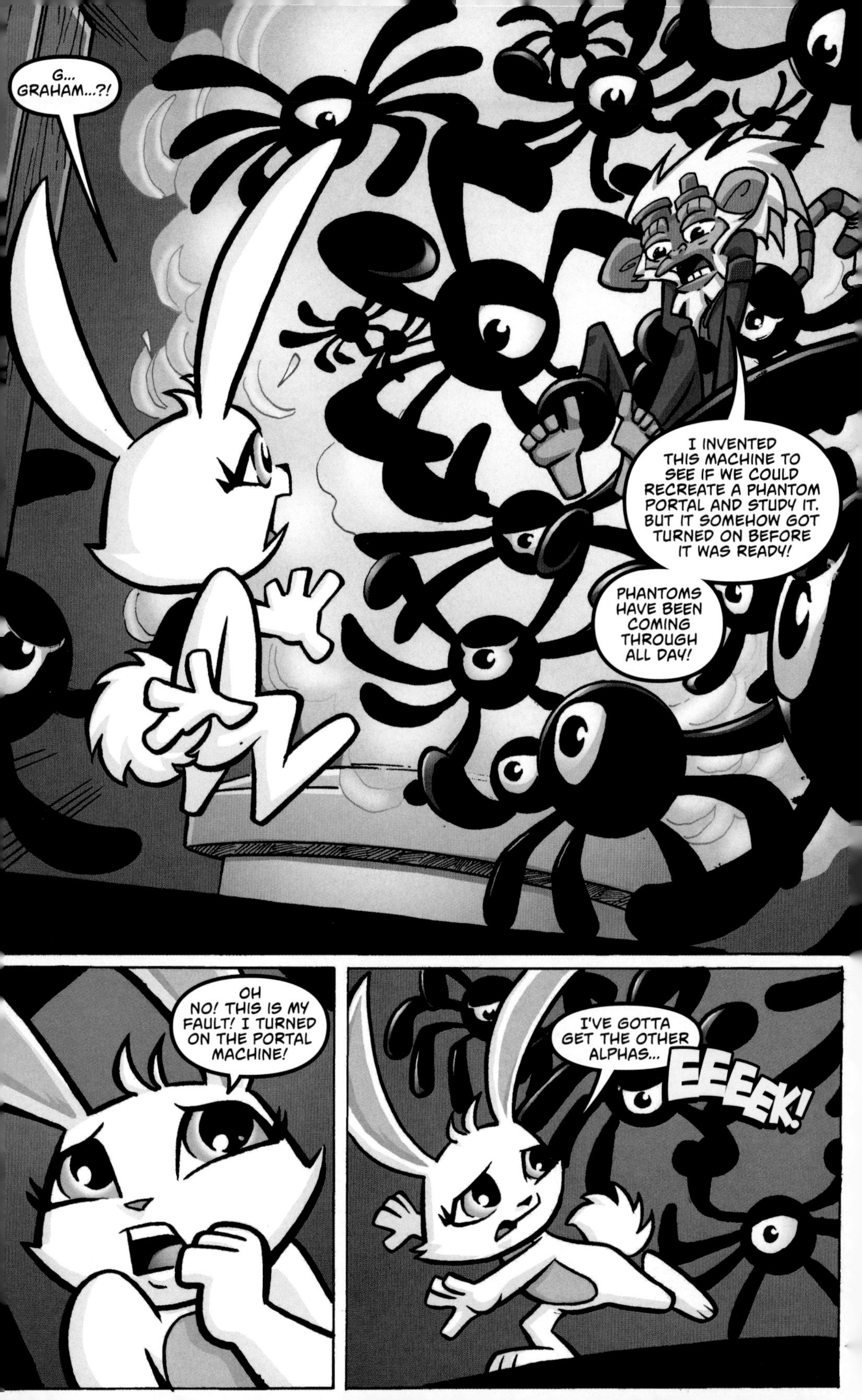
G... GRAHAM...?!
I INVENTED THIS MACHINE TO SEE IF WE COULD RECREATE A PHANTOM PORTAL AND STUDY IT. BUT IT SOMEHOW GOT TURNED ON BEFORE IT WAS READY!
PHANTOMS HAVE BEEN COMING THROUGH ALL DAY!
OH NO! THIS IS MY FAULT! I TURNED ON THE PORTAL MACHINE!
I'VE GOTTA GET THE OTHER ALPHAS...
EEEEK!

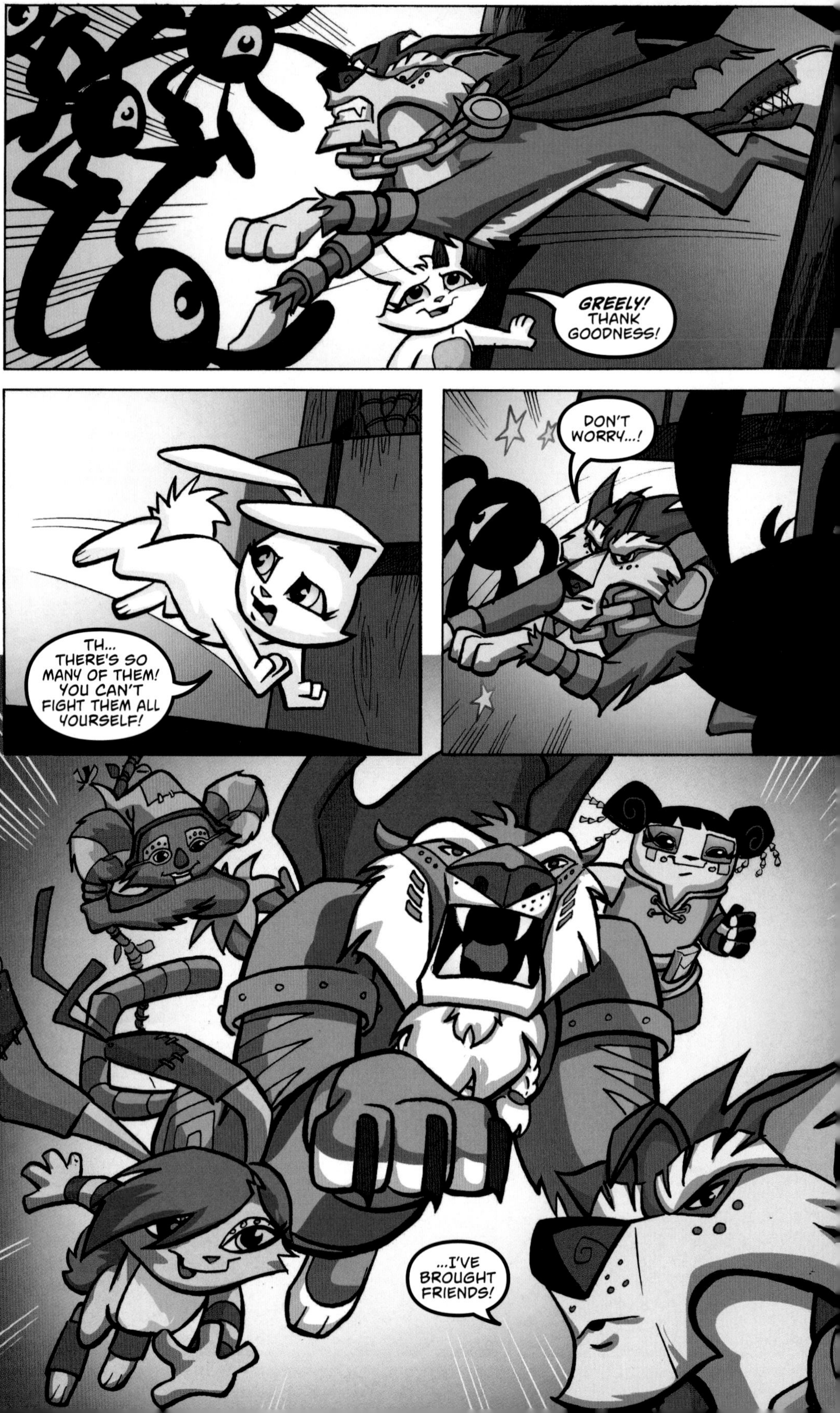
GREELY! THANK GOODNESS!
TH... THERE'S SO MANY OF THEM! YOU CAN'T FIGHT THEM ALL YOURSELF!
DON'T WORRY...!
...I'VE BROUGHT FRIENDS!

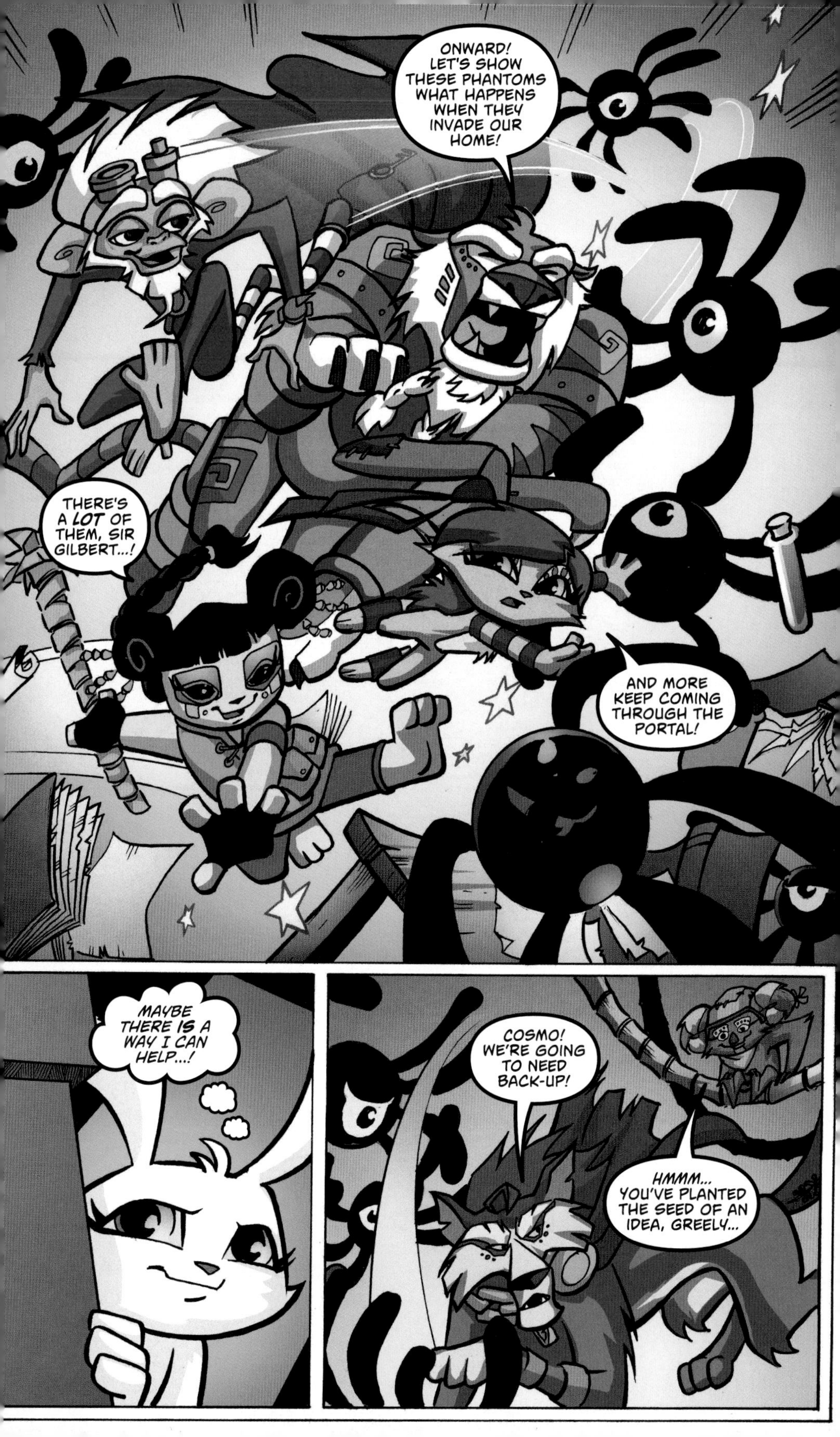
ONWARD! LET'S SHOW THESE PHANTOMS WHAT HAPPENS WHEN THEY INVADE OUR HOME!
THERE'S A *LOT* OF THEM, SIR GILBERT...!
AND MORE KEEP COMING THROUGH THE PORTAL!
*MAYBE THERE **IS** A WAY I CAN HELP...!*
COSMO! WE'RE GOING TO NEED BACK-UP!
HMMM... YOU'VE PLANTED THE SEED OF AN IDEA, GREELY...

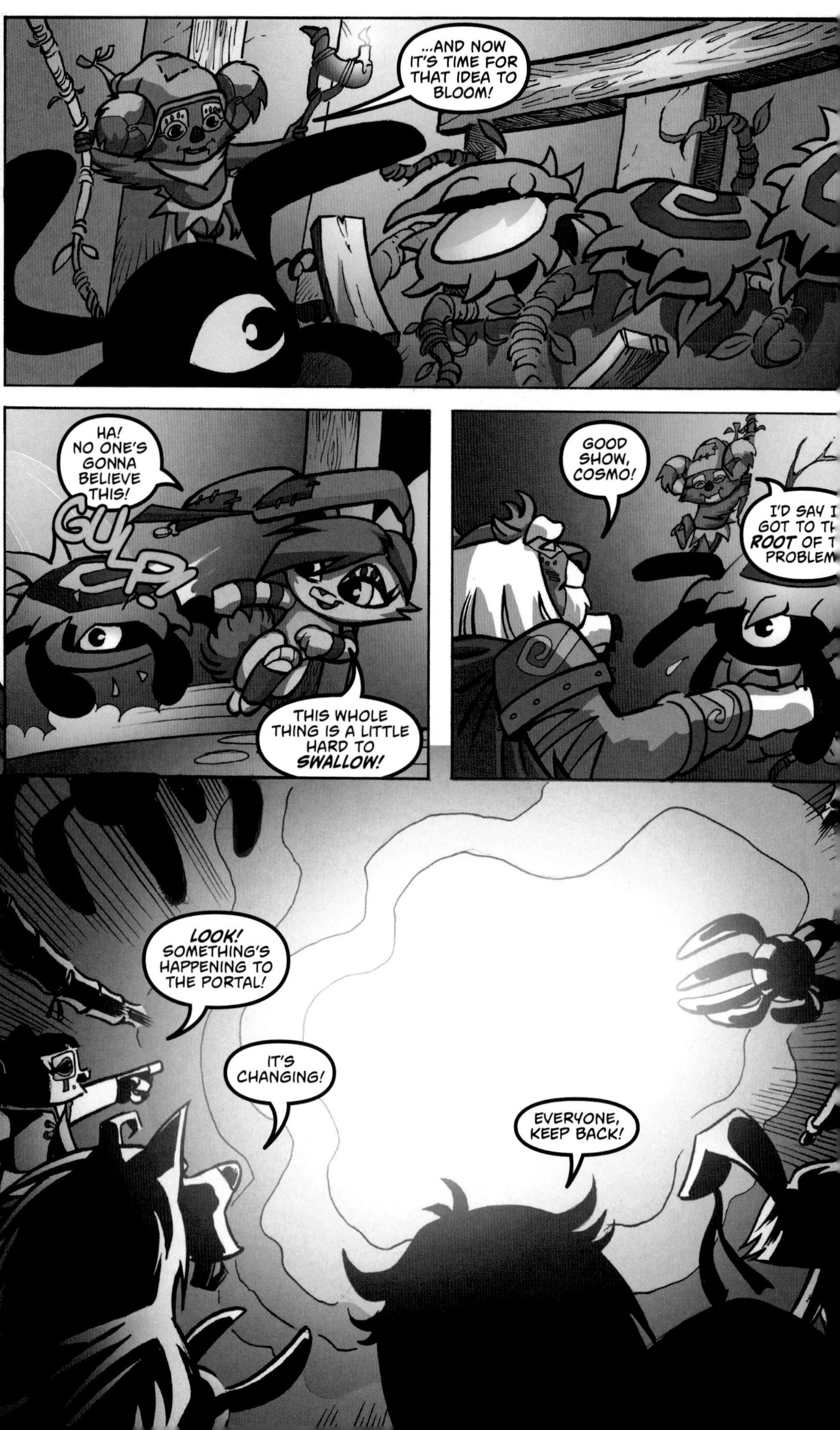
...AND NOW IT'S TIME FOR THAT IDEA TO BLOOM!
HA! NO ONE'S GONNA BELIEVE THIS!
GULP!
THIS WHOLE THING IS A LITTLE HARD TO **SWALLOW!**
GOOD SHOW, COSMO!
I'D SAY I GOT TO TH **ROOT** OF T PROBLEM
LOOK! SOMETHING'S HAPPENING TO THE PORTAL!
IT'S CHANGING!
EVERYONE, KEEP BACK!

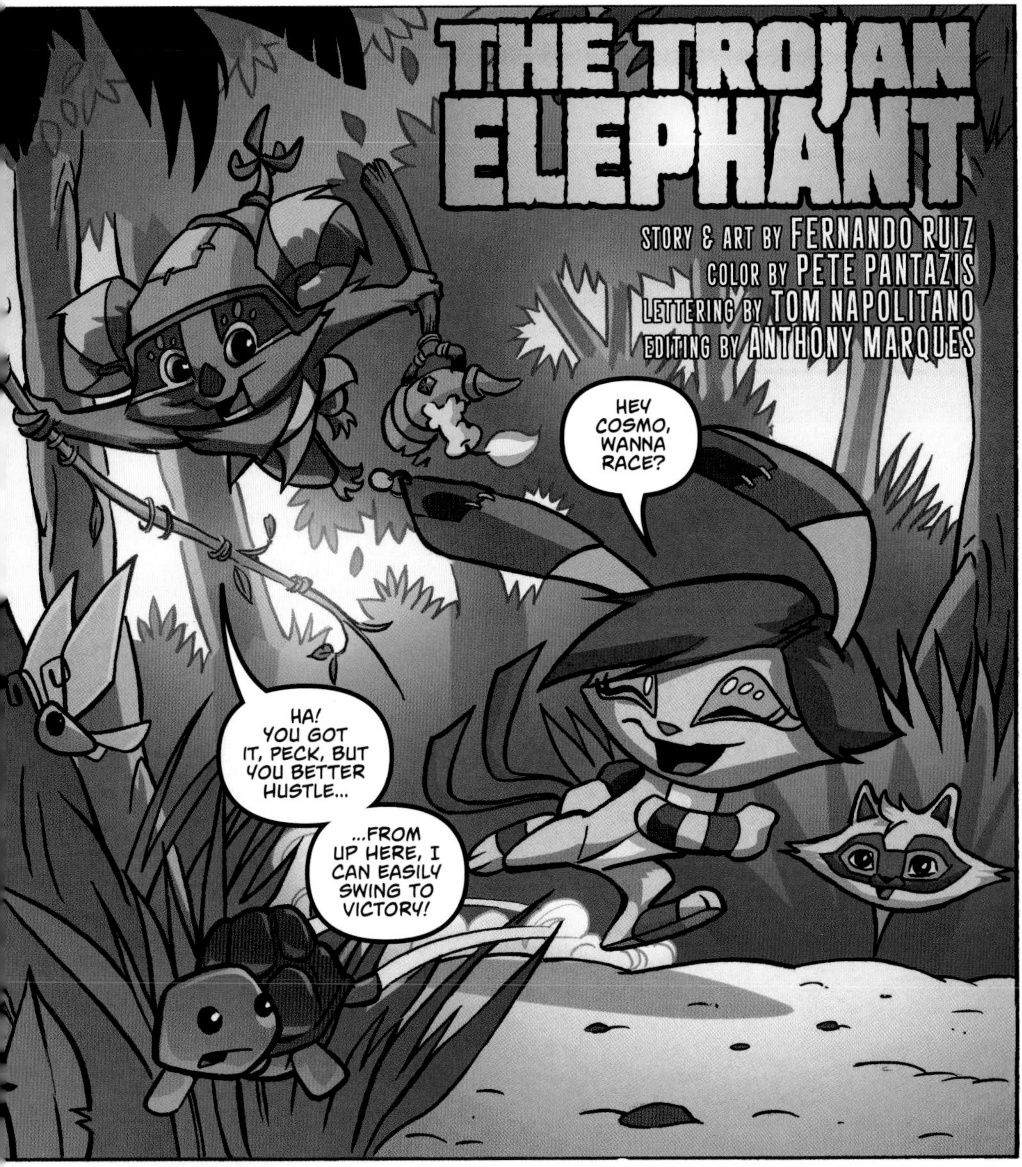
THE TROJAN ELEPHANT
STORY & ART BY FERNANDO RUIZ
COLOR BY PETE PANTAZIS
LETTERING BY TOM NAPOLITANO
EDITING BY ANTHONY MARQUES
HEY COSMO, WANNA RACE?
HA! YOU GOT IT, PECK, BUT YOU BETTER HUSTLE...
...FROM UP HERE, I CAN EASILY SWING TO VICTORY!

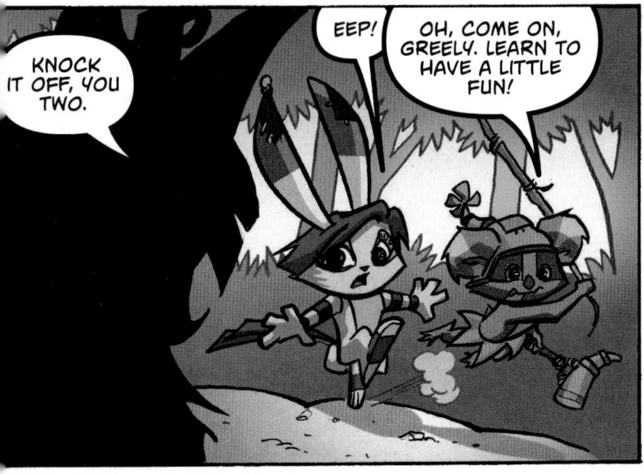
KNOCK IT OFF, YOU TWO.
EEP!
OH, COME ON, GREELY. LEARN TO HAVE A LITTLE FUN!

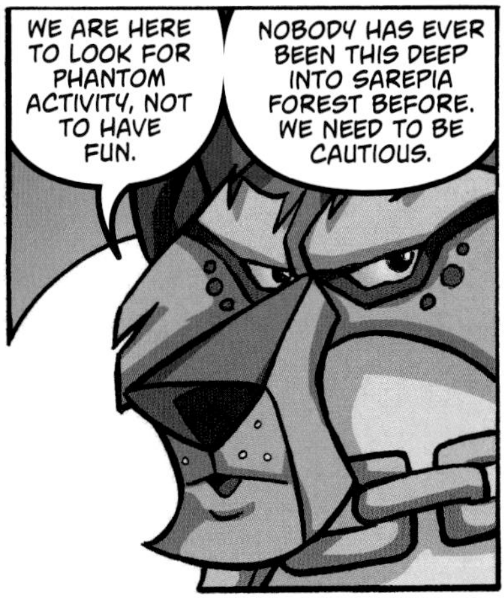
WE ARE HERE TO LOOK FOR PHANTOM ACTIVITY, NOT TO HAVE FUN.
NOBODY HAS EVER BEEN THIS DEEP INTO SAREPIA FOREST BEFORE. WE NEED TO BE CAUTIOUS.

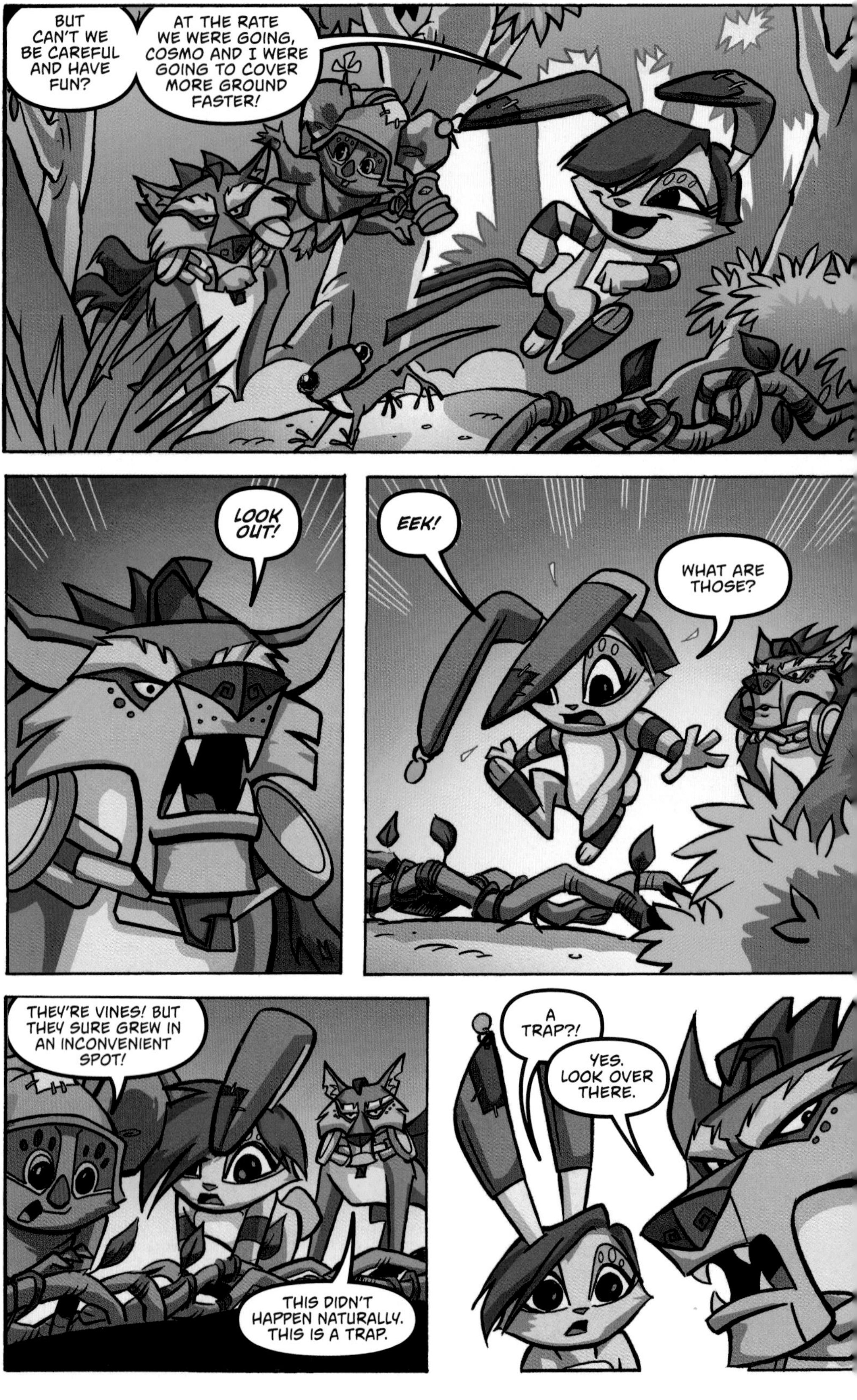
BUT CAN'T WE BE CAREFUL AND HAVE FUN?
AT THE RATE WE WERE GOING, COSMO AND I WERE GOING TO COVER MORE GROUND FASTER!
LOOK OUT!
EEK!
WHAT ARE THOSE?
THEY'RE VINES! BUT THEY SURE GREW IN AN INCONVENIENT SPOT!
THIS DIDN'T HAPPEN NATURALLY. THIS IS A TRAP.
A TRAP?!
YES. LOOK OVER THERE.

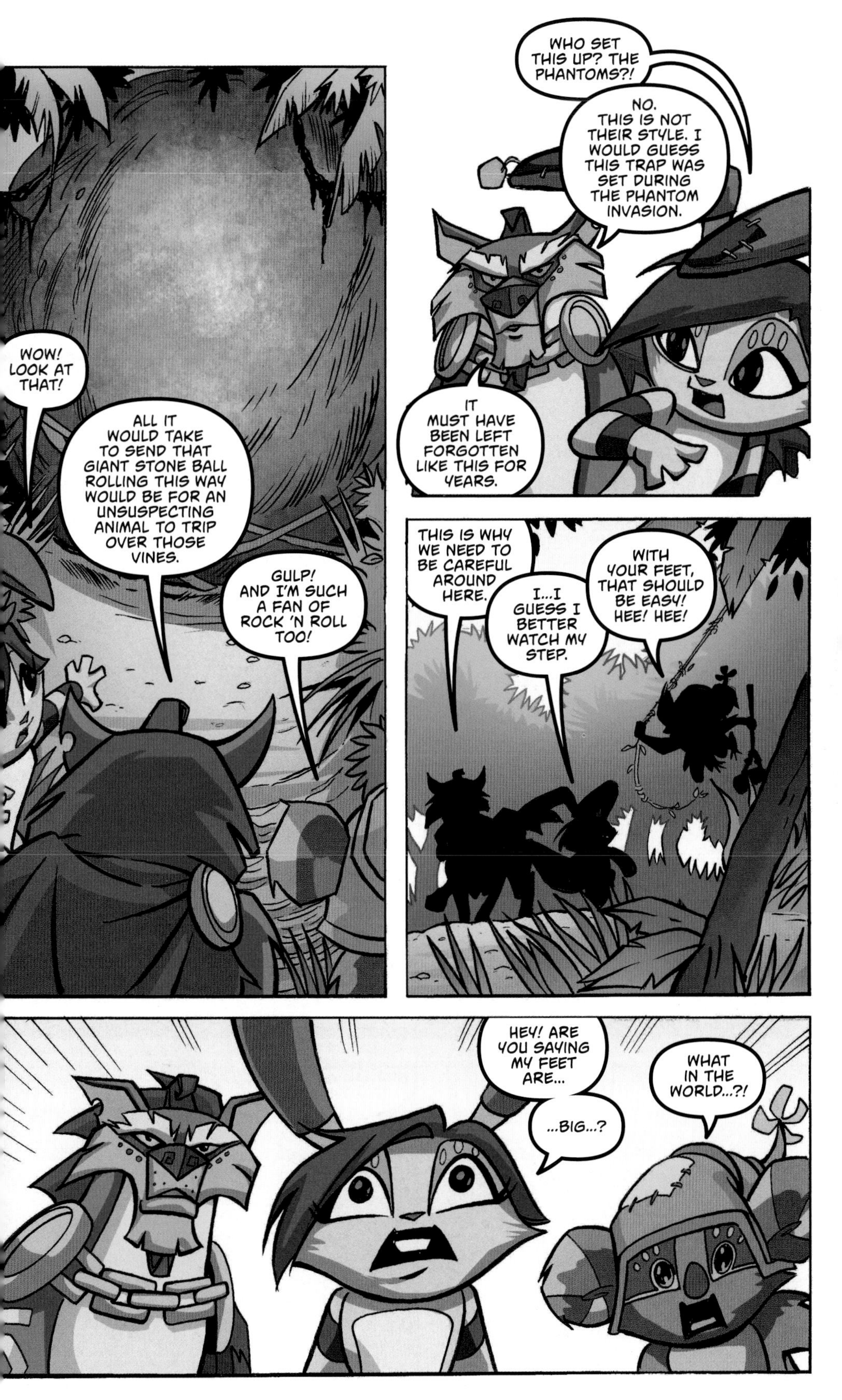
WOW! LOOK AT THAT!
ALL IT WOULD TAKE TO SEND THAT GIANT STONE BALL ROLLING THIS WAY WOULD BE FOR AN UNSUSPECTING ANIMAL TO TRIP OVER THOSE VINES.
GULP! AND I'M SUCH A FAN OF ROCK 'N ROLL TOO!
WHO SET THIS UP? THE PHANTOMS?!
NO. THIS IS NOT THEIR STYLE. I WOULD GUESS THIS TRAP WAS SET DURING THE PHANTOM INVASION.
IT MUST HAVE BEEN LEFT FORGOTTEN LIKE THIS FOR YEARS.
THIS IS WHY WE NEED TO BE CAREFUL AROUND HERE.
I...I GUESS I BETTER WATCH MY STEP.
WITH YOUR FEET, THAT SHOULD BE EASY! HEE! HEE!
HEY! ARE YOU SAYING MY FEET ARE...
...BIG...?
WHAT IN THE WORLD...?!

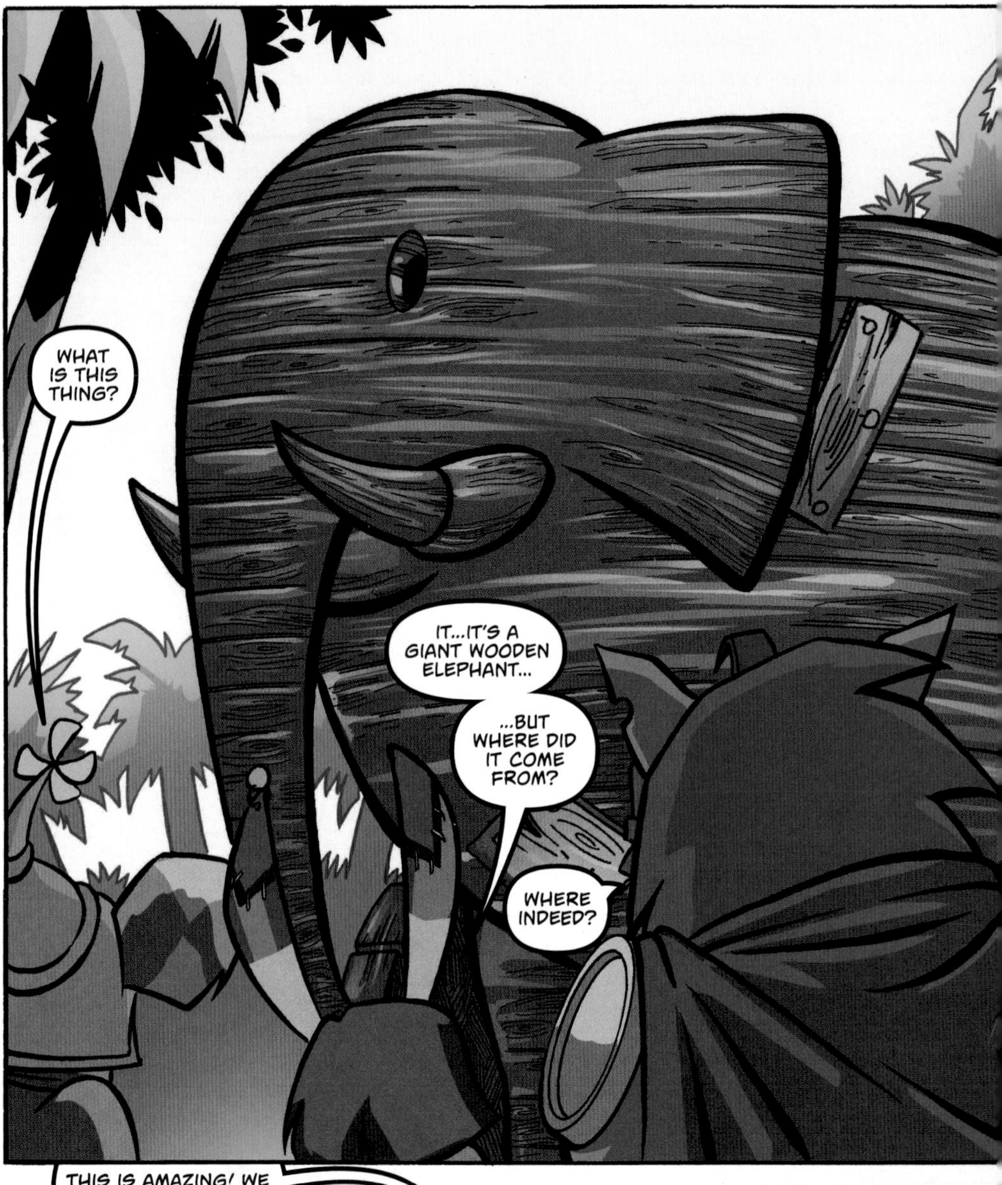
WHAT IS THIS THING?
IT...IT'S A GIANT WOODEN ELEPHANT...
...BUT WHERE DID IT COME FROM?
WHERE INDEED?

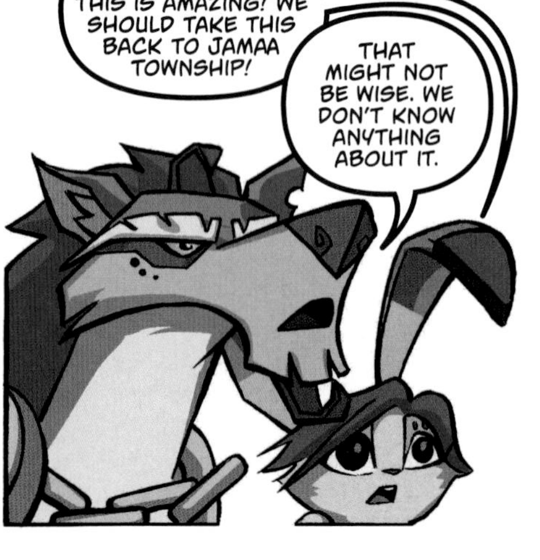
THIS IS AMAZING! WE SHOULD TAKE THIS BACK TO JAMAA TOWNSHIP!
THAT MIGHT NOT BE WISE. WE DON'T KNOW ANYTHING ABOUT IT.

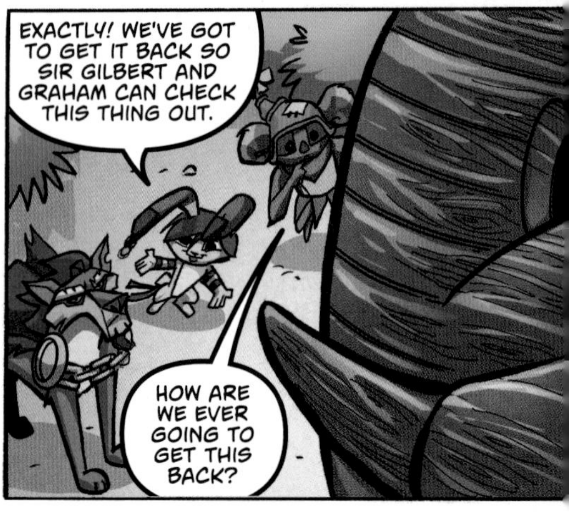
EXACTLY! WE'VE GOT TO GET IT BACK SO SIR GILBERT AND GRAHAM CAN CHECK THIS THING OUT.
HOW ARE WE EVER GOING TO GET THIS BACK?

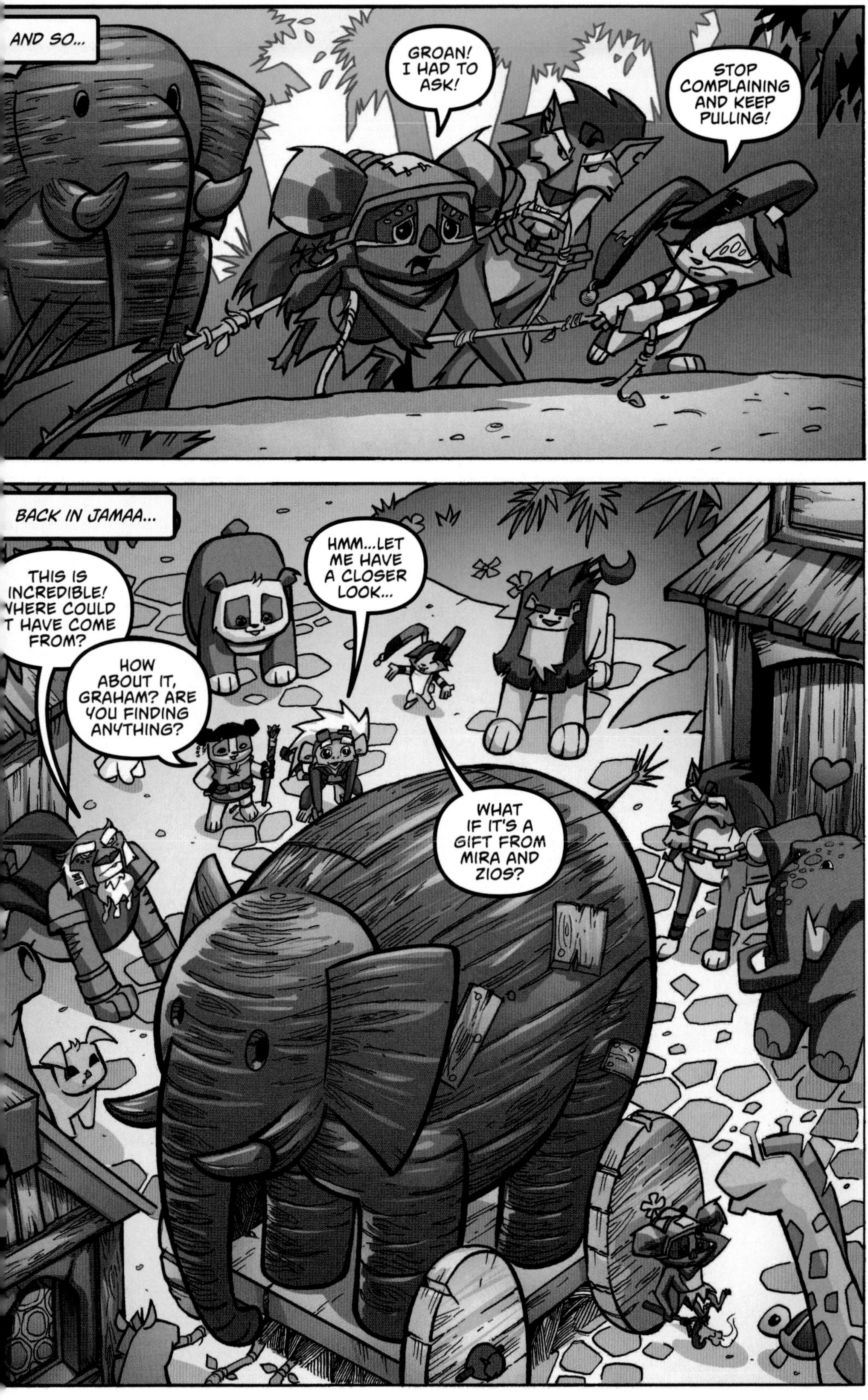
AND SO...
GROAN! I HAD TO ASK!
STOP COMPLAINING AND KEEP PULLING!
BACK IN JAMAA...
THIS IS INCREDIBLE! VHERE COULD T HAVE COME FROM?
HMM...LET ME HAVE A CLOSER LOOK...
HOW ABOUT IT, GRAHAM? ARE YOU FINDING ANYTHING?
WHAT IF IT'S A GIFT FROM MIRA AND ZIOS?

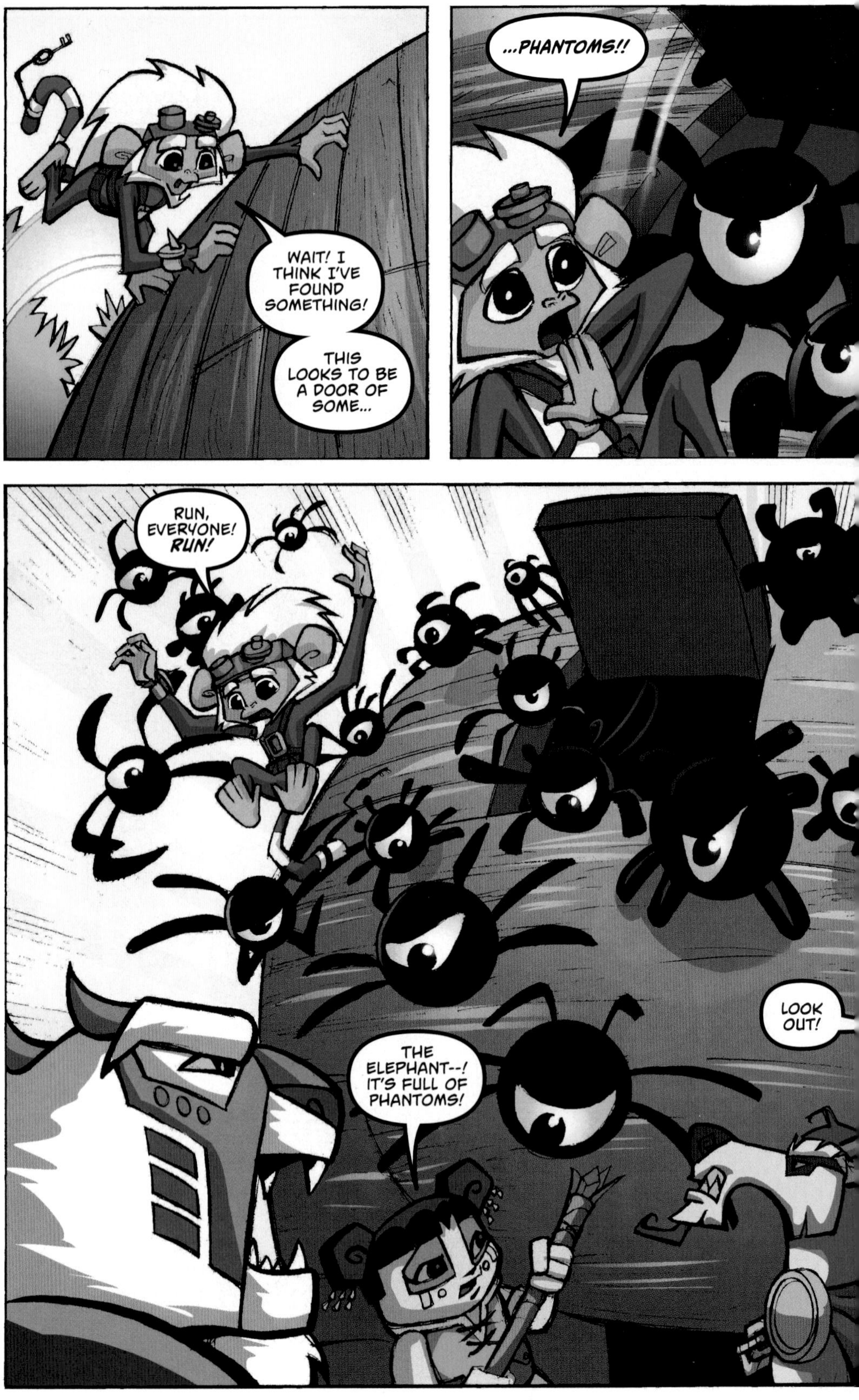
WAIT! I THINK I'VE FOUND SOMETHING!
THIS LOOKS TO BE A DOOR OF SOME...
...PHANTOMS!!
RUN, EVERYONE! RUN!
LOOK OUT!
THE ELEPHANT--! IT'S FULL OF PHANTOMS!

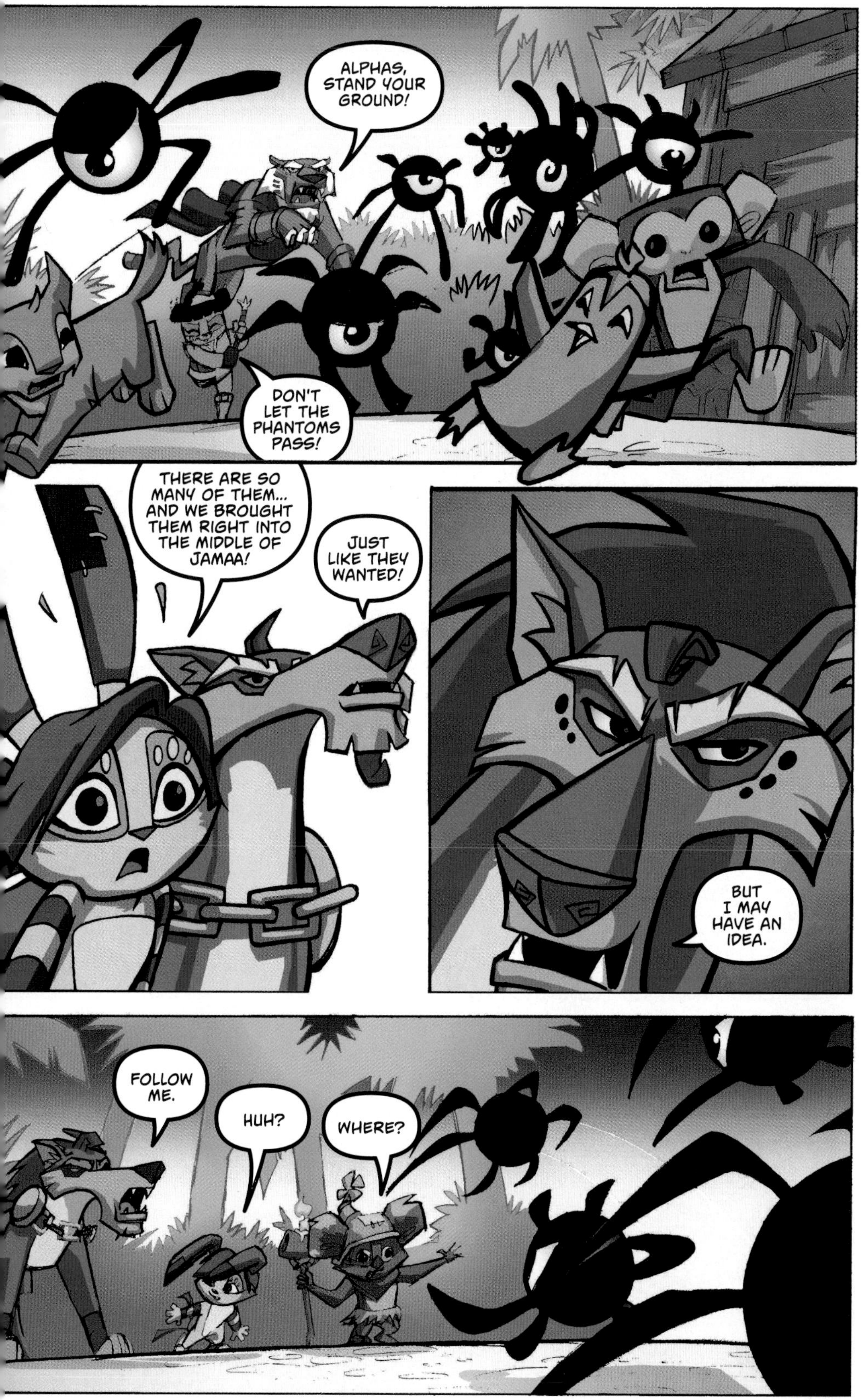
ALPHAS, STAND YOUR GROUND!
DON'T LET THE PHANTOMS PASS!
THERE ARE SO MANY OF THEM... AND WE BROUGHT THEM RIGHT INTO THE MIDDLE OF JAMAA!
JUST LIKE THEY WANTED!
BUT I MAY HAVE AN IDEA.
FOLLOW ME.
HUH?
WHERE?

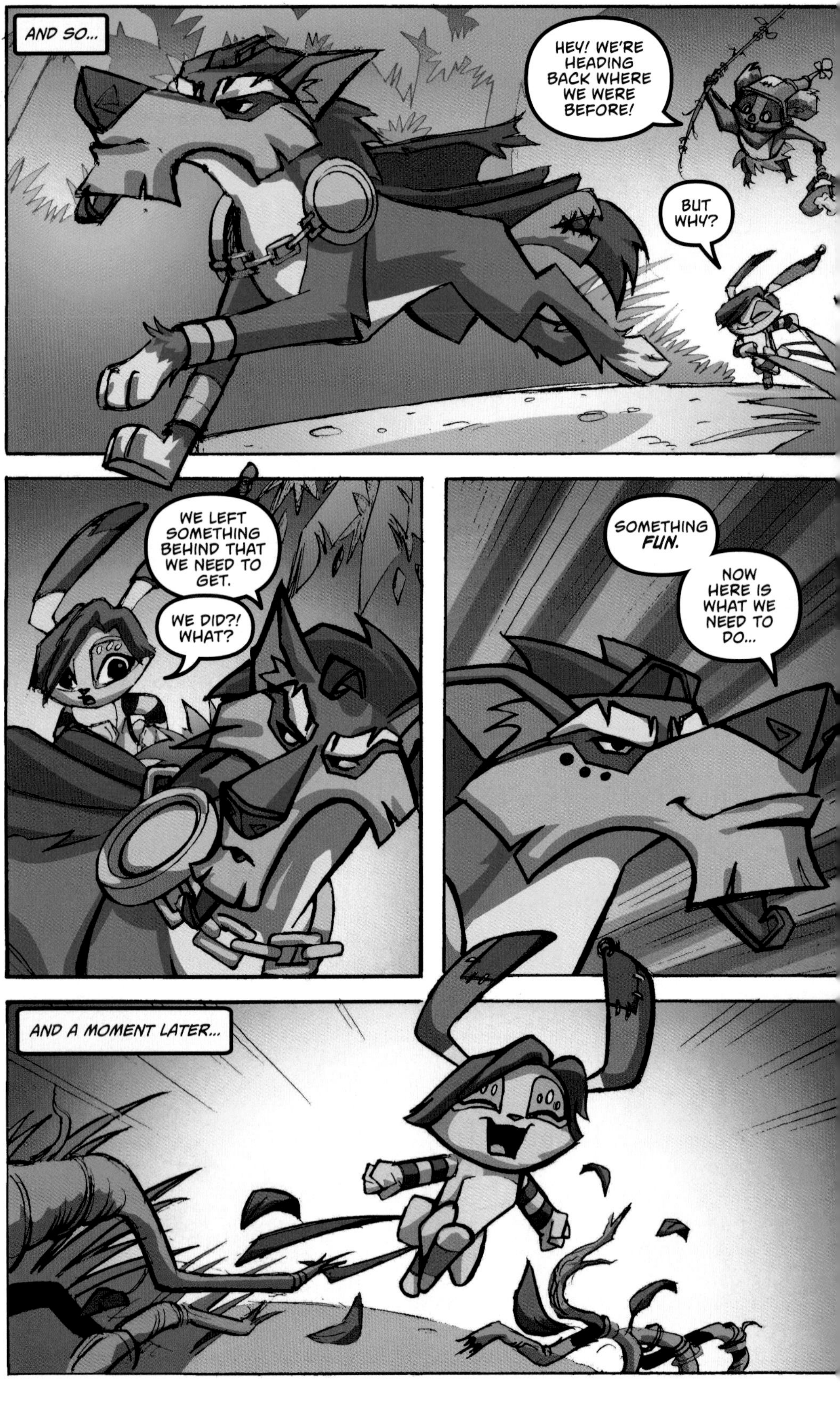
AND SO...
HEY! WE'RE HEADING BACK WHERE WE WERE BEFORE!
BUT WHY?
WE LEFT SOMETHING BEHIND THAT WE NEED TO GET.
WE DID?! WHAT?
SOMETHING FUN.
NOW HERE IS WHAT WE NEED TO DO...
AND A MOMENT LATER...

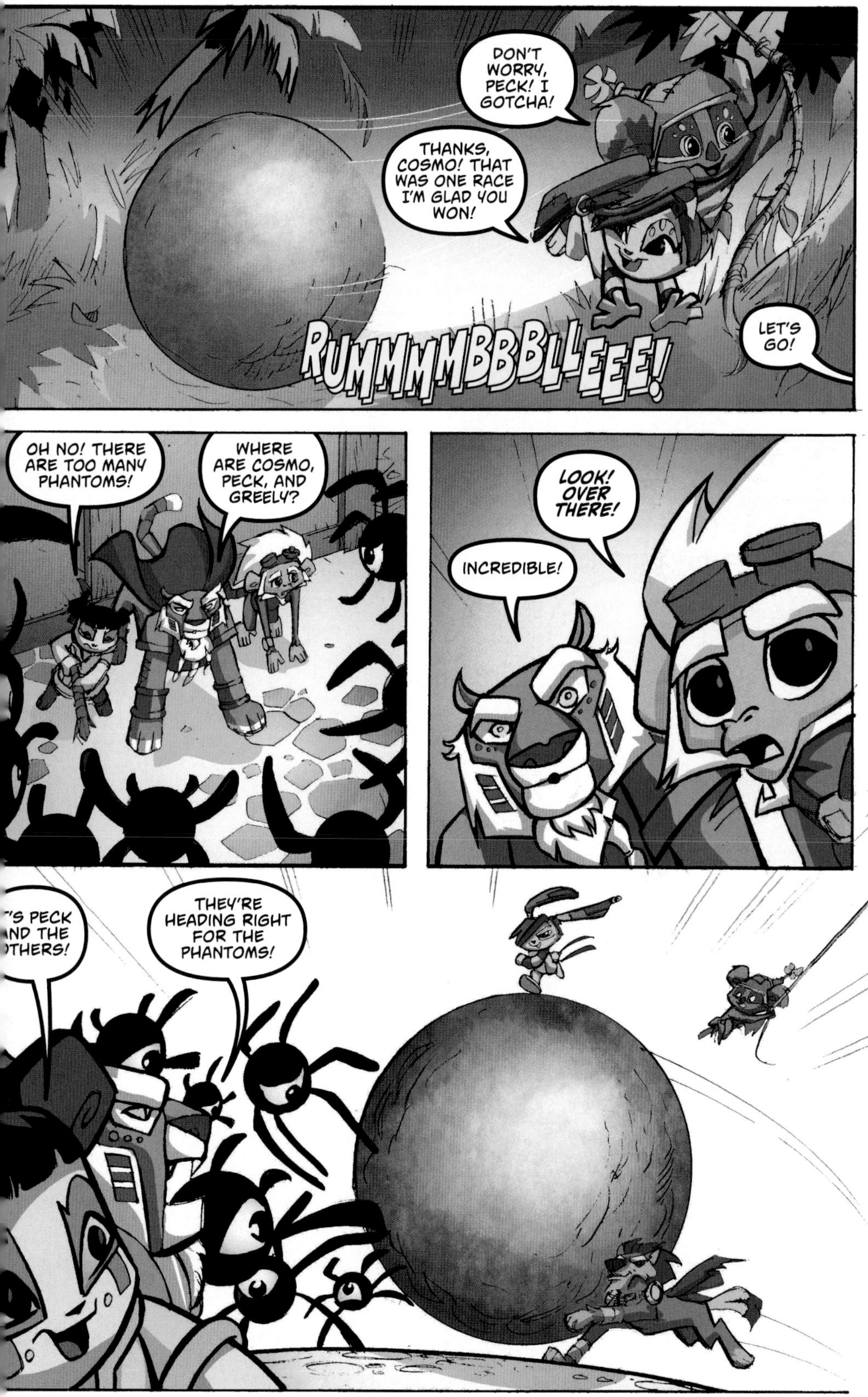
DON'T WORRY, PECK! I GOTCHA!
THANKS, COSMO! THAT WAS ONE RACE I'M GLAD YOU WON!
RUMMMMBBBLLEEE!
LET'S GO!
OH NO! THERE ARE TOO MANY PHANTOMS!
WHERE ARE COSMO, PECK, AND GREELY?
LOOK! OVER THERE!
INCREDIBLE!
'S PECK ND THE THERS!
THEY'RE HEADING RIGHT FOR THE PHANTOMS!

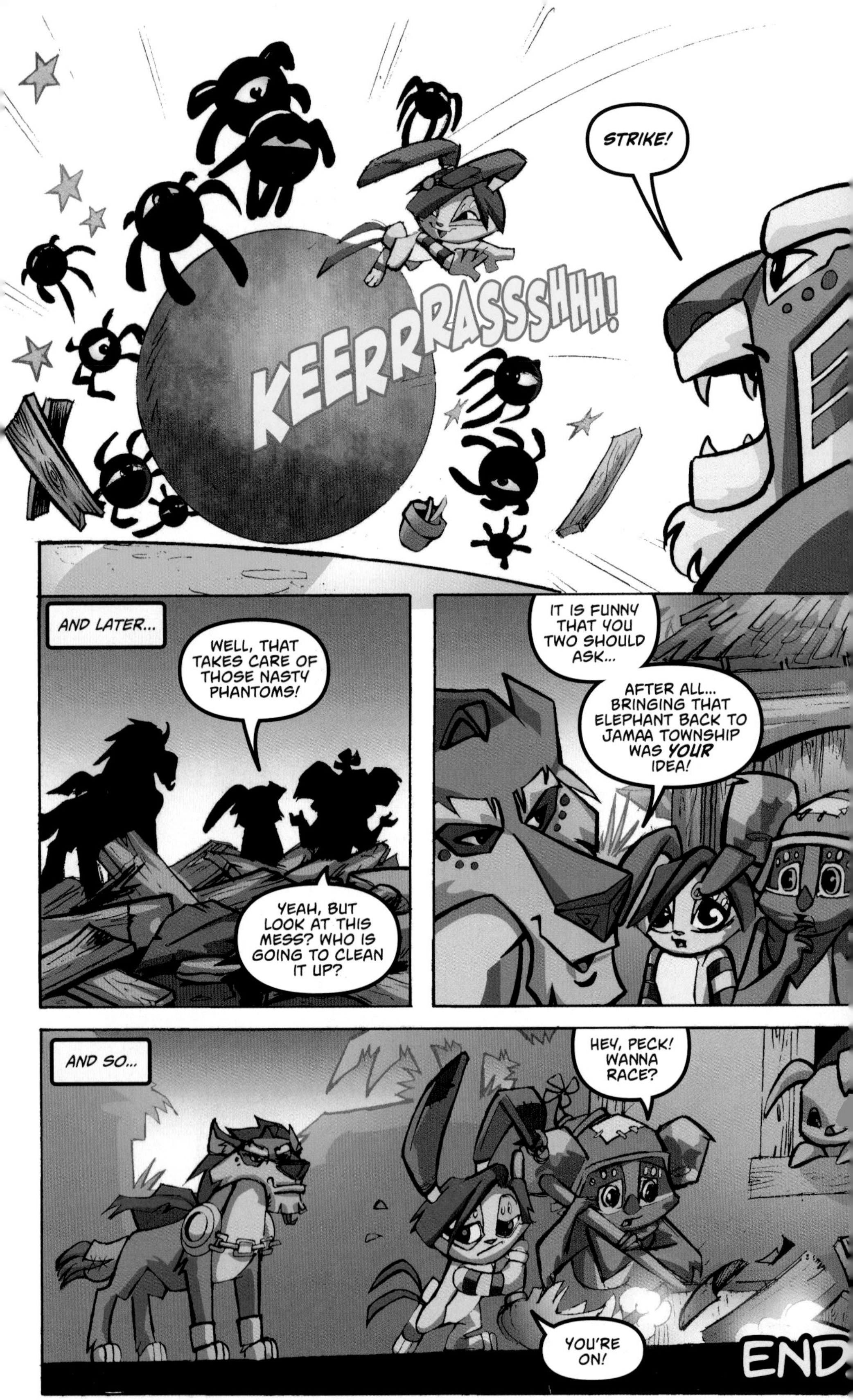
STRIKE!
KEERRRASSSHHH!
AND LATER...
WELL, THAT TAKES CARE OF THOSE NASTY PHANTOMS!
YEAH, BUT LOOK AT THIS MESS? WHO IS GOING TO CLEAN IT UP?
IT IS FUNNY THAT YOU TWO SHOULD ASK...
AFTER ALL... BRINGING THAT ELEPHANT BACK TO JAMAA TOWNSHIP WAS YOUR IDEA!
AND SO...
HEY, PECK! WANNA RACE?
YOU'RE ON!
END

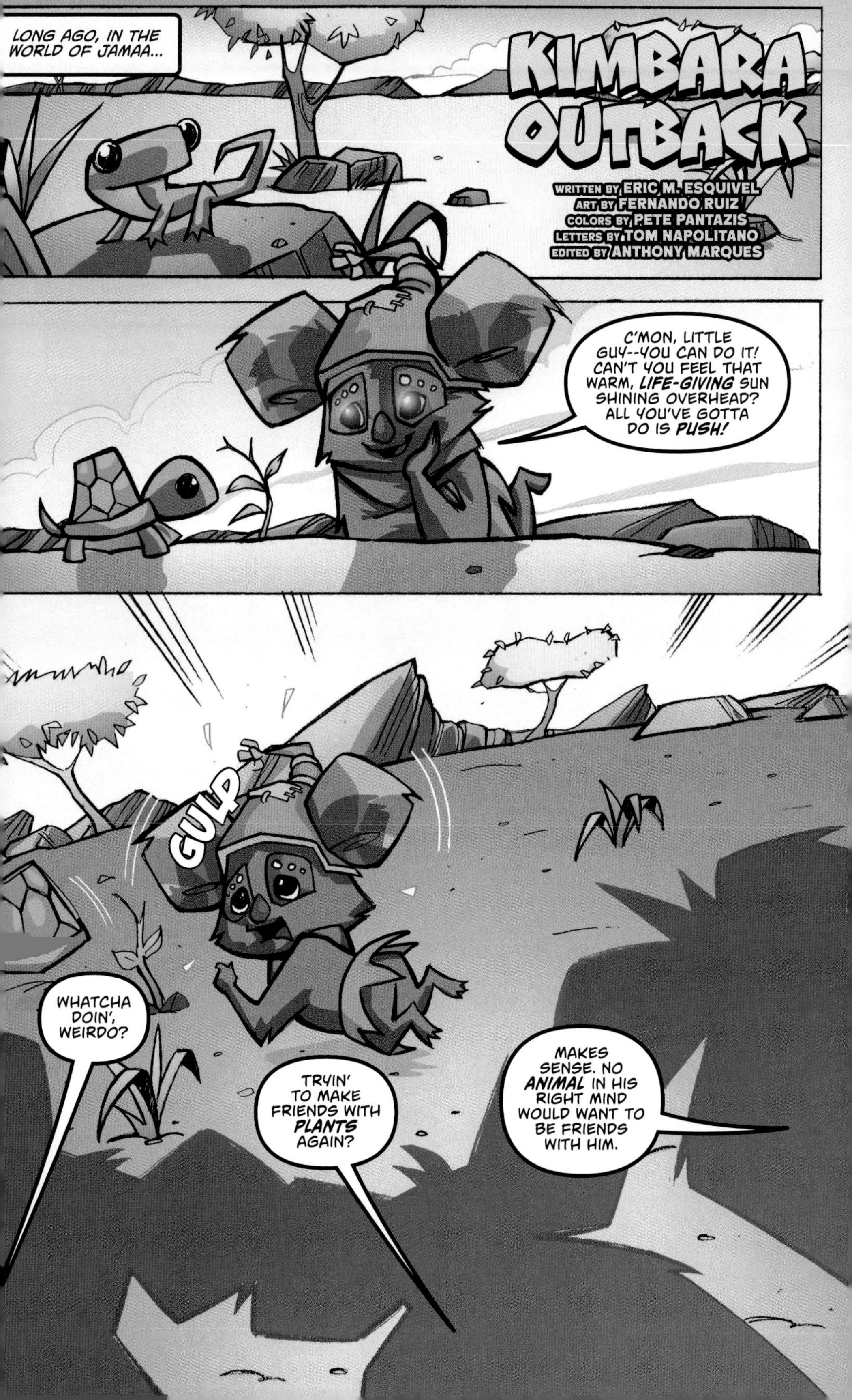
LONG AGO, IN THE WORLD OF JAMAA...
KIMBARA OUTBACK
WRITTEN BY ERIC M. ESQUIVEL
ART BY FERNANDO RUIZ
COLORS BY PETE PANTAZIS
LETTERS BY TOM NAPOLITANO
EDITED BY ANTHONY MARQUES
C'MON, LITTLE GUY--YOU CAN DO IT! CAN'T YOU FEEL THAT WARM, LIFE-GIVING SUN SHINING OVERHEAD? ALL YOU'VE GOTTA DO IS PUSH!
GULP
WHATCHA DOIN', WEIRDO?
TRYIN' TO MAKE FRIENDS WITH PLANTS AGAIN?
MAKES SENSE. NO ANIMAL IN HIS RIGHT MIND WOULD WANT TO BE FRIENDS WITH HIM.

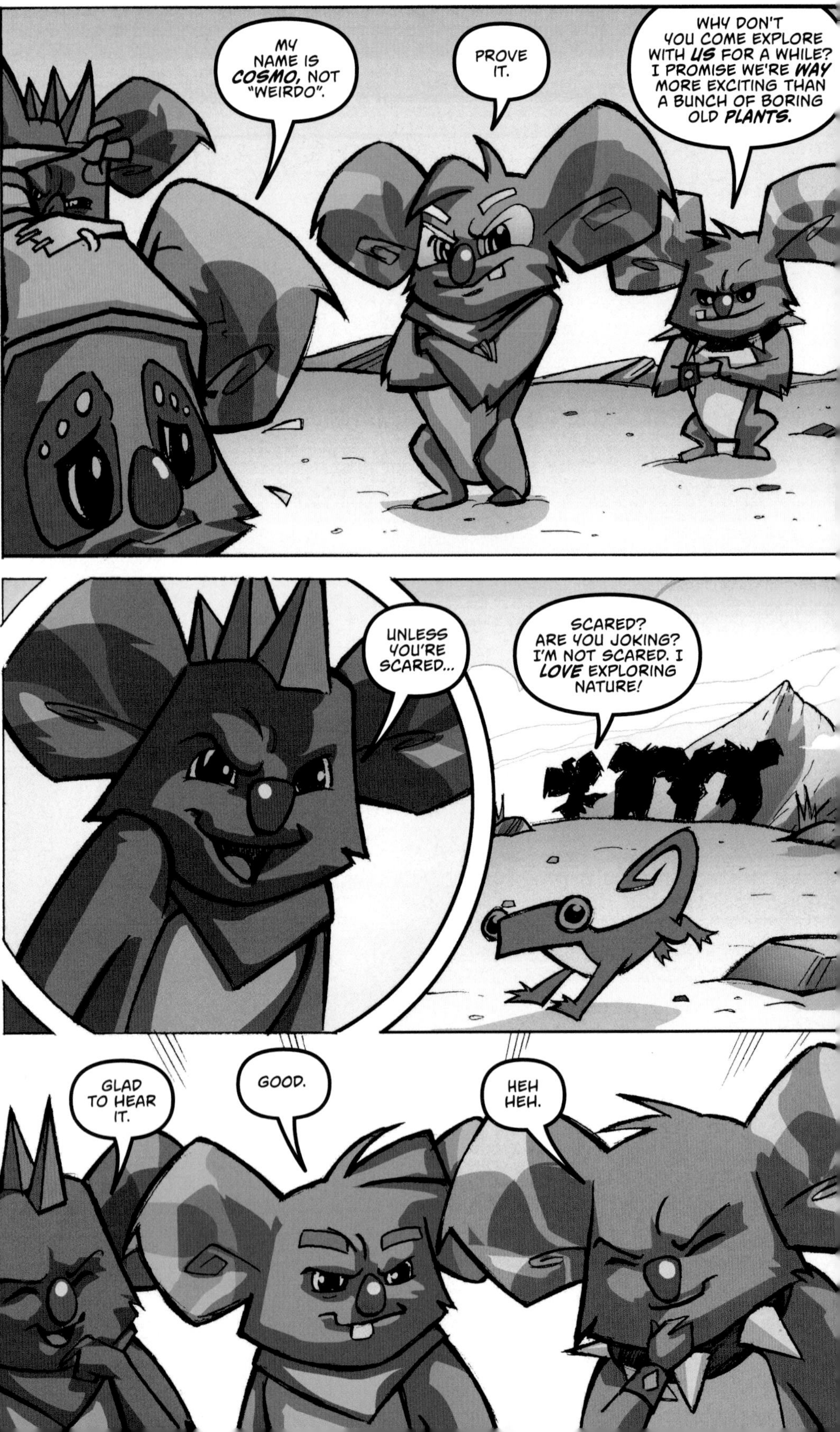
MY NAME IS COSMO, NOT "WEIRDO".
PROVE IT.
WHY DON'T YOU COME EXPLORE WITH US FOR A WHILE? I PROMISE WE'RE WAY MORE EXCITING THAN A BUNCH OF BORING OLD PLANTS.
UNLESS YOU'RE SCARED...
SCARED? ARE YOU JOKING? I'M NOT SCARED. I LOVE EXPLORING NATURE!
GLAD TO HEAR IT.
GOOD.
HEH HEH.

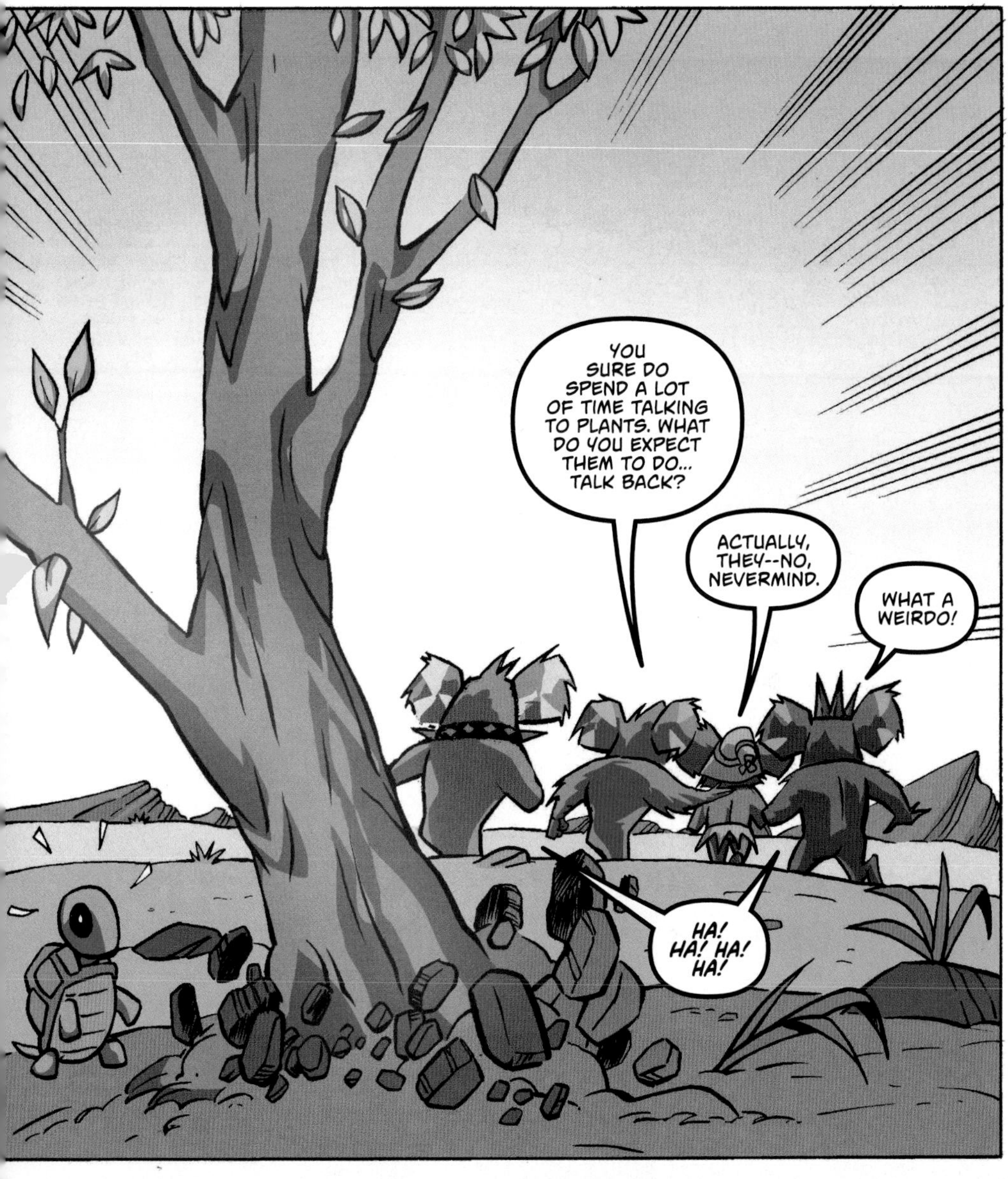
YOU SURE DO SPEND A LOT OF TIME TALKING TO PLANTS. WHAT DO YOU EXPECT THEM TO DO... TALK BACK?
ACTUALLY, THEY--NO, NEVERMIND.
WHAT A WEIRDO!
HA! HA! HA! HA!

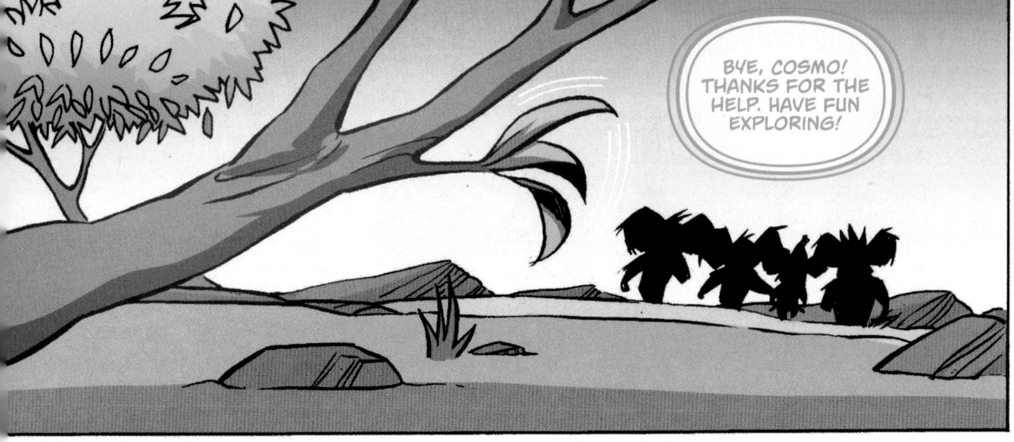
BYE, COSMO! THANKS FOR THE HELP. HAVE FUN EXPLORING!

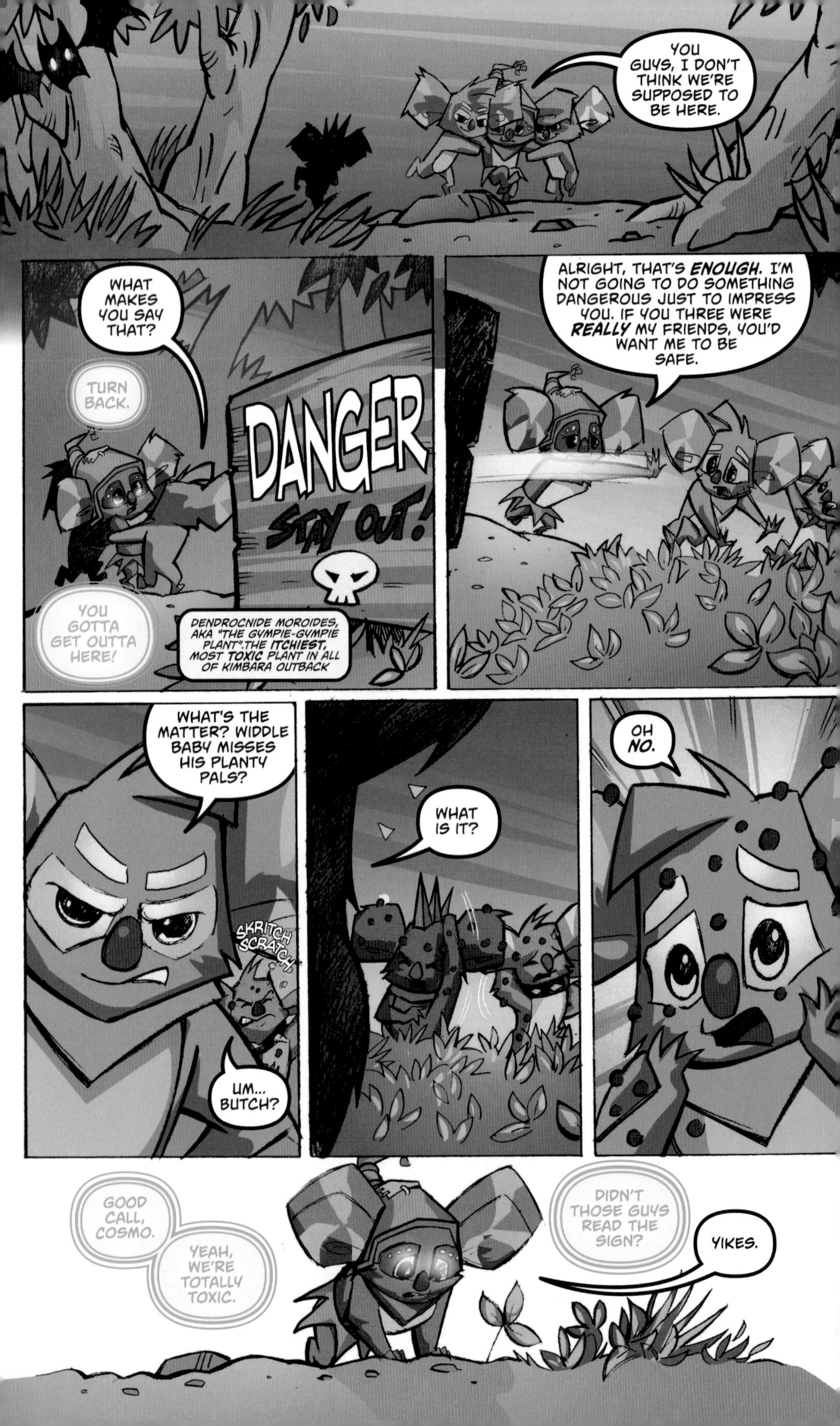
YOU GUYS, I DON'T THINK WE'RE SUPPOSED TO BE HERE.
WHAT MAKES YOU SAY THAT?
TURN BACK.
DANGER
STAY OUT!
YOU GOTTA GET OUTTA HERE!
DENDROCNIDE MOROIDES, AKA "THE GYMPIE-GYMPIE PLANT". THE ITCHIEST, MOST TOXIC PLANT IN ALL OF KIMBARA OUTBACK
ALRIGHT, THAT'S ENOUGH. I'M NOT GOING TO DO SOMETHING DANGEROUS JUST TO IMPRESS YOU. IF YOU THREE WERE REALLY MY FRIENDS, YOU'D WANT ME TO BE SAFE.
WHAT'S THE MATTER? WIDDLE BABY MISSES HIS PLANTY PALS?
SKRITCH SCRATCH
UM... BUTCH?
WHAT IS IT?
OH NO.
GOOD CALL, COSMO.
YEAH, WE'RE TOTALLY TOXIC.
DIDN'T THOSE GUYS READ THE SIGN?
YIKES.

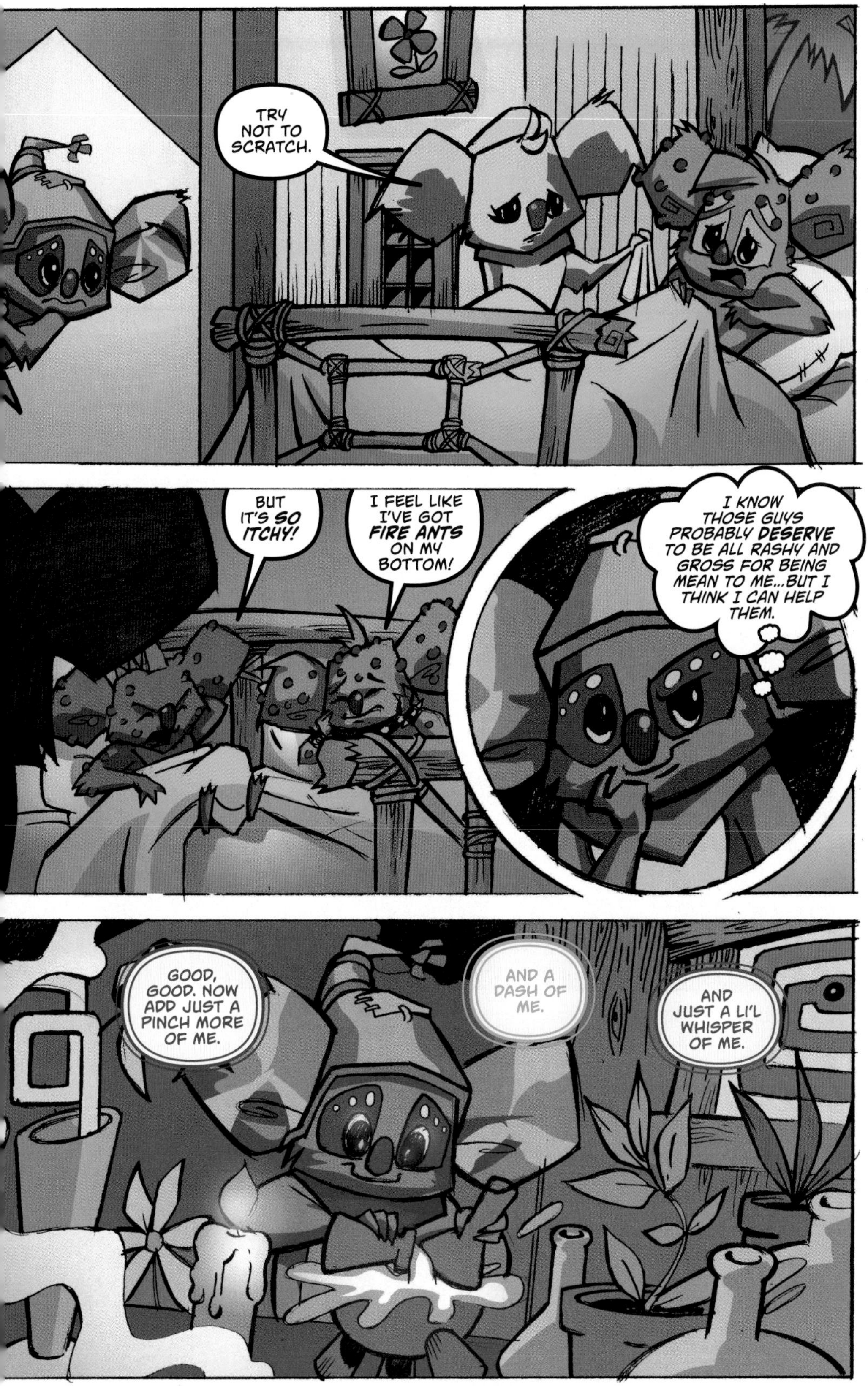
TRY NOT TO SCRATCH.
BUT IT'S **SO** ***ITCHY!***
I FEEL LIKE I'VE GOT ***FIRE ANTS*** ON MY BOTTOM!
*I KNOW THOSE GUYS PROBABLY **DESERVE** TO BE ALL RASHY AND GROSS FOR BEING MEAN TO ME...BUT I THINK I CAN HELP THEM.*
GOOD, GOOD. NOW ADD JUST A PINCH MORE OF ME.
AND A DASH OF ME.
AND JUST A LI'L WHISPER OF ME.

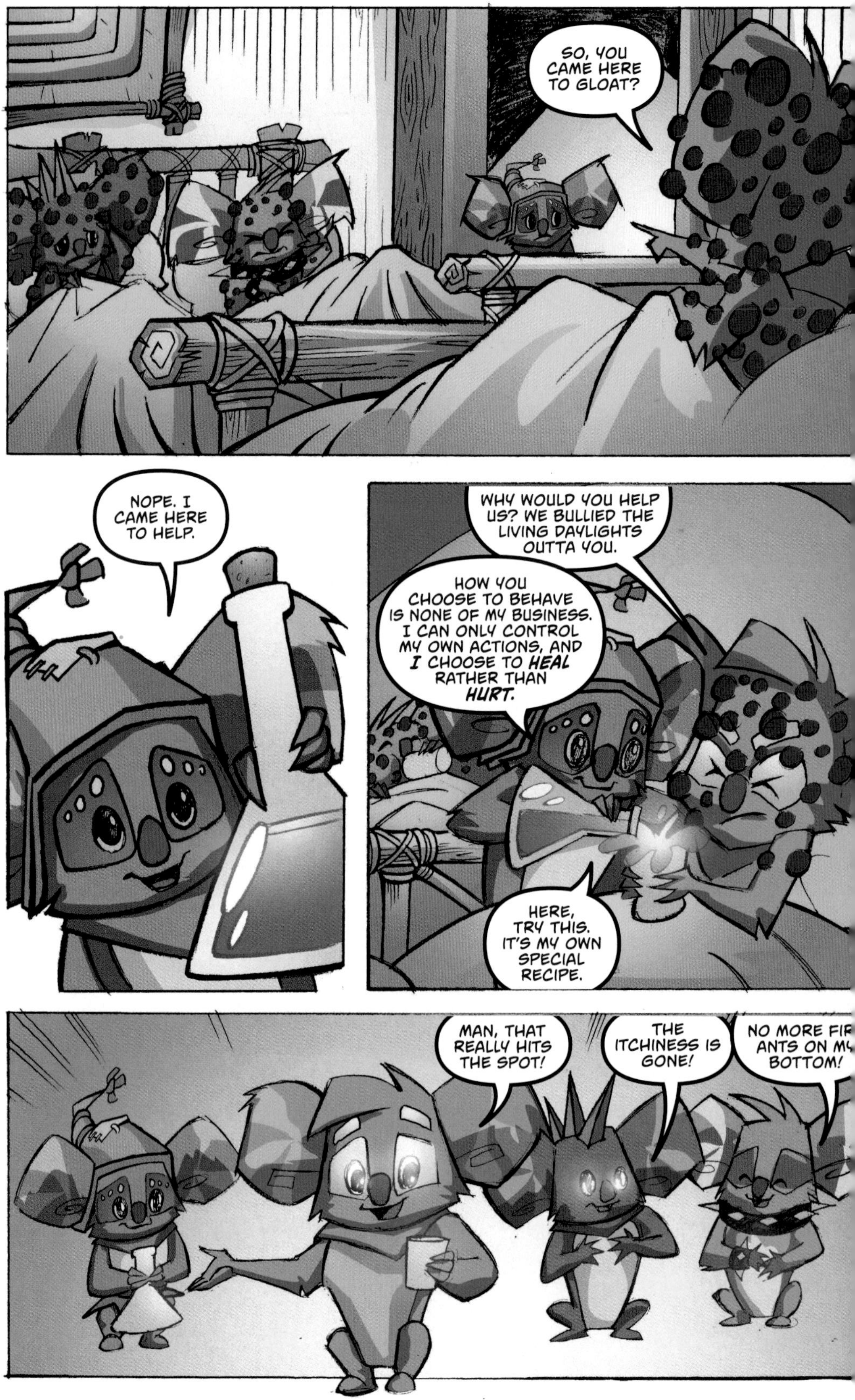
SO, YOU CAME HERE TO GLOAT?
NOPE. I CAME HERE TO HELP.
WHY WOULD YOU HELP US? WE BULLIED THE LIVING DAYLIGHTS OUTTA YOU.
HOW YOU CHOOSE TO BEHAVE IS NONE OF MY BUSINESS. I CAN ONLY CONTROL MY OWN ACTIONS, AND *I* CHOOSE TO ***HEAL*** RATHER THAN ***HURT.***
HERE, TRY THIS. IT'S MY OWN SPECIAL RECIPE.
MAN, THAT REALLY HITS THE SPOT!
THE ITCHINESS IS GONE!
NO MORE FIR
ANTS ON MY
BOTTOM!

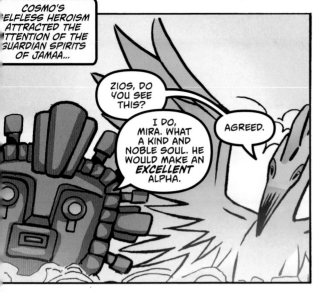

COSMO'S SELFLESS HEROISM ATTRACTED THE ATTENTION OF THE GUARDIAN SPIRITS OF JAMAA...
ZIOS, DO YOU SEE THIS?
I DO, MIRA. WHAT A KIND AND NOBLE SOUL. HE WOULD MAKE AN EXCELLENT ALPHA.
AGREED.
WHAT CAN I DO TO REPAY YOU?
MAYBE BE NICE TO EVERYONE FROM NOW ON? NO MORE BULLYING?
YOU GOT IT, COSMO!
GREETINGS!
MIRA! ZIOS! WHAT ARE THE GUARDIAN SPIRITS OF JAMAA DOING HERE?!
LOOKING FOR HEROES. AND WE BELIEVE WE'VE FOUND ONE...
WE HAVE OBSERVED YOUR NOBLE DEEDS COSMO, AND WE WOULD LIKE YOU TO HELP US ON A QUEST TO SAVE JAMAA AND ALL WHO LIVE HERE.
ME? ARE YOU SURE?
GO GET 'EM, COSMO!
YOU TOTALLY GOT THIS!
DO IT!
ALRIGHT, I'M IN!
A CHANCE TO HELP ALL THE ANIMALS IN JAMAA? HOW'D I GET SO LUCKY?

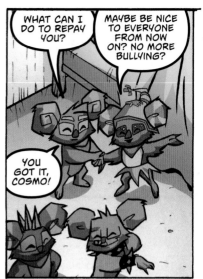

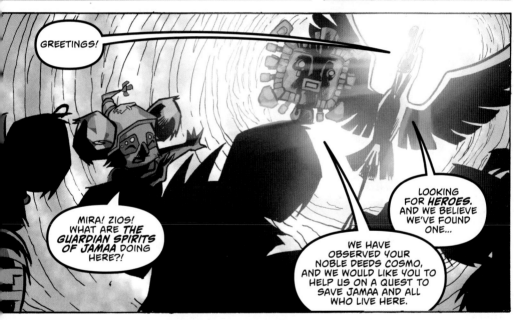

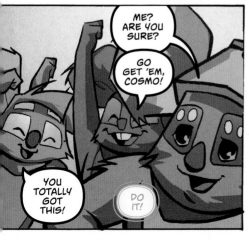

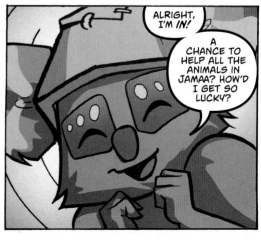

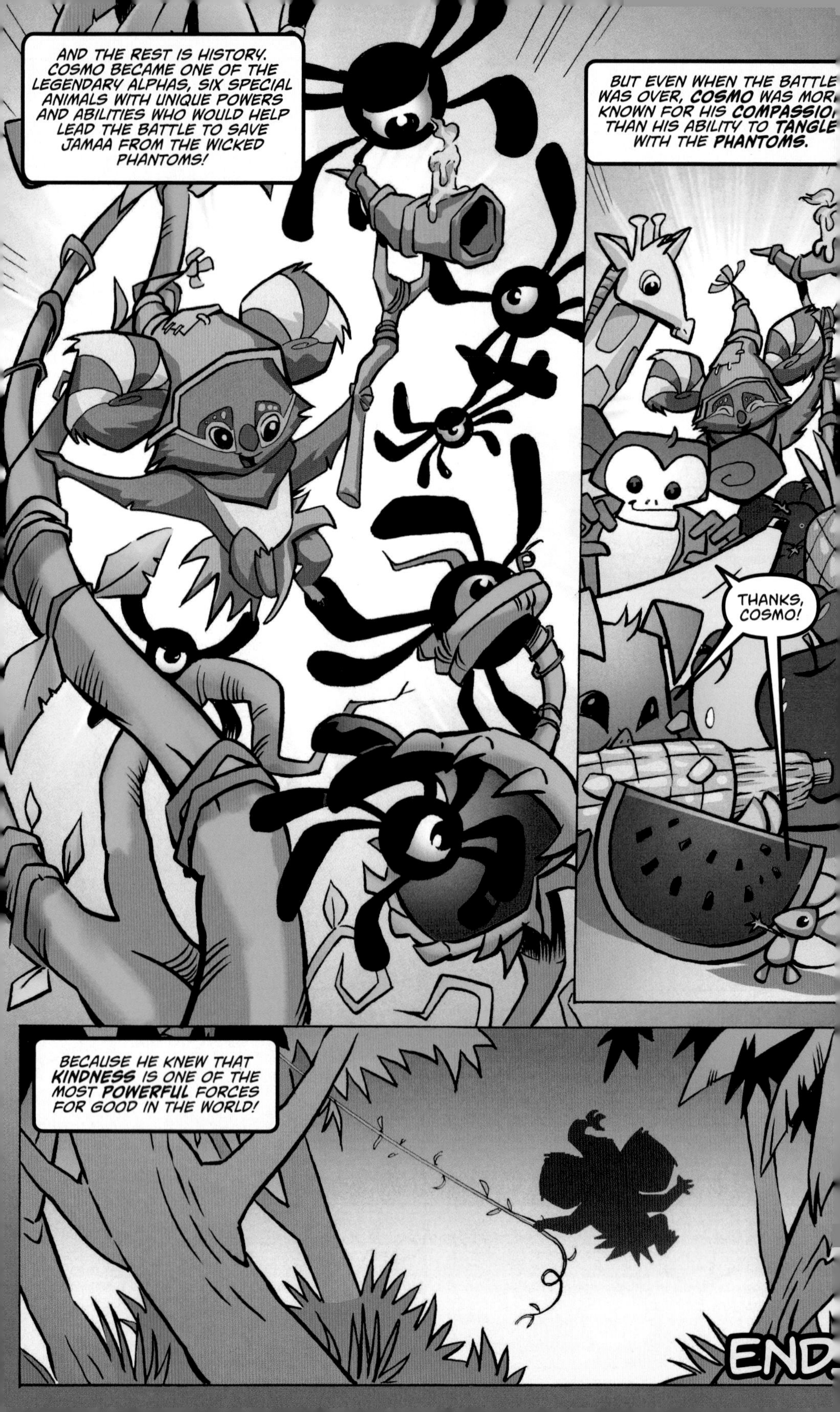
AND THE REST IS HISTORY. COSMO BECAME ONE OF THE LEGENDARY ALPHAS, SIX SPECIAL ANIMALS WITH UNIQUE POWERS AND ABILITIES WHO WOULD HELP LEAD THE BATTLE TO SAVE JAMAA FROM THE WICKED PHANTOMS!
BUT EVEN WHEN THE BATTLE WAS OVER, COSMO WAS MOR KNOWN FOR HIS COMPASSIO THAN HIS ABILITY TO TANGLE WITH THE PHANTOMS.
THANKS, COSMO!
BECAUSE HE KNEW THAT KINDNESS IS ONE OF THE MOST POWERFUL FORCES FOR GOOD IN THE WORLD!
END

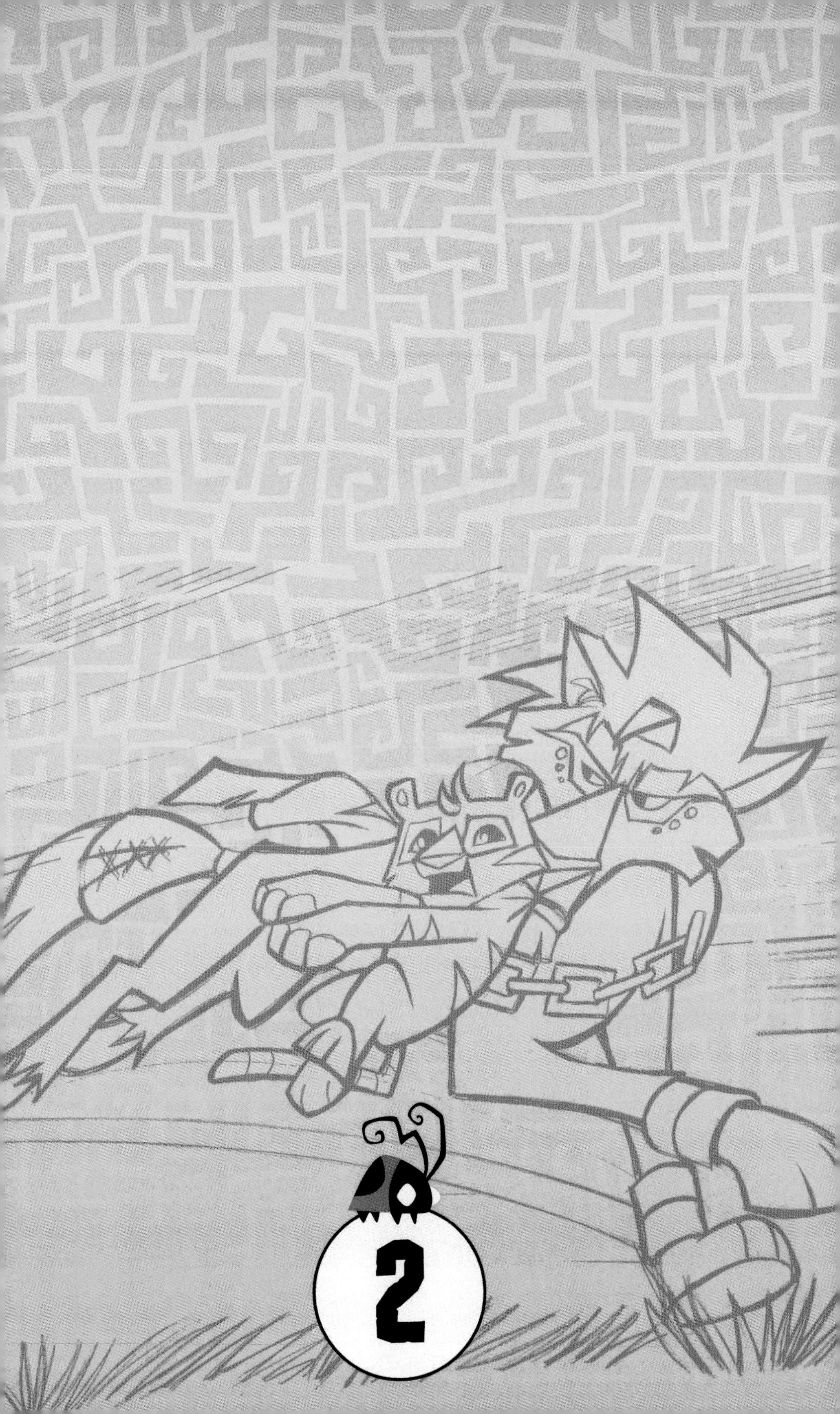
2

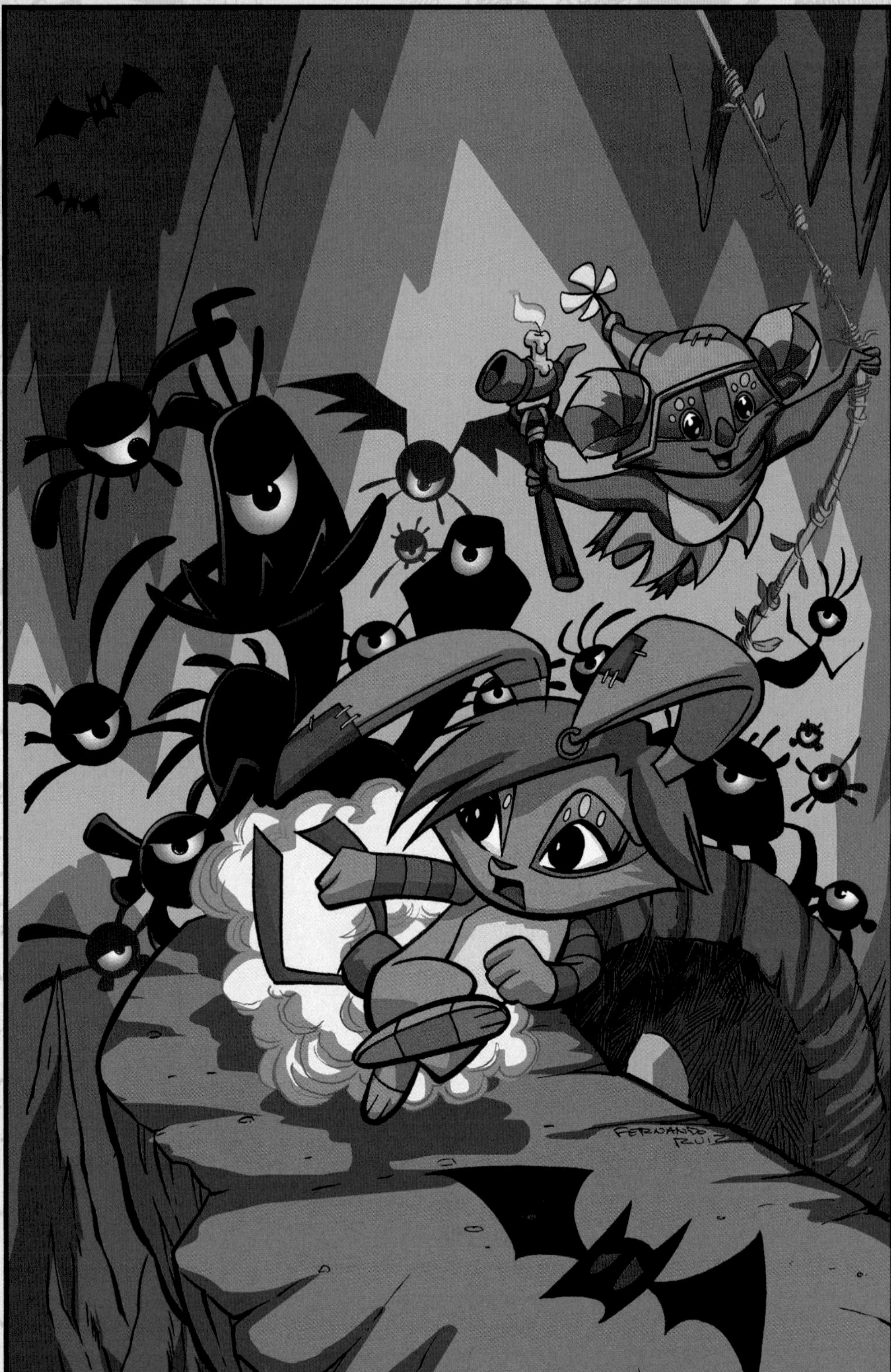
FERNANDO RUIZ

Issue #2: Cover Art by FERNANDO RUIZ & PETE PANTAZIS

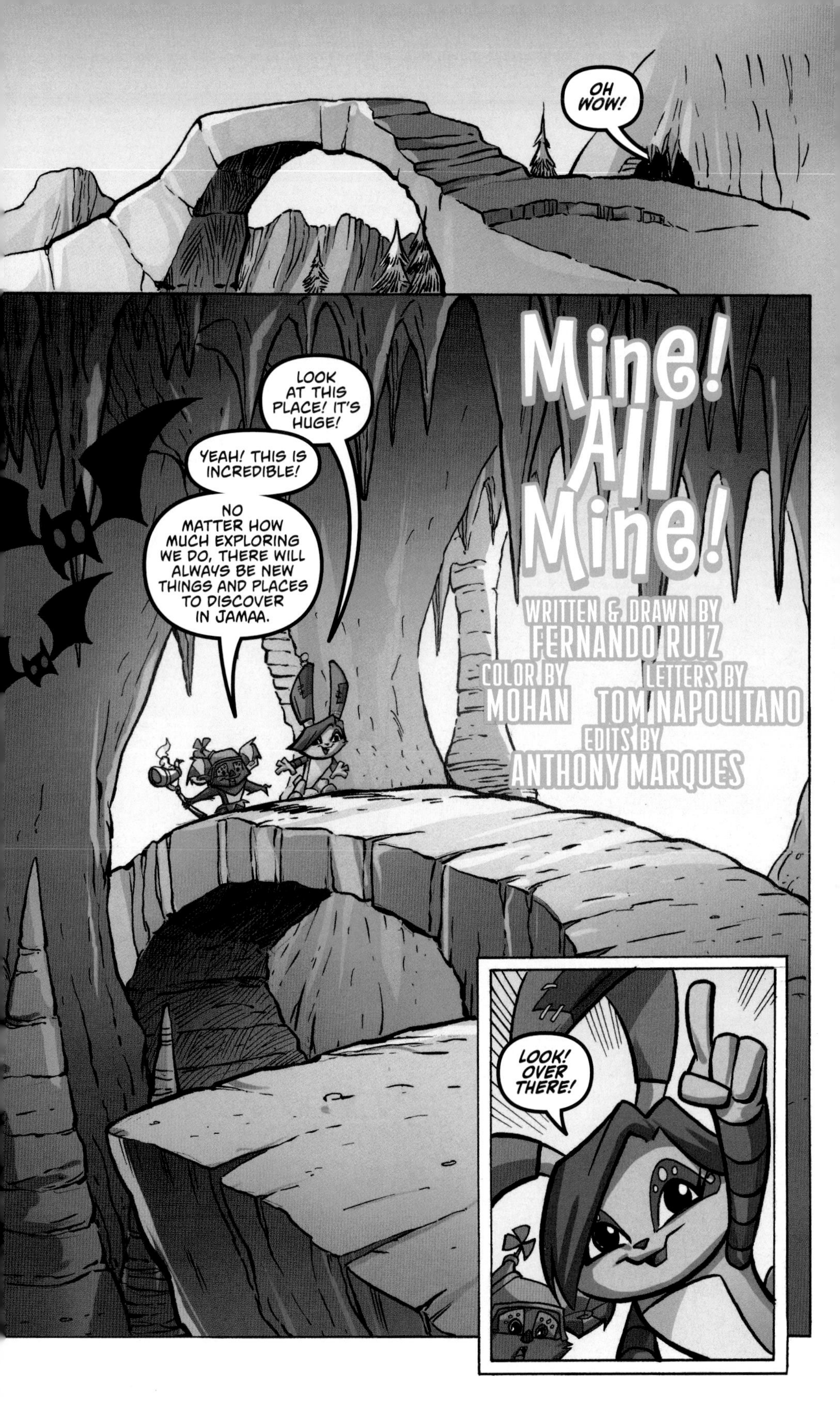
OH WOW!
LOOK AT THIS PLACE! IT'S HUGE!
YEAH! THIS IS INCREDIBLE!
NO MATTER HOW MUCH EXPLORING WE DO, THERE WILL ALWAYS BE NEW THINGS AND PLACES TO DISCOVER IN JAMAA.
Mine! All Mine!
WRITTEN & DRAWN BY FERNANDO RUIZ
COLOR BY MOHAN
LETTERS BY TOM NAPOLITANO
EDITS BY ANTHONY MARQUES
LOOK! OVER THERE!

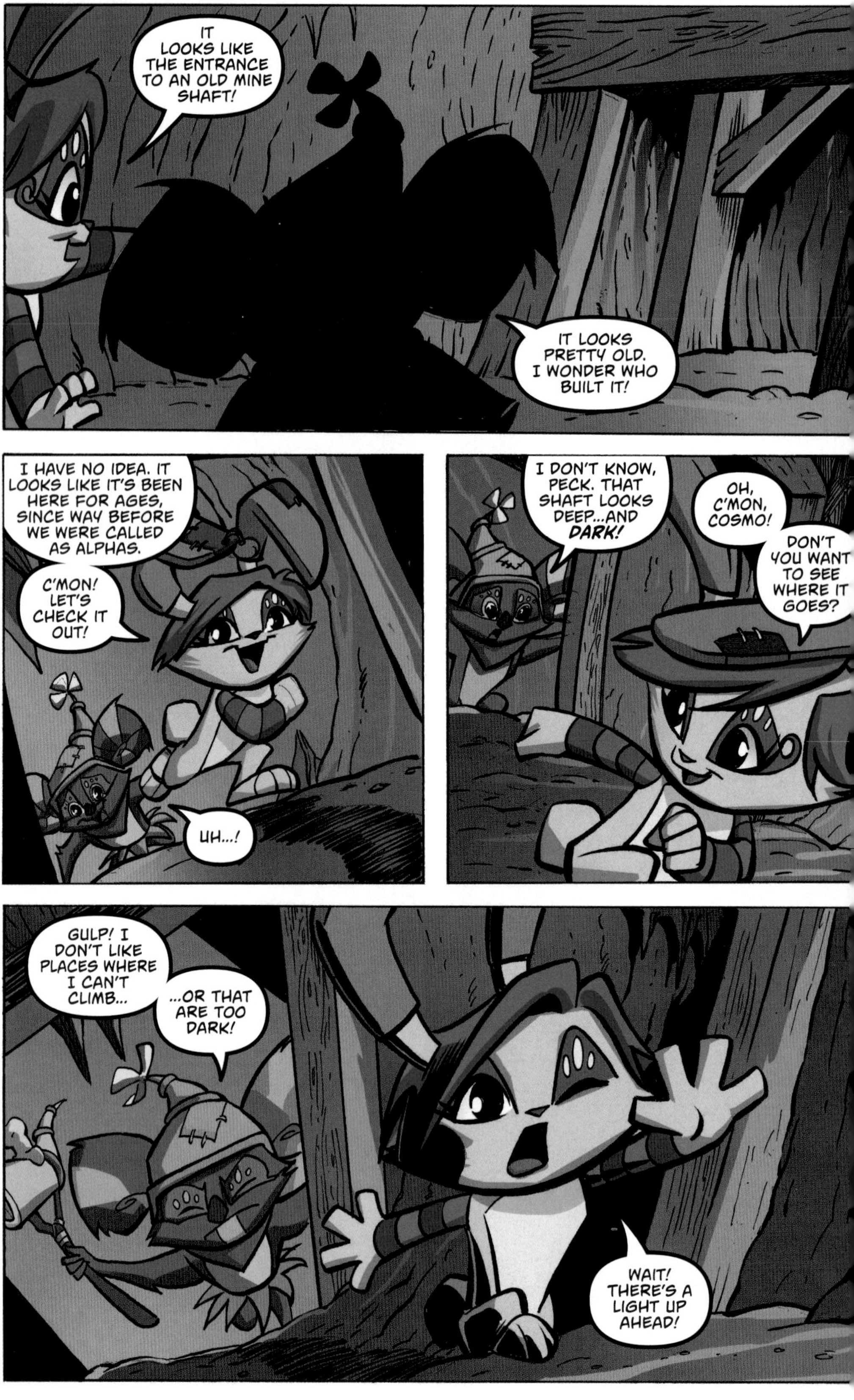

IT LOOKS LIKE THE ENTRANCE TO AN OLD MINE SHAFT!
IT LOOKS PRETTY OLD. I WONDER WHO BUILT IT!
I HAVE NO IDEA. IT LOOKS LIKE IT'S BEEN HERE FOR AGES, SINCE WAY BEFORE WE WERE CALLED AS ALPHAS.
C'MON! LET'S CHECK IT OUT!
UH...!
I DON'T KNOW, PECK. THAT SHAFT LOOKS DEEP...AND DARK!
OH, C'MON, COSMO!
DON'T YOU WANT TO SEE WHERE IT GOES?
GULP! I DON'T LIKE PLACES WHERE I CAN'T CLIMB...
...OR THAT ARE TOO DARK!
WAIT! THERE'S A LIGHT UP AHEAD!

COSMO! LOOK! IT'S A JEWEL OF SOME KIND...AND IT GLOWS!

IT'S BEAUTIFUL. I WONDER...

UH, PECK...? WHAT'S *THAT?*

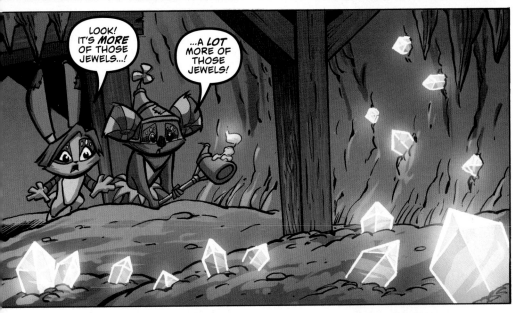

LOOK! IT'S *MORE* OF THOSE JEWELS...!

...A *LOT* MORE OF THOSE JEWELS!

JUST IMAGINE ALL THE FUN WE COULD HAVE WITH THESE IF WE TOOK THEM BACK TO JAMAA TOWNSHIP!

EVERYONE WOULD LOOK SO COOL WEARING THEM!

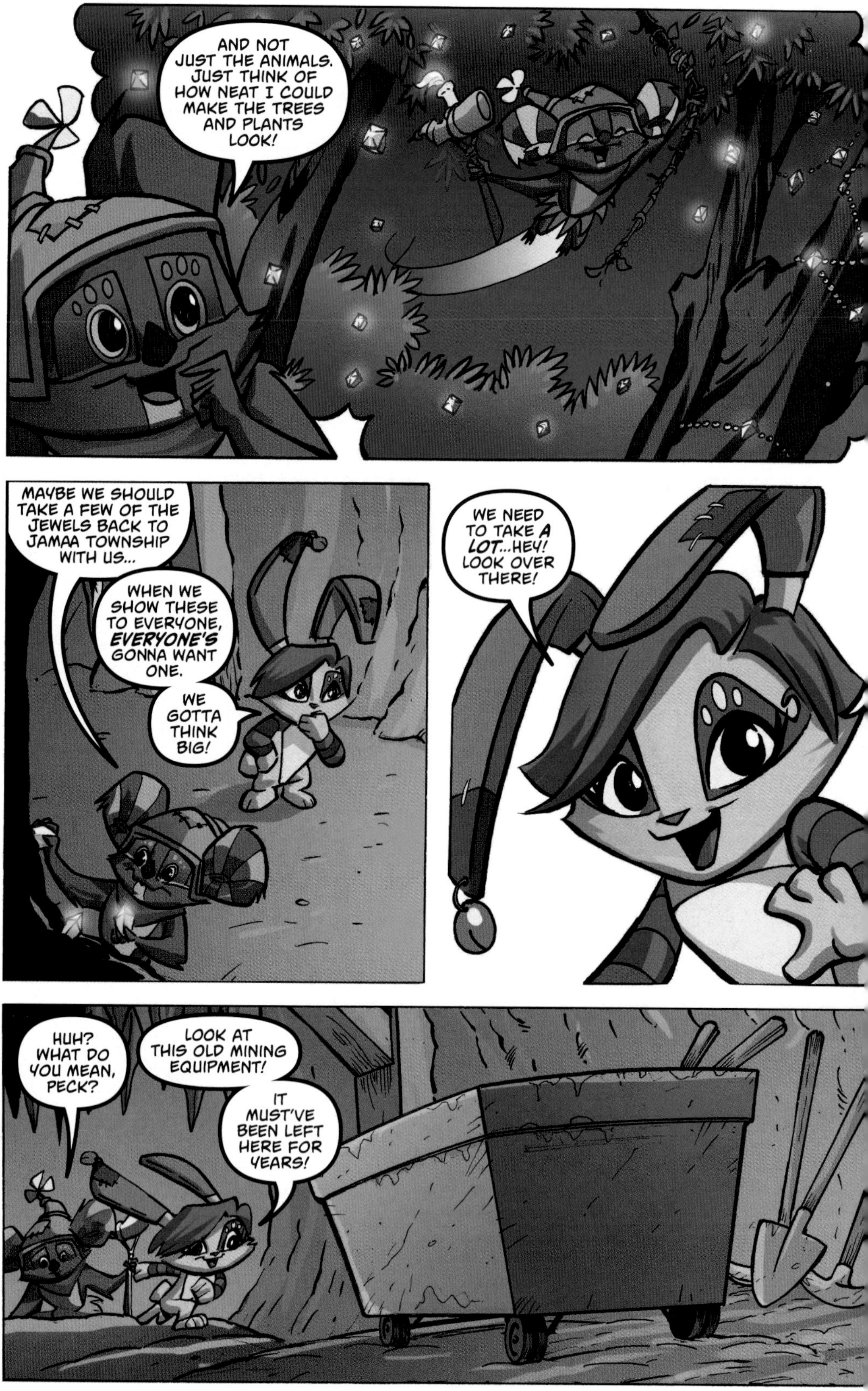
AND NOT JUST THE ANIMALS. JUST THINK OF HOW NEAT I COULD MAKE THE TREES AND PLANTS LOOK!
MAYBE WE SHOULD TAKE A FEW OF THE JEWELS BACK TO JAMAA TOWNSHIP WITH US...
WHEN WE SHOW THESE TO EVERYONE, EVERYONE'S GONNA WANT ONE.
WE GOTTA THINK BIG!
WE NEED TO TAKE A LOT...HEY! LOOK OVER THERE!
HUH? WHAT DO YOU MEAN, PECK?
LOOK AT THIS OLD MINING EQUIPMENT!
IT MUST'VE BEEN LEFT HERE FOR YEARS!

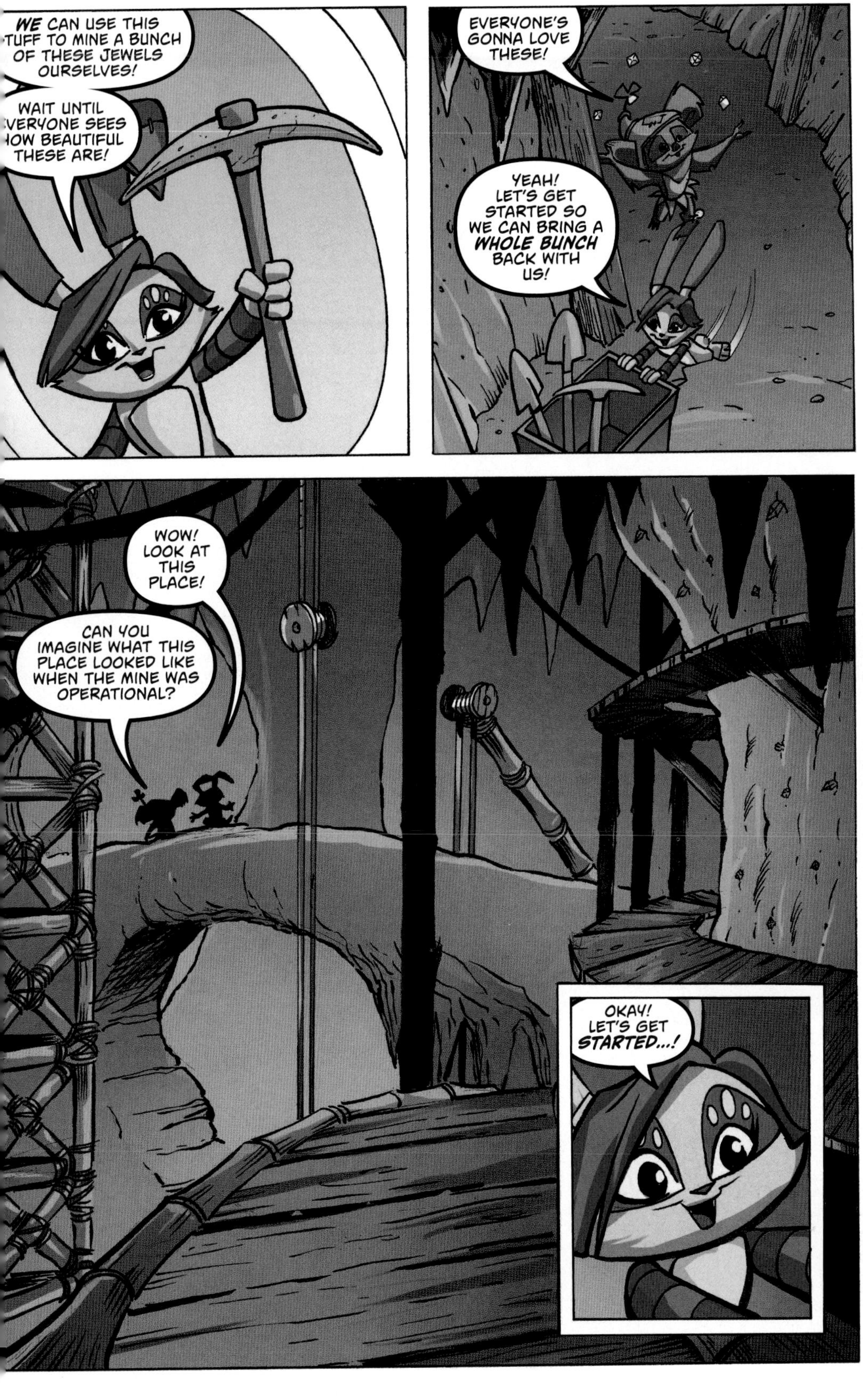
WE CAN USE THIS TUFF TO MINE A BUNCH OF THESE JEWELS OURSELVES!
WAIT UNTIL EVERYONE SEES HOW BEAUTIFUL THESE ARE!
EVERYONE'S GONNA LOVE THESE!
YEAH! LET'S GET STARTED SO WE CAN BRING A WHOLE BUNCH BACK WITH US!
WOW! LOOK AT THIS PLACE!
CAN YOU IMAGINE WHAT THIS PLACE LOOKED LIKE WHEN THE MINE WAS OPERATIONAL?
OKAY! LET'S GET STARTED...!

AND LATER...
OH BOY! WHATTA HAUL!
WE'VE COLLECTED ENOUGH JEWELS FOR ALL OF OUR BUDDIES BACK HOME!
NOT JUST OUR BUDDIES. WE HAVE ENOUGH FOR EVERYONE!
MAYBE WE SHOULD PACK OF FEW OF THESE JEWELS ASIDE FOR A PEACE OFFERING THE NEXT TIME WE'RE ATTACKED BY...
...PHANTOMS!!!
PHANTOMS! LOTS OF 'EM!
LET'S GET OUTTA HERE!
MAYBE WE SHOULD TRY YOUR PEACE OFFERING IDEA!

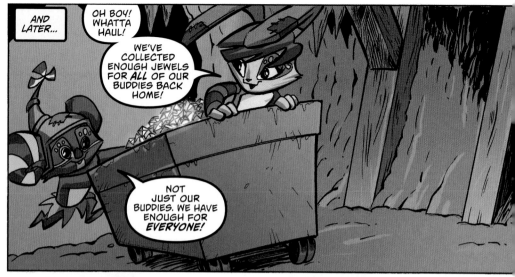

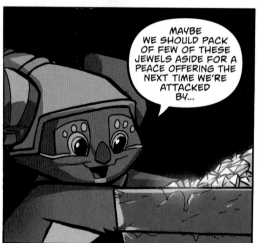

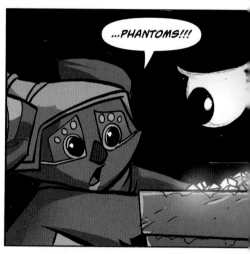

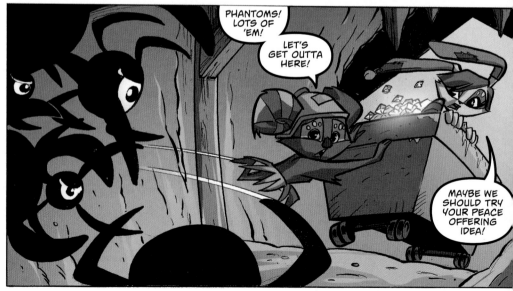

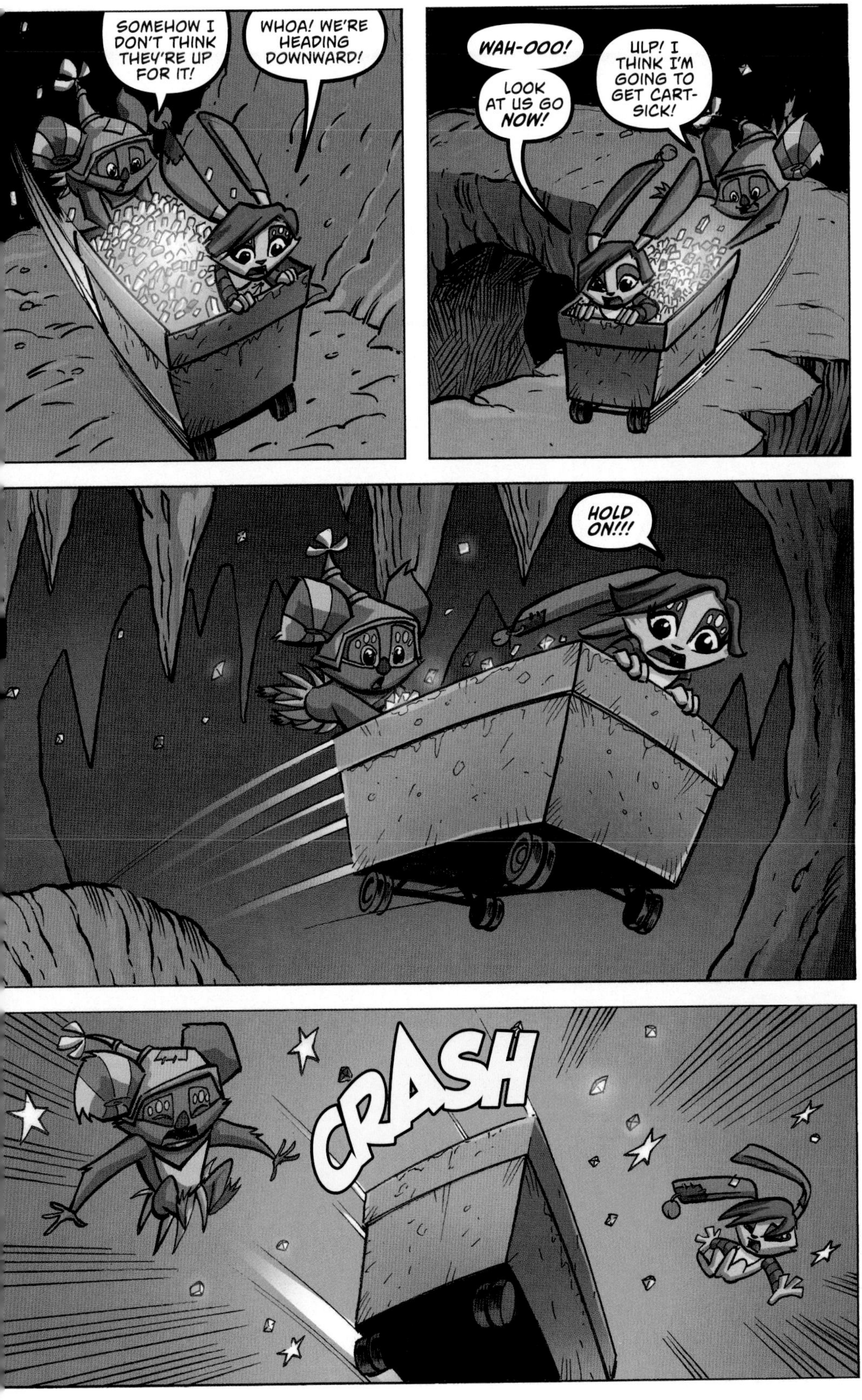
SOMEHOW I DON'T THINK THEY'RE UP FOR IT!
WHOA! WE'RE HEADING DOWNWARD!
WAH-OOO!
LOOK AT US GO NOW!
ULP! I THINK I'M GOING TO GET CART-SICK!
HOLD ON!!!
CRASH

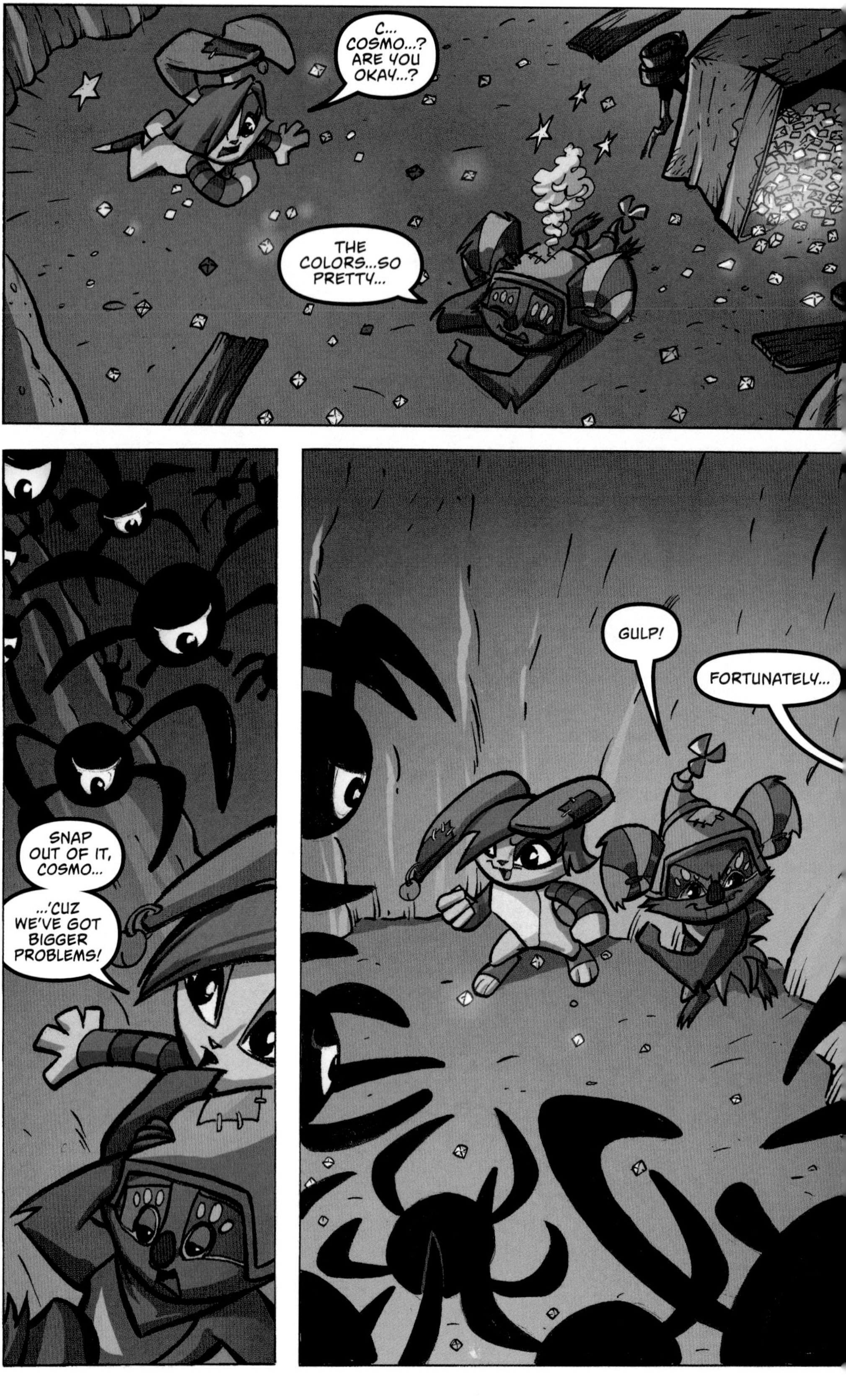
C... COSMO...? ARE YOU OKAY...?
THE COLORS...SO PRETTY...
SNAP OUT OF IT, COSMO...
...'CUZ WE'VE GOT BIGGER PROBLEMS!
GULP!
FORTUNATELY...

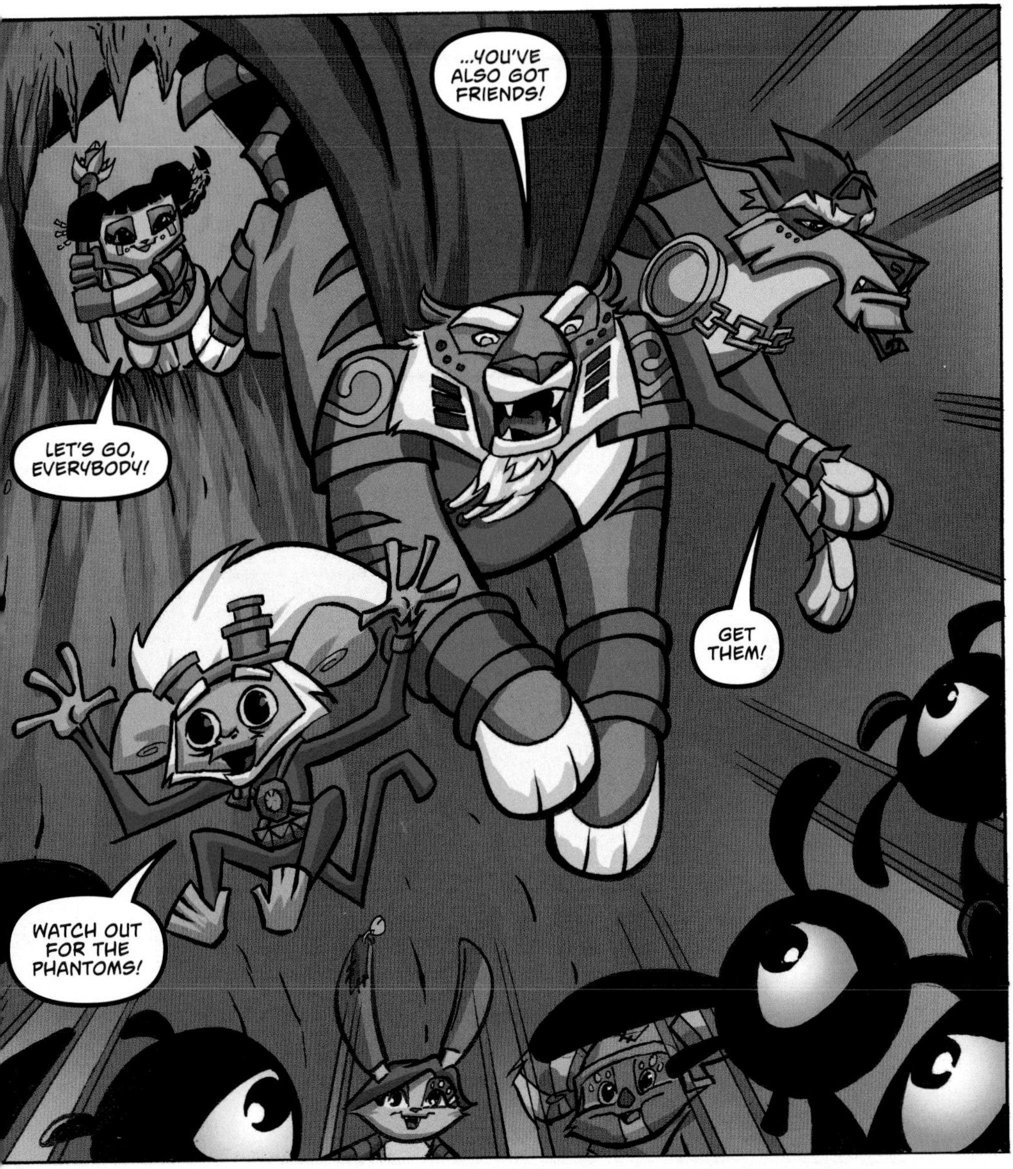
...YOU'VE ALSO GOT FRIENDS!
LET'S GO, EVERYBODY!
GET THEM!
WATCH OUT FOR THE PHANTOMS!

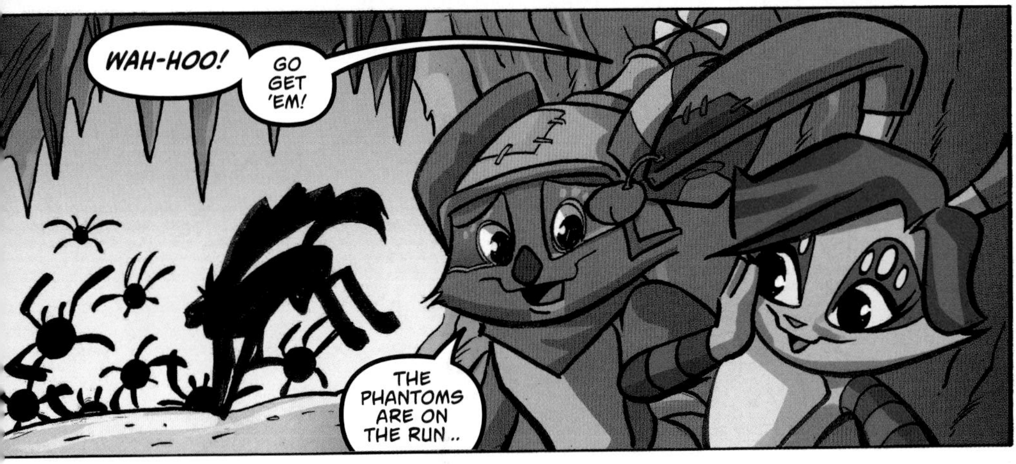
WAH-HOO!
GO GET 'EM!
THE PHANTOMS ARE ON THE RUN ..

THEY NO DOUBT WILL MAKE A STRATEGIC WITHDRAWAL!

SIR GILBERT! BUT HOW DID YOU KNOW WE WERE IN TROUBLE?

SOME OF OUR FRIENDS TOLD US WHAT YOU TWO WERE UP TO.

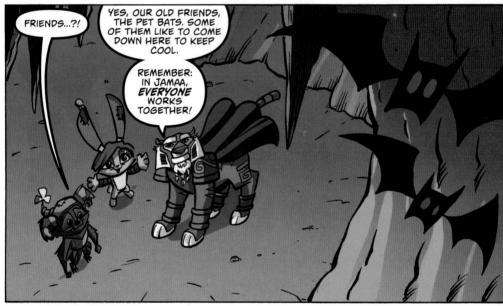

FRIENDS...?!

YES, OUR OLD FRIENDS, THE PET BATS. SOME OF THEM LIKE TO COME DOWN HERE TO KEEP COOL.

REMEMBER: IN JAMAA, *EVERYONE* WORKS TOGETHER!

I GUESS WE FORGOT ALL ABOUT TEAMWORK!

...AND OF HOW WE CAN COME TOGETHER FOR EACH OTHER WHEN WE NEED TO.

NOW REALIZING *THAT* IS A *REAL* TREASURE!

YEAH! AND WE CAN GET THAT ONE WITH A WHOLE LOT LESS DIGGING!

END

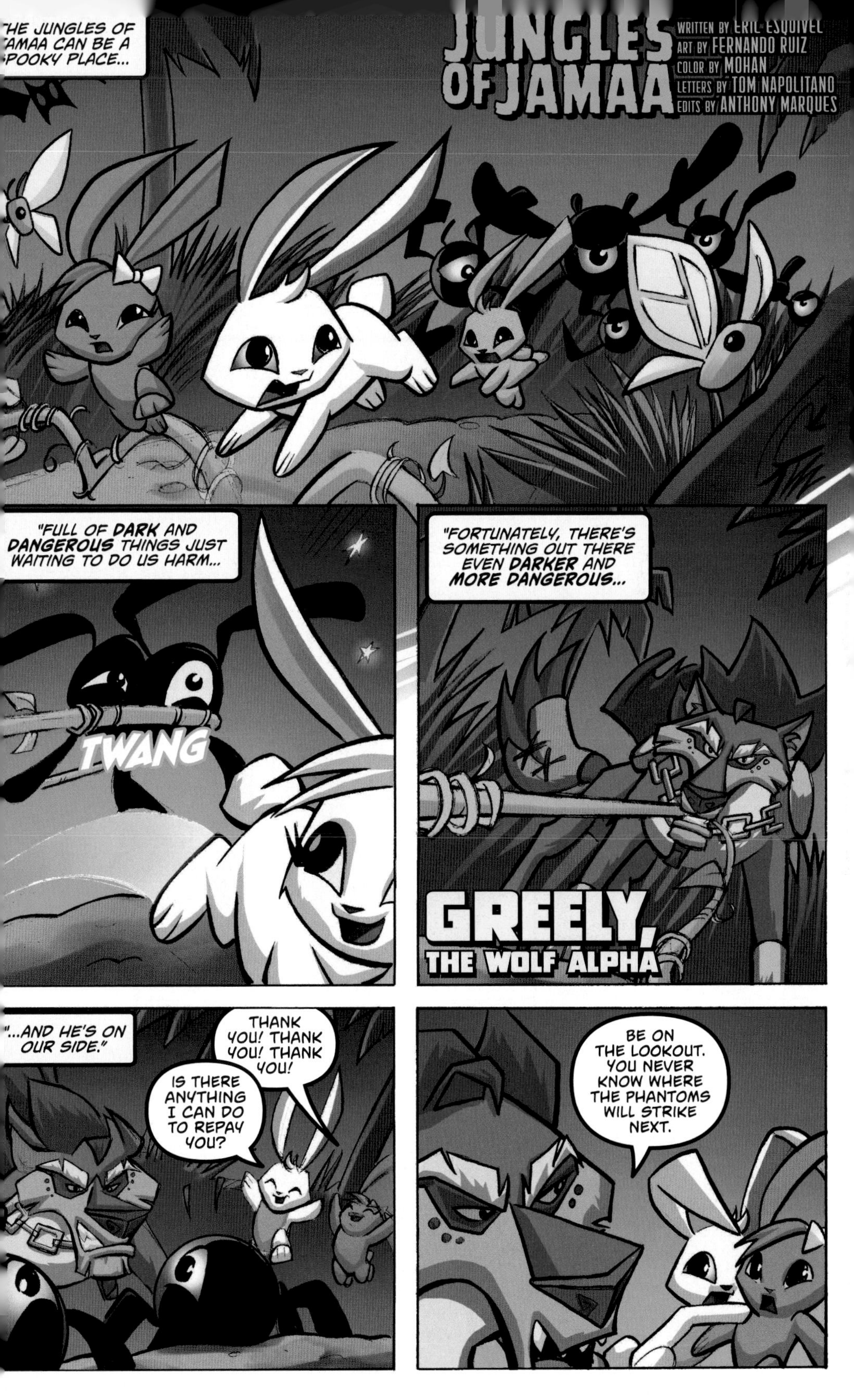

THE JUNGLES OF JAMAA CAN BE A SPOOKY PLACE...
JUNGLES OF JAMAA
WRITTEN BY ERIC ESQUIVEL
ART BY FERNANDO RUIZ
COLOR BY MOHAN
LETTERS BY TOM NAPOLITANO
EDITS BY ANTHONY MARQUES
"FULL OF DARK AND DANGEROUS THINGS JUST WAITING TO DO US HARM...
TWANG
"FORTUNATELY, THERE'S SOMETHING OUT THERE EVEN DARKER AND MORE DANGEROUS...
GREELY, THE WOLF ALPHA
"...AND HE'S ON OUR SIDE."
THANK YOU! THANK YOU! THANK YOU!
IS THERE ANYTHING I CAN DO TO REPAY YOU?
BE ON THE LOOKOUT. YOU NEVER KNOW WHERE THE PHANTOMS WILL STRIKE NEXT.

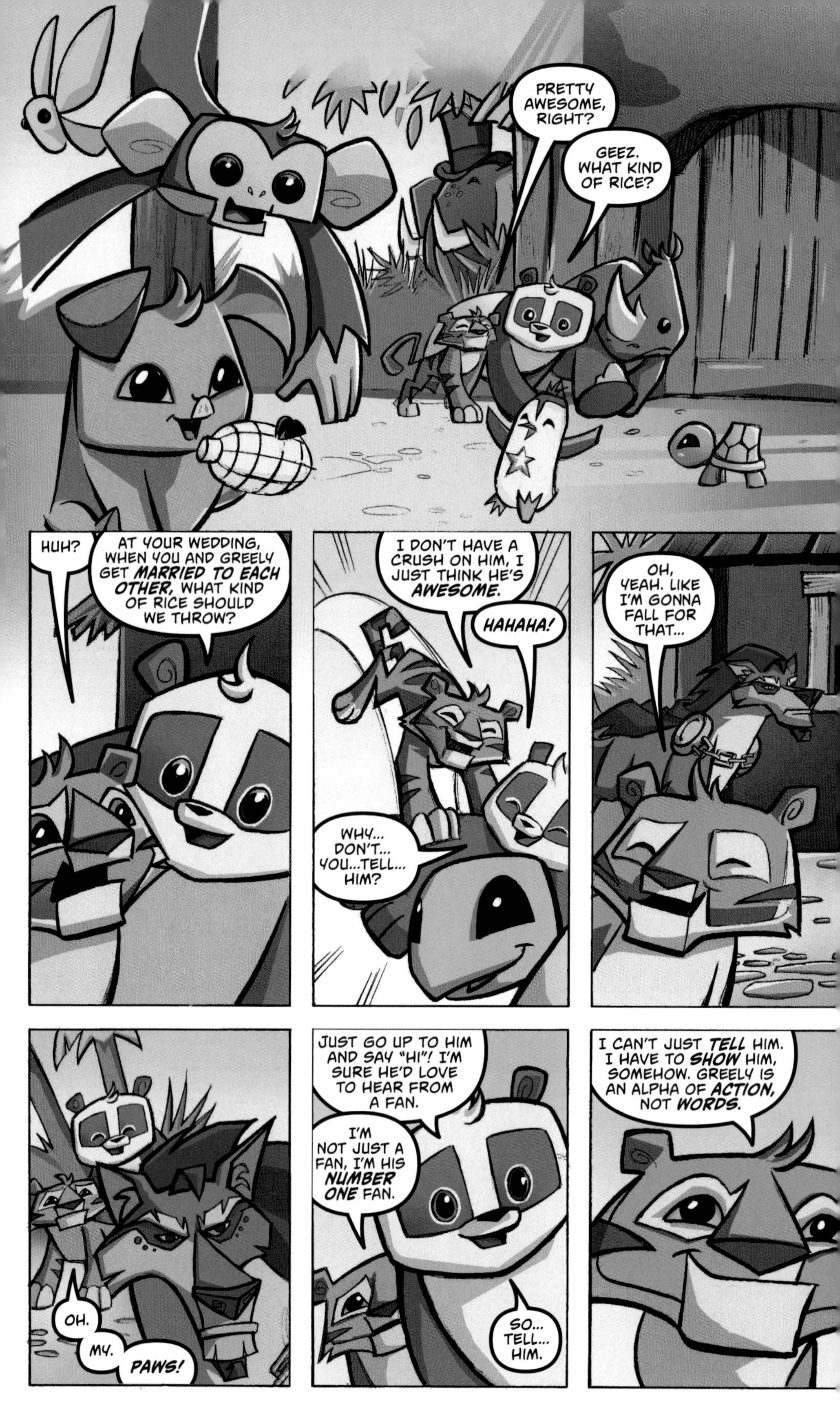
PRETTY AWESOME, RIGHT?
GEEZ. WHAT KIND OF RICE?
HUH?
AT YOUR WEDDING, WHEN YOU AND GREELY GET MARRIED TO EACH OTHER, WHAT KIND OF RICE SHOULD WE THROW?
I DON'T HAVE A CRUSH ON HIM, I JUST THINK HE'S AWESOME.
HAHAHA!
WHY... DON'T... YOU...TELL... HIM?
OH, YEAH. LIKE I'M GONNA FALL FOR THAT...
OH.
MY.
PAWS!
JUST GO UP TO HIM AND SAY "HI"! I'M SURE HE'D LOVE TO HEAR FROM A FAN.
I'M NOT JUST A FAN, I'M HIS NUMBER ONE FAN.
SO... TELL... HIM.
I CAN'T JUST TELL HIM. I HAVE TO SHOW HIM, SOMEHOW. GREELY IS AN ALPHA OF ACTION, NOT WORDS.

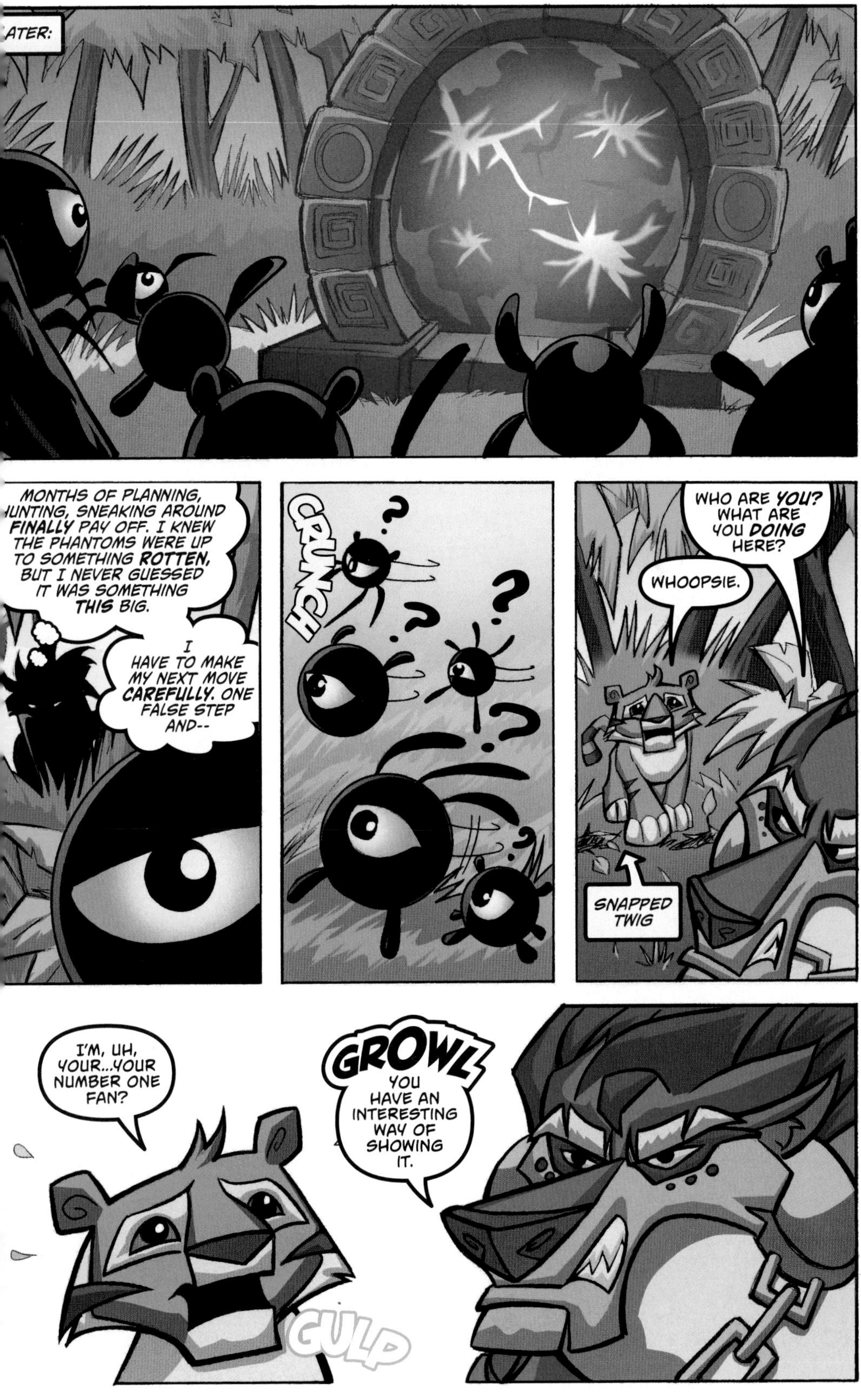
ATER:
MONTHS OF PLANNING, HUNTING, SNEAKING AROUND FINALLY PAY OFF. I KNEW THE PHANTOMS WERE UP TO SOMETHING ROTTEN, BUT I NEVER GUESSED IT WAS SOMETHING THIS BIG.
I HAVE TO MAKE MY NEXT MOVE CAREFULLY. ONE FALSE STEP AND--
CRUNCH
WHO ARE YOU? WHAT ARE YOU DOING HERE?
WHOOPSIE.
SNAPPED TWIG
I'M, UH, YOUR...YOUR NUMBER ONE FAN?
GROWL
YOU HAVE AN INTERESTING WAY OF SHOWING IT.
GULP

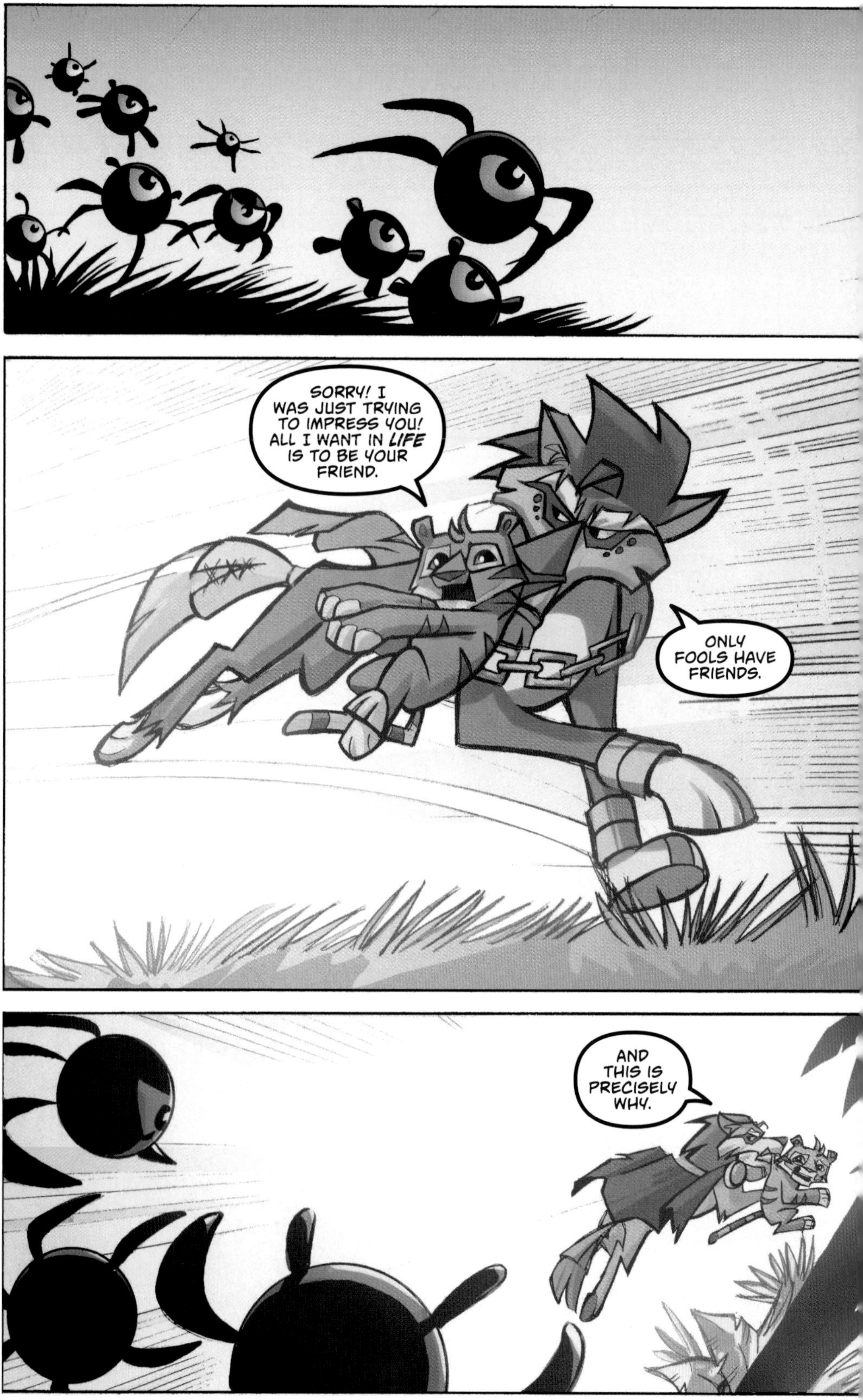
SORRY! I WAS JUST TRYING TO IMPRESS YOU! ALL I WANT IN LIFE IS TO BE YOUR FRIEND.
ONLY FOOLS HAVE FRIENDS.
AND THIS IS PRECISELY WHY.

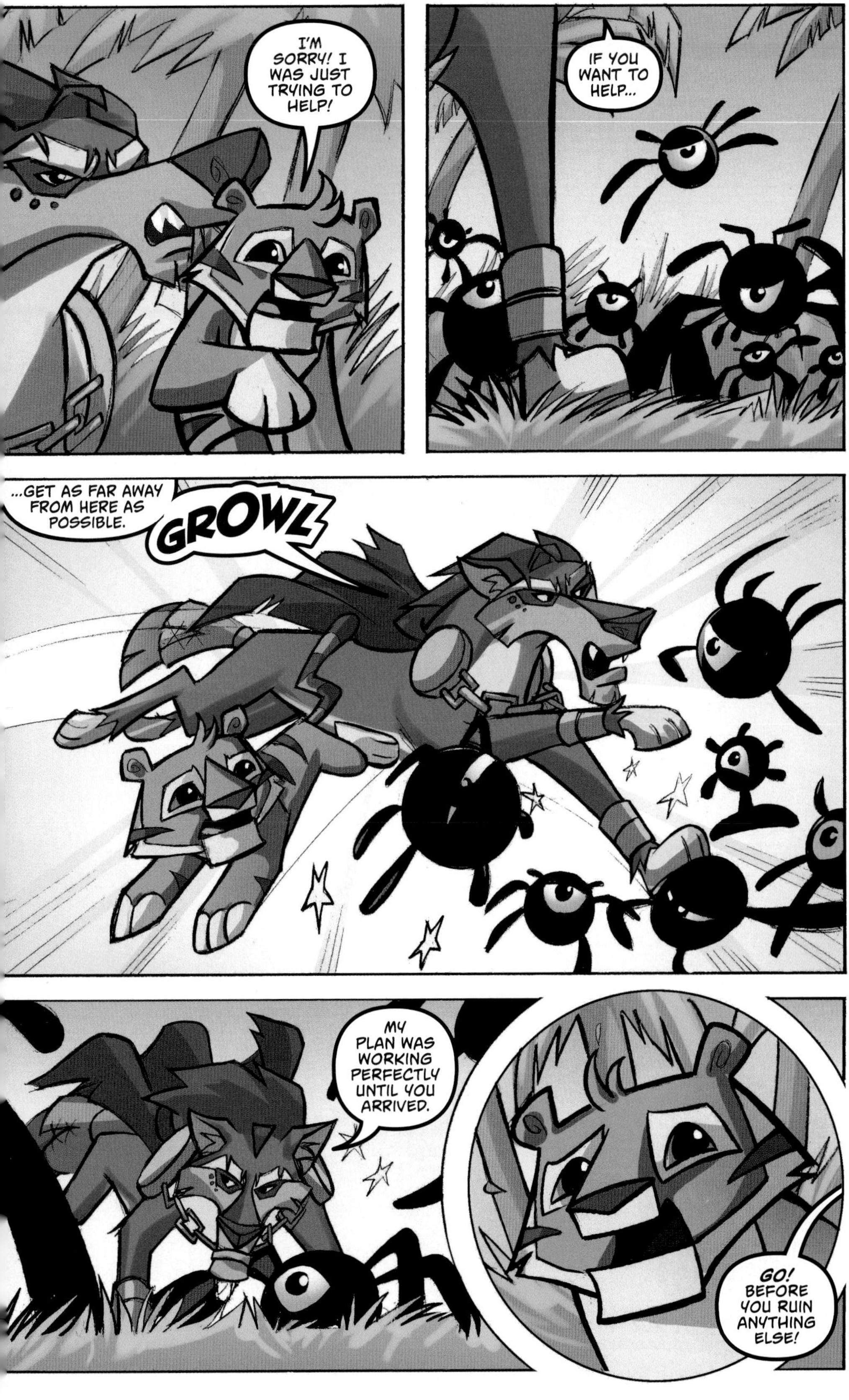
I'M SORRY! I WAS JUST TRYING TO HELP!
IF YOU WANT TO HELP...
...GET AS FAR AWAY FROM HERE AS POSSIBLE.
GROWL
MY PLAN WAS WORKING PERFECTLY UNTIL YOU ARRIVED.
GO! BEFORE YOU RUIN ANYTHING ELSE!

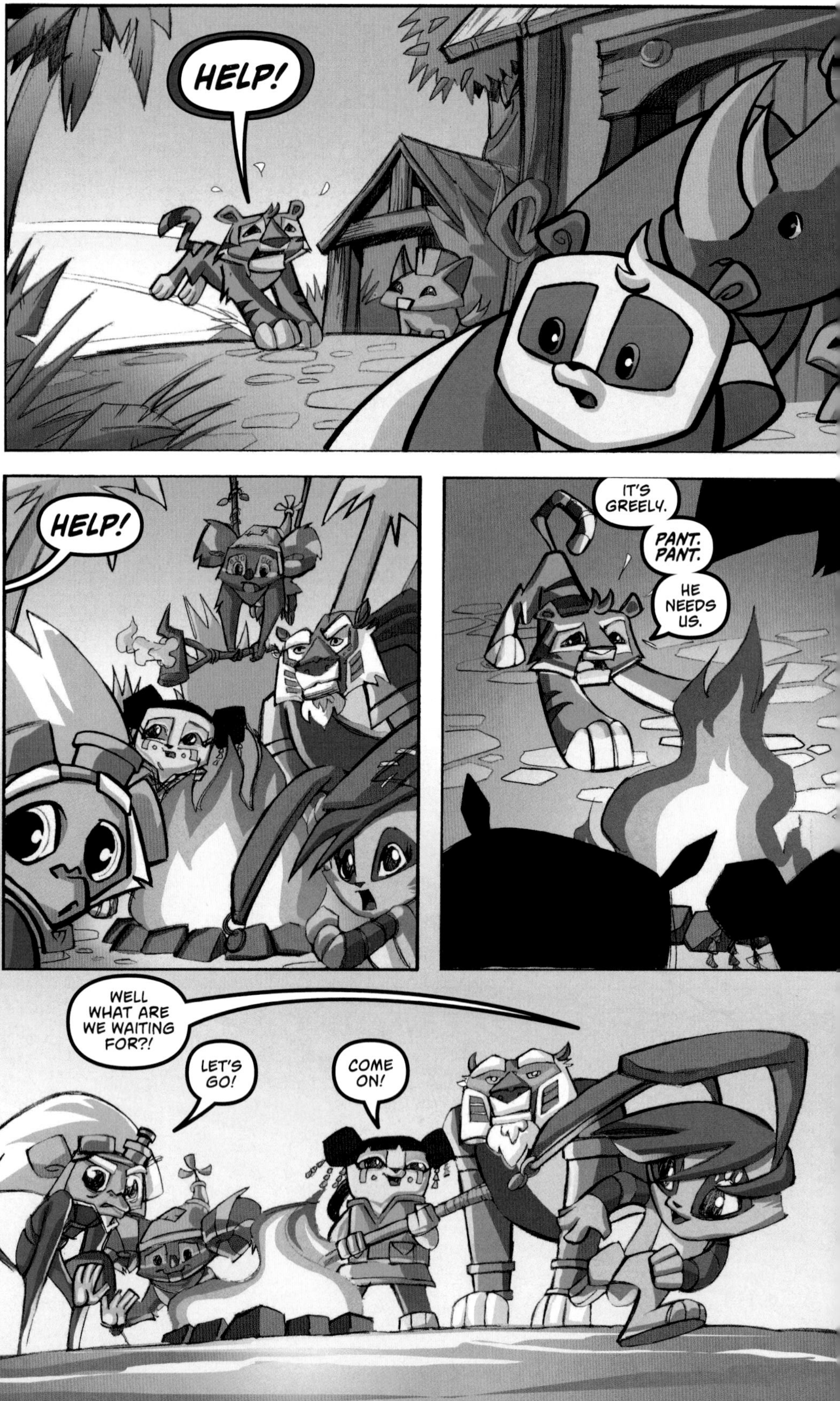
HELP!
HELP!
IT'S GREELY.
PANT. PANT.
HE NEEDS US.
WELL WHAT ARE WE WAITING FOR?!
LET'S GO!
COME ON!

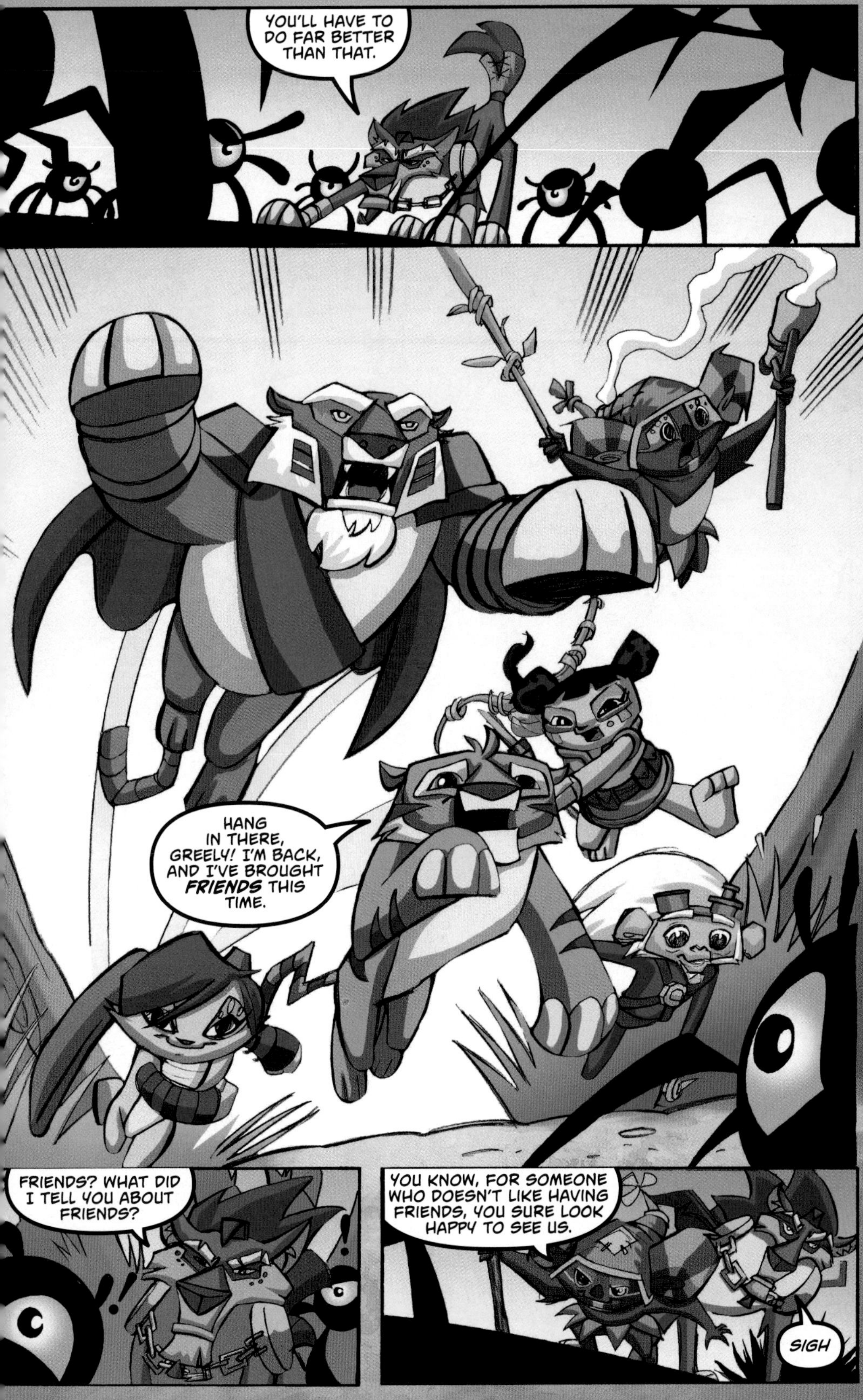
YOU'LL HAVE TO DO FAR BETTER THAN THAT.
HANG IN THERE, GREELY! I'M BACK, AND I'VE BROUGHT *FRIENDS* THIS TIME.
FRIENDS? WHAT DID I TELL YOU ABOUT FRIENDS?
YOU KNOW, FOR SOMEONE WHO DOESN'T LIKE HAVING FRIENDS, YOU SURE LOOK HAPPY TO SEE US.
SIGH

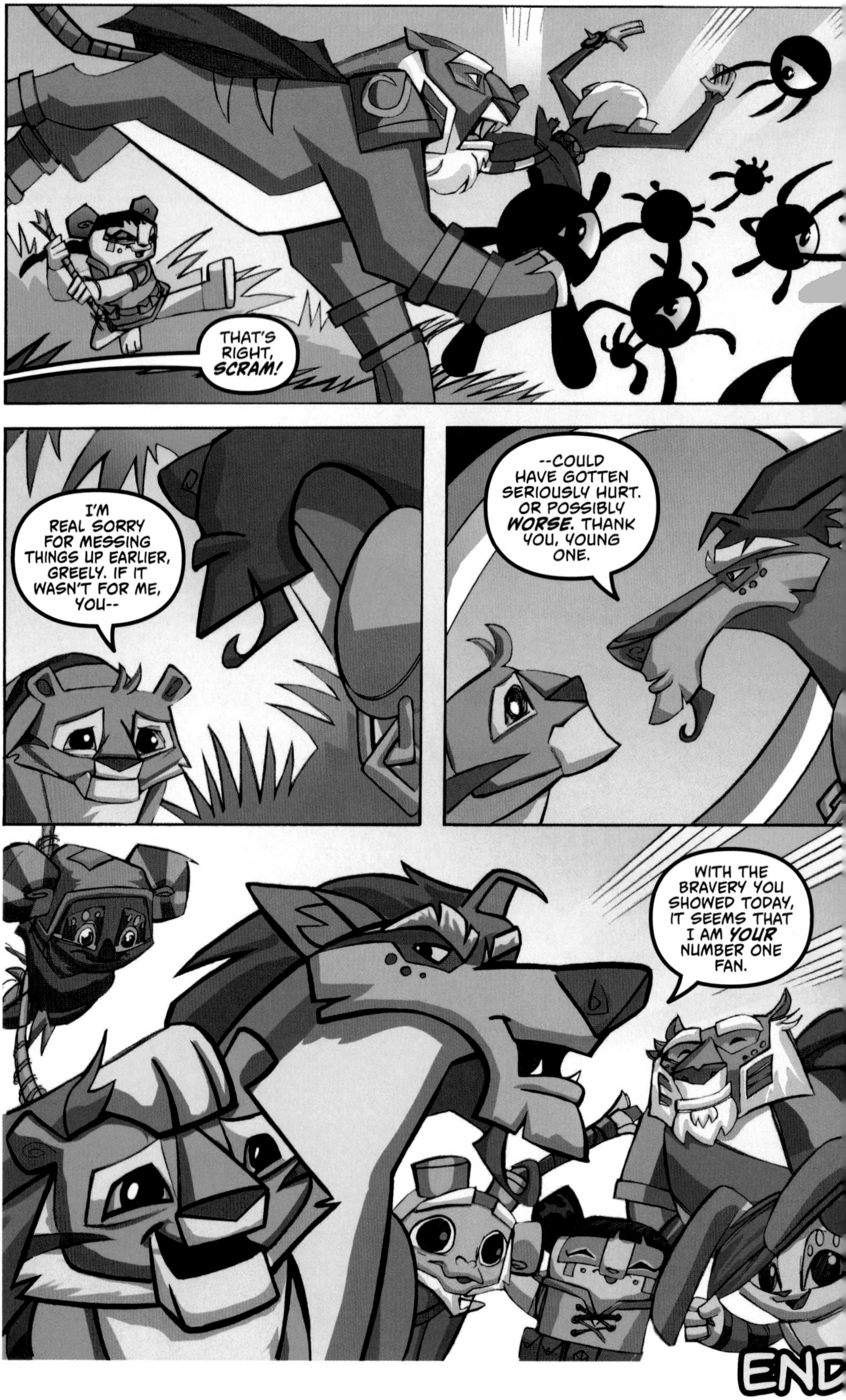
THAT'S RIGHT, SCRAM!
I'M REAL SORRY FOR MESSING THINGS UP EARLIER, GREELY. IF IT WASN'T FOR ME, YOU--
--COULD HAVE GOTTEN SERIOUSLY HURT. OR POSSIBLY WORSE. THANK YOU, YOUNG ONE.
WITH THE BRAVERY YOU SHOWED TODAY, IT SEEMS THAT I AM YOUR NUMBER ONE FAN.
END

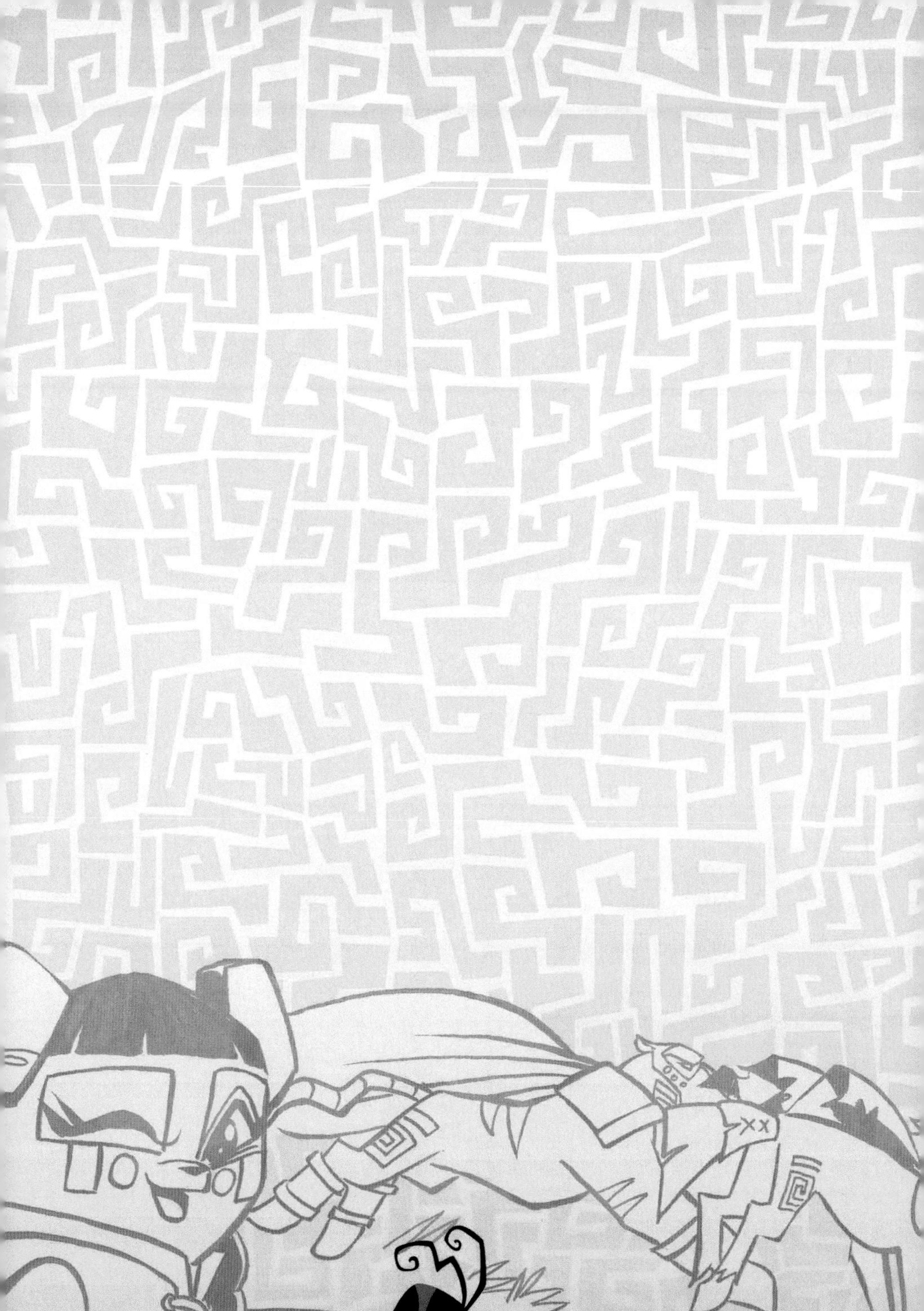

3

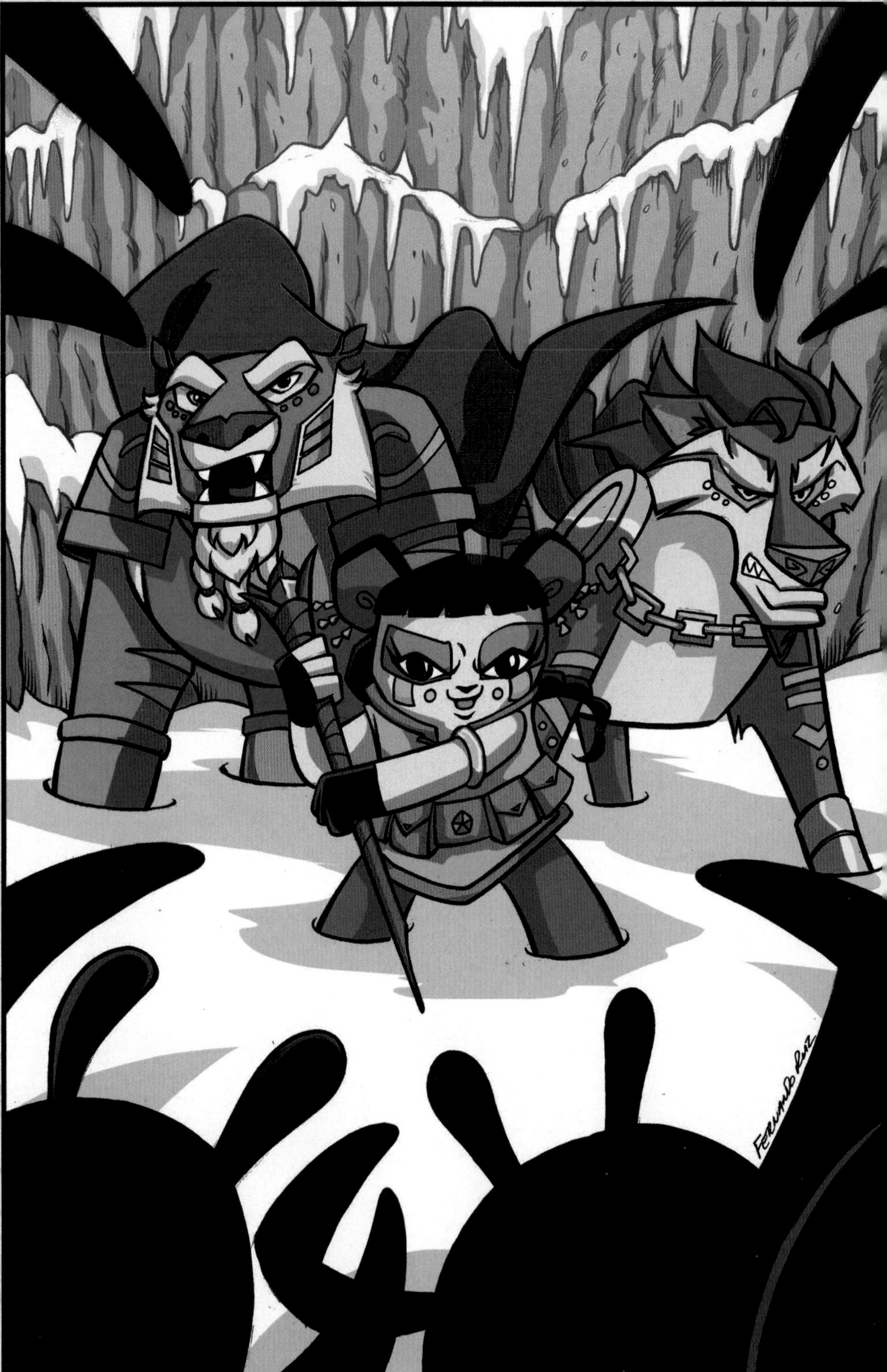
FERNANDO RUIZ

Issue #3: Cover Art by **FERNANDO RUIZ & PETE PANTAZIS**

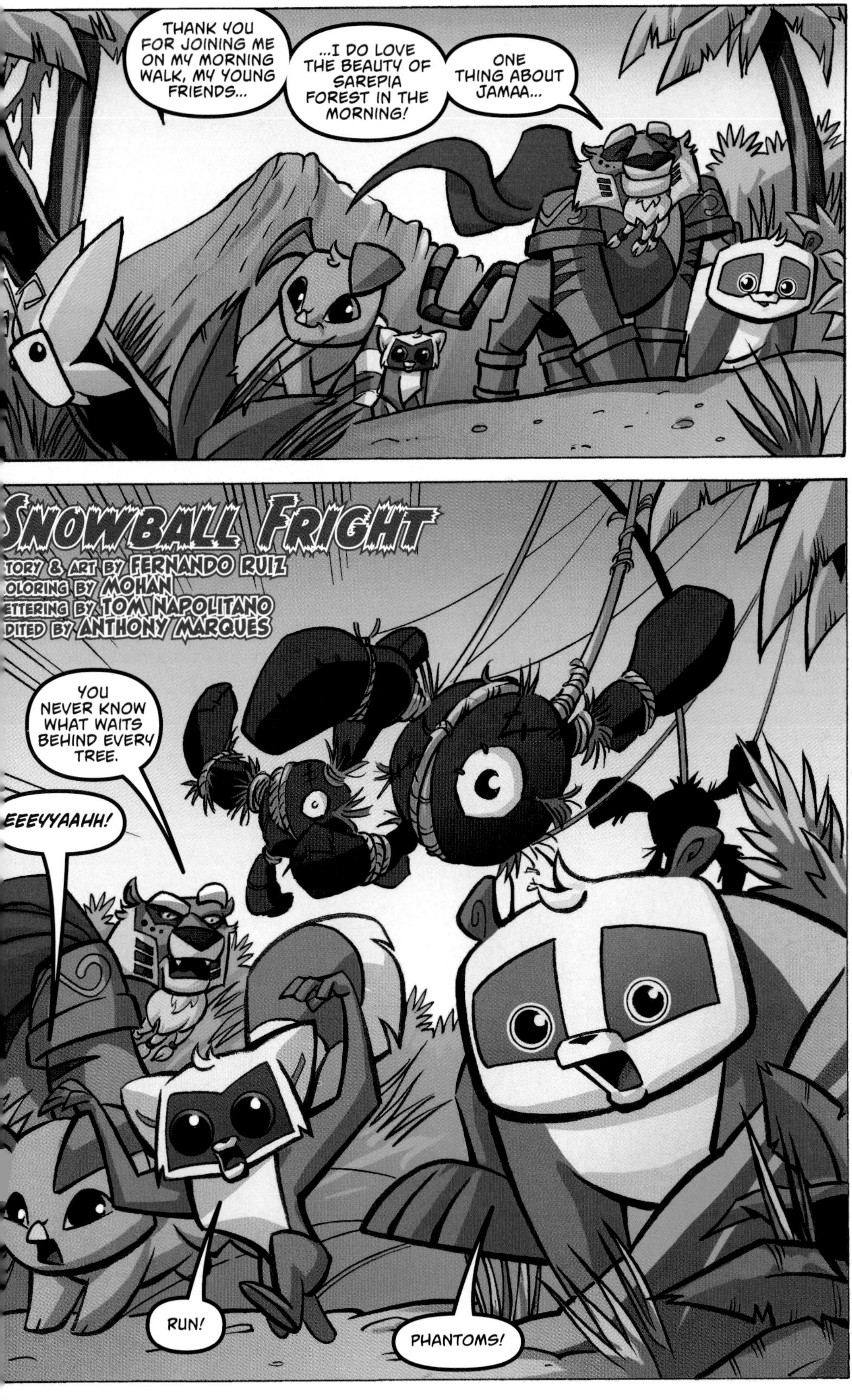
THANK YOU FOR JOINING ME ON MY MORNING WALK, MY YOUNG FRIENDS...
...I DO LOVE THE BEAUTY OF SAREPIA FOREST IN THE MORNING!
ONE THING ABOUT JAMAA...
SNOWBALL FRIGHT
TORY & ART BY FERNANDO RUIZ
OLORING BY MOHAN
ETTERING BY TOM NAPOLITANO
DITED BY ANTHONY MARQUES
YOU NEVER KNOW WHAT WAITS BEHIND EVERY TREE.
EEEYYAAHH!
RUN!
PHANTOMS!

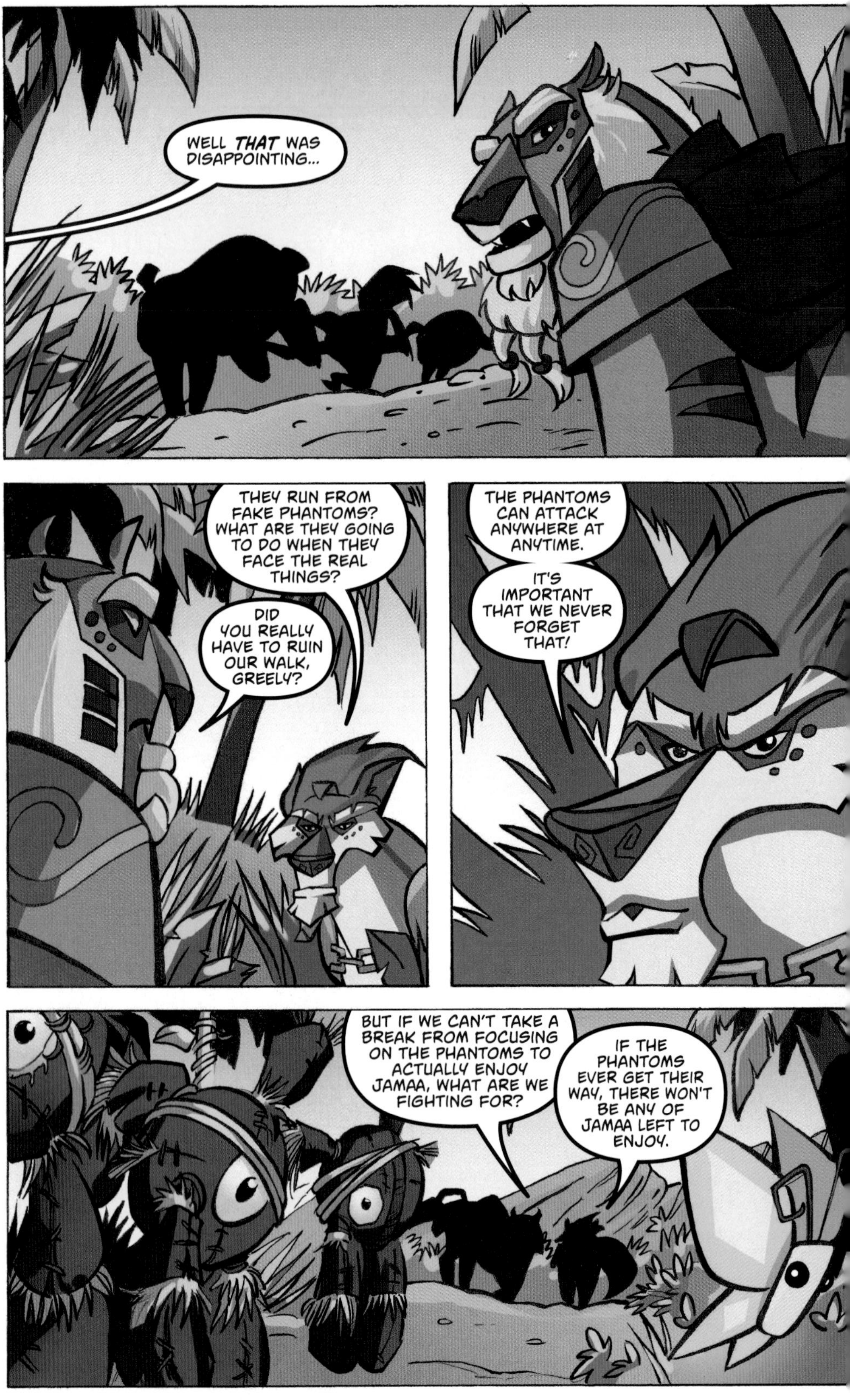
WELL *THAT* WAS DISAPPOINTING...
THEY RUN FROM FAKE PHANTOMS? WHAT ARE THEY GOING TO DO WHEN THEY FACE THE REAL THINGS?
DID YOU REALLY HAVE TO RUIN OUR WALK, GREELY?
THE PHANTOMS CAN ATTACK ANYWHERE AT ANYTIME.
IT'S IMPORTANT THAT WE NEVER FORGET THAT!
BUT IF WE CAN'T TAKE A BREAK FROM FOCUSING ON THE PHANTOMS TO ACTUALLY ENJOY JAMAA, WHAT ARE WE FIGHTING FOR?
IF THE PHANTOMS EVER GET THEIR WAY, THERE WON'T BE ANY OF JAMAA LEFT TO ENJOY.

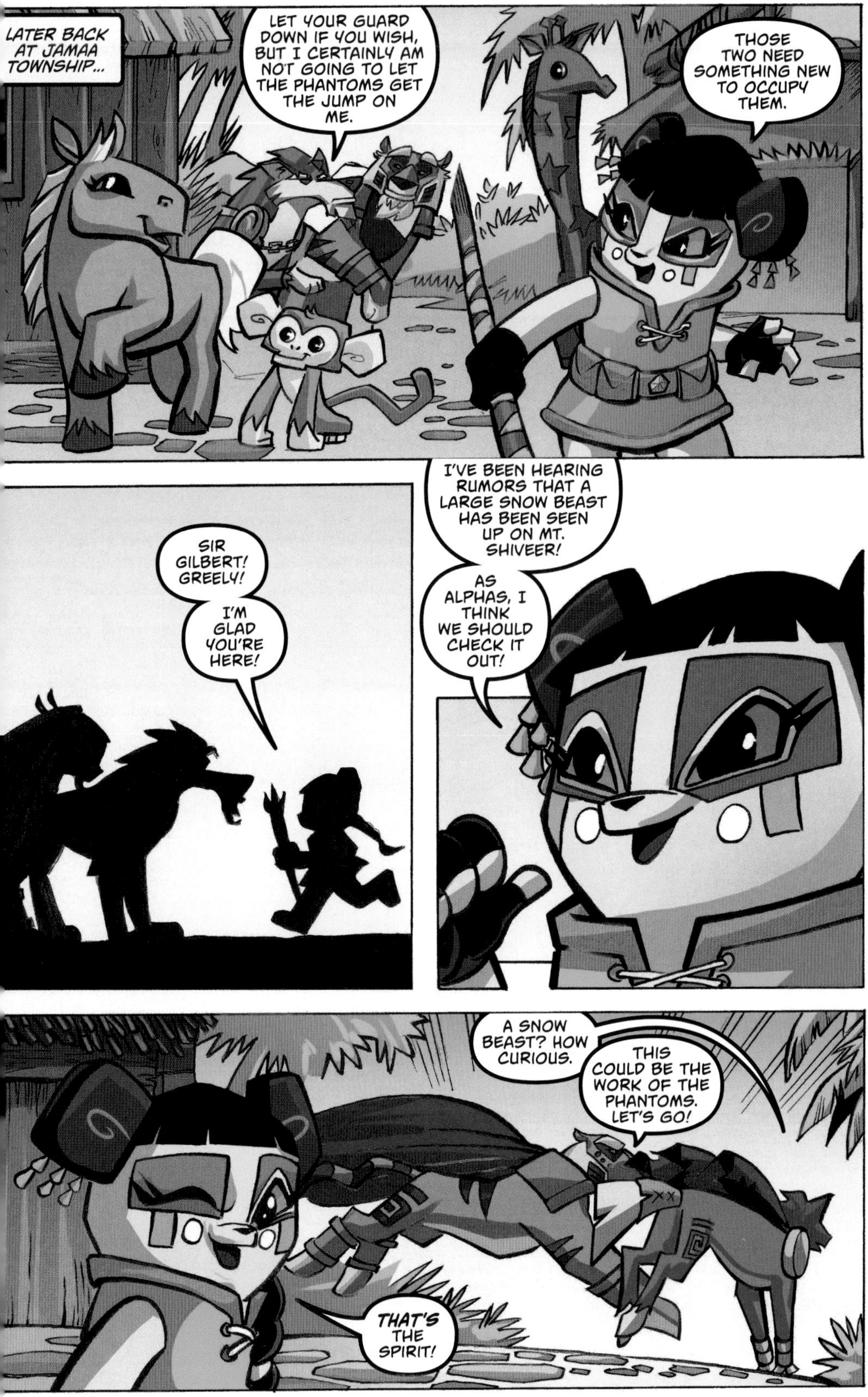
LATER BACK AT JAMAA TOWNSHIP...
LET YOUR GUARD DOWN IF YOU WISH, BUT I CERTAINLY AM NOT GOING TO LET THE PHANTOMS GET THE JUMP ON ME.
THOSE TWO NEED SOMETHING NEW TO OCCUPY THEM.
SIR GILBERT! GREELY!
I'M GLAD YOU'RE HERE!
I'VE BEEN HEARING RUMORS THAT A LARGE SNOW BEAST HAS BEEN SEEN UP ON MT. SHIVEER!
AS ALPHAS, I THINK WE SHOULD CHECK IT OUT!
A SNOW BEAST? HOW CURIOUS.
THIS COULD BE THE WORK OF THE PHANTOMS. LET'S GO!
THAT'S THE SPIRIT!

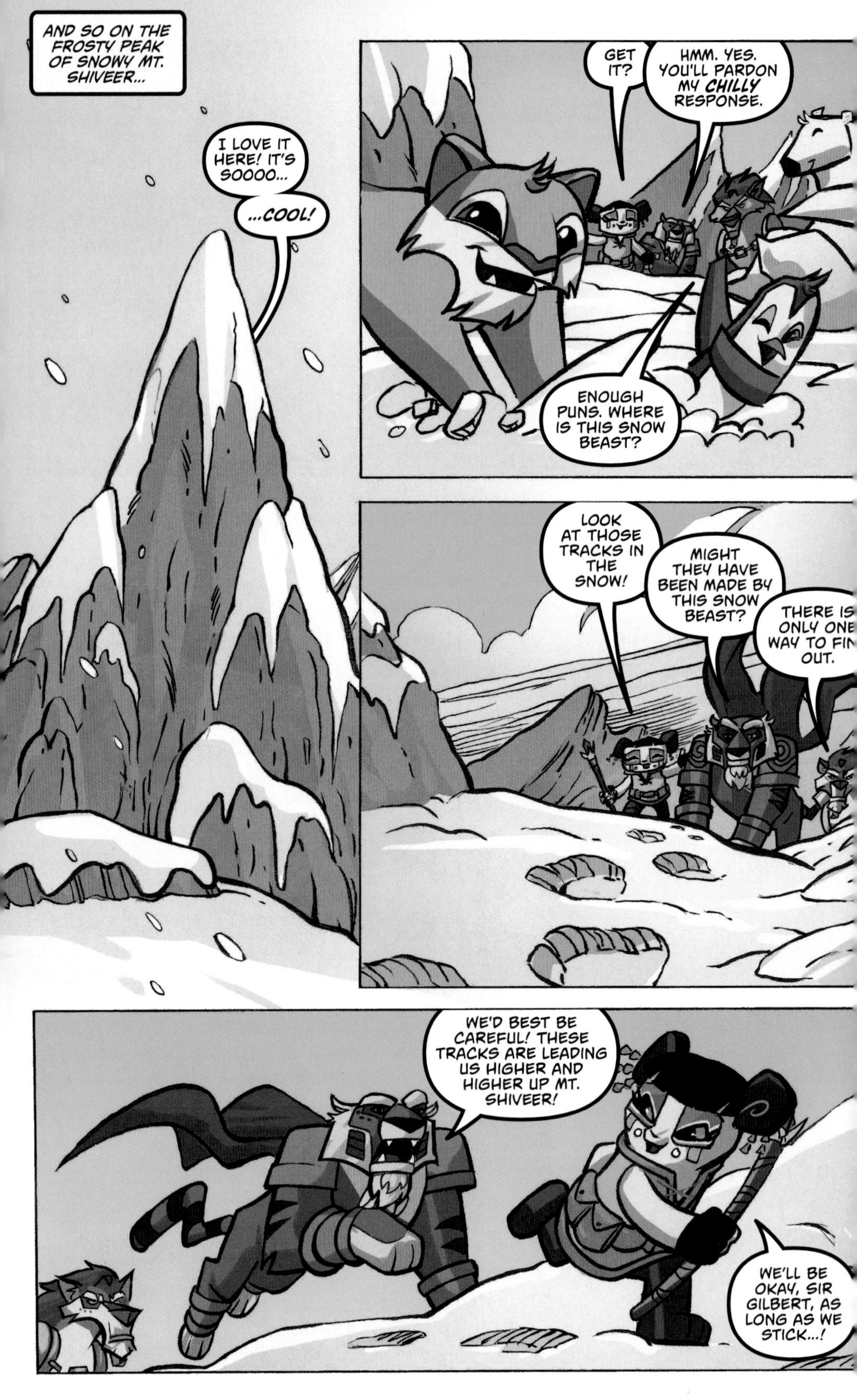
AND SO ON THE FROSTY PEAK OF SNOWY MT. SHIVEER...
I LOVE IT HERE! IT'S SOOOO...
...COOL!
GET IT?
HMM. YES. YOU'LL PARDON MY CHILLY RESPONSE.
ENOUGH PUNS. WHERE IS THIS SNOW BEAST?
LOOK AT THOSE TRACKS IN THE SNOW!
MIGHT THEY HAVE BEEN MADE BY THIS SNOW BEAST?
THERE IS ONLY ONE WAY TO FIN OUT.
WE'D BEST BE CAREFUL! THESE TRACKS ARE LEADING US HIGHER AND HIGHER UP MT. SHIVEER!
WE'LL BE OKAY, SIR GILBERT, AS LONG AS WE STICK...!

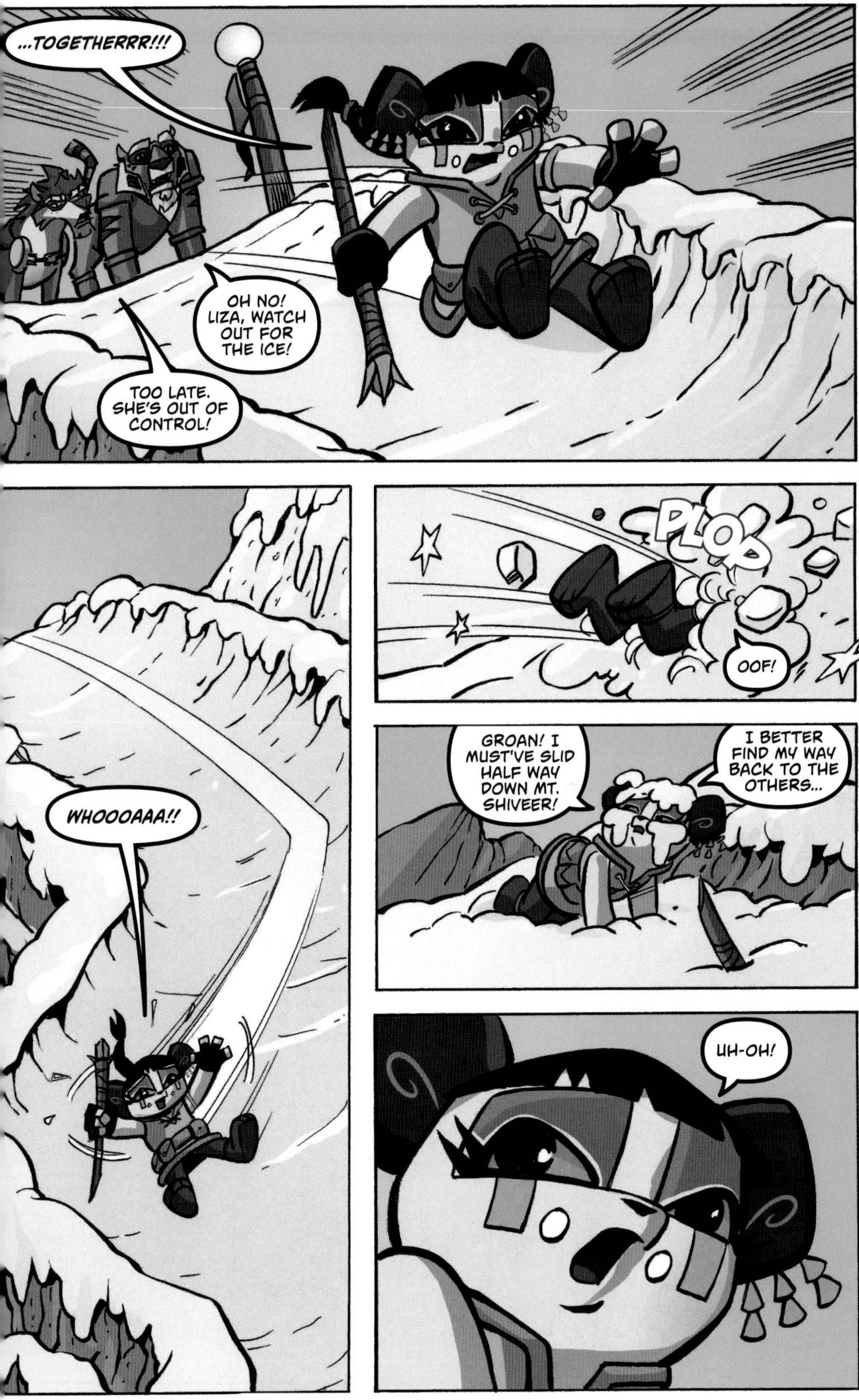
...TOGETHERRR!!!
OH NO! LIZA, WATCH OUT FOR THE ICE!
TOO LATE. SHE'S OUT OF CONTROL!
WHOOOAAA!!
PLOP
OOF!
GROAN! I MUST'VE SLID HALF WAY DOWN MT. SHIVEER!
I BETTER FIND MY WAY BACK TO THE OTHERS...
UH-OH!

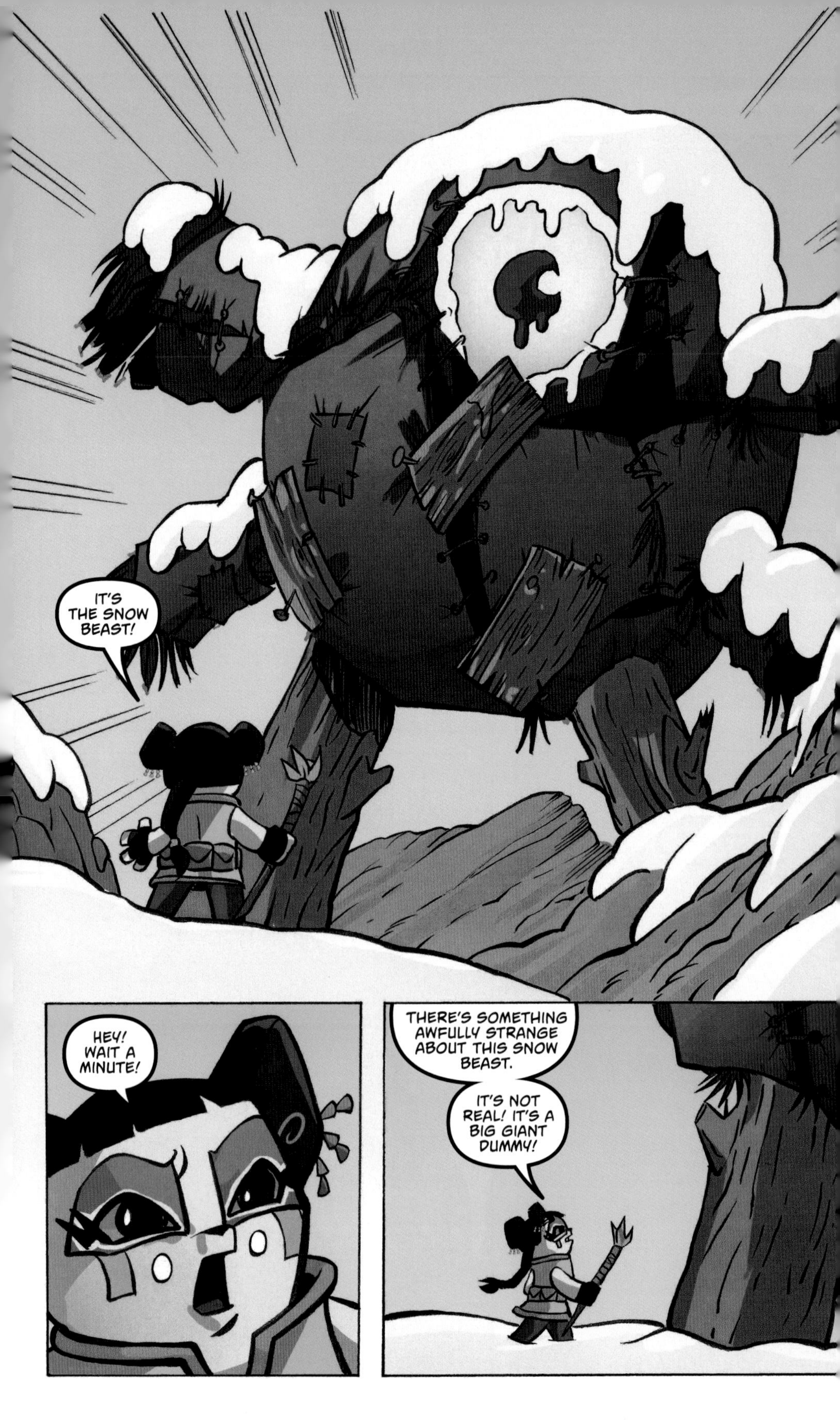
IT'S THE SNOW BEAST!
HEY! WAIT A MINUTE!
THERE'S SOMETHING AWFULLY STRANGE ABOUT THIS SNOW BEAST.
IT'S NOT REAL! IT'S A BIG GIANT DUMMY!

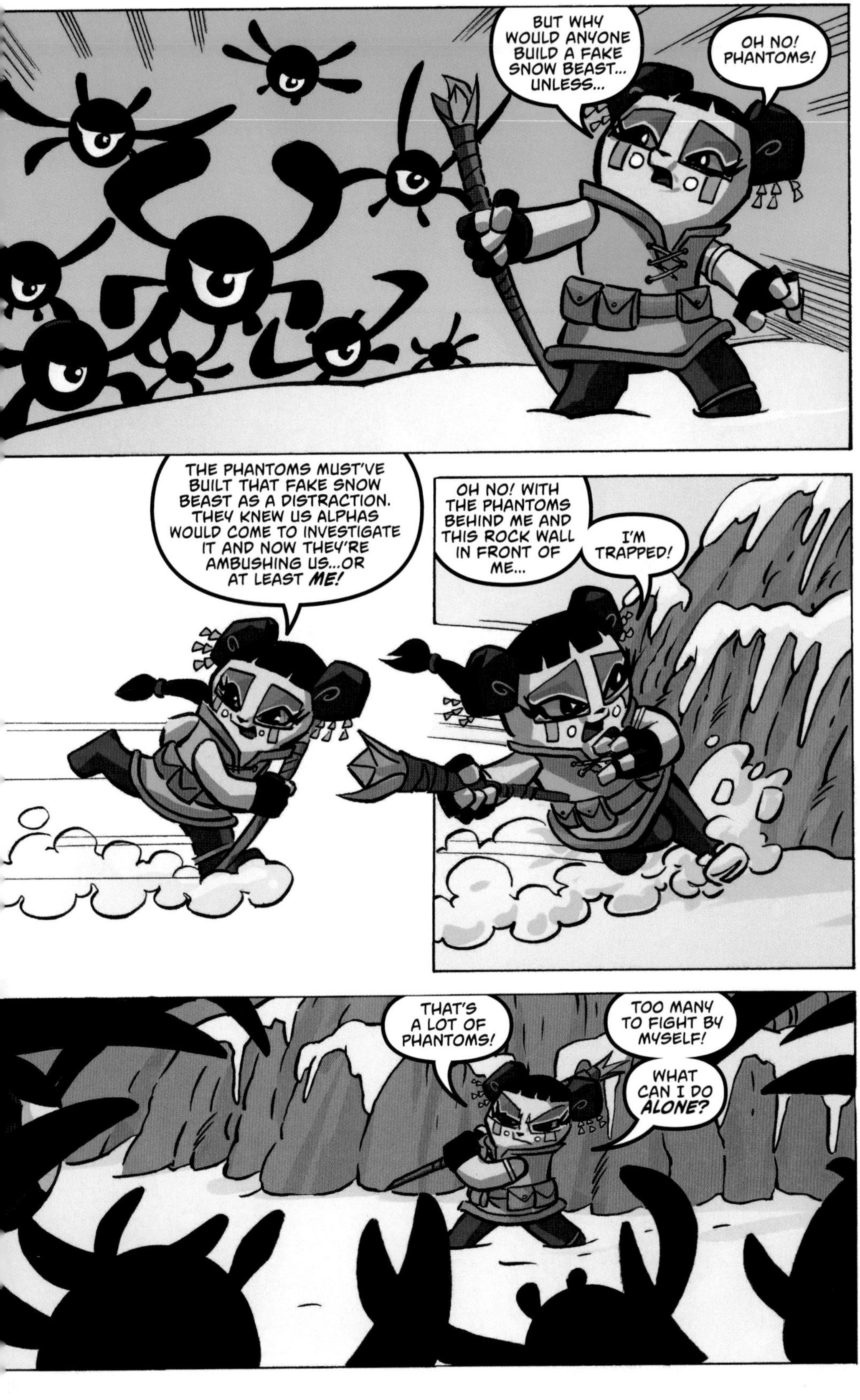
BUT WHY WOULD ANYONE BUILD A FAKE SNOW BEAST... UNLESS...
OH NO! PHANTOMS!
THE PHANTOMS MUST'VE BUILT THAT FAKE SNOW BEAST AS A DISTRACTION. THEY KNEW US ALPHAS WOULD COME TO INVESTIGATE IT AND NOW THEY'RE AMBUSHING US...OR AT LEAST ME!
OH NO! WITH THE PHANTOMS BEHIND ME AND THIS ROCK WALL IN FRONT OF ME...
I'M TRAPPED!
THAT'S A LOT OF PHANTOMS!
TOO MANY TO FIGHT BY MYSELF!
WHAT CAN I DO ALONE?

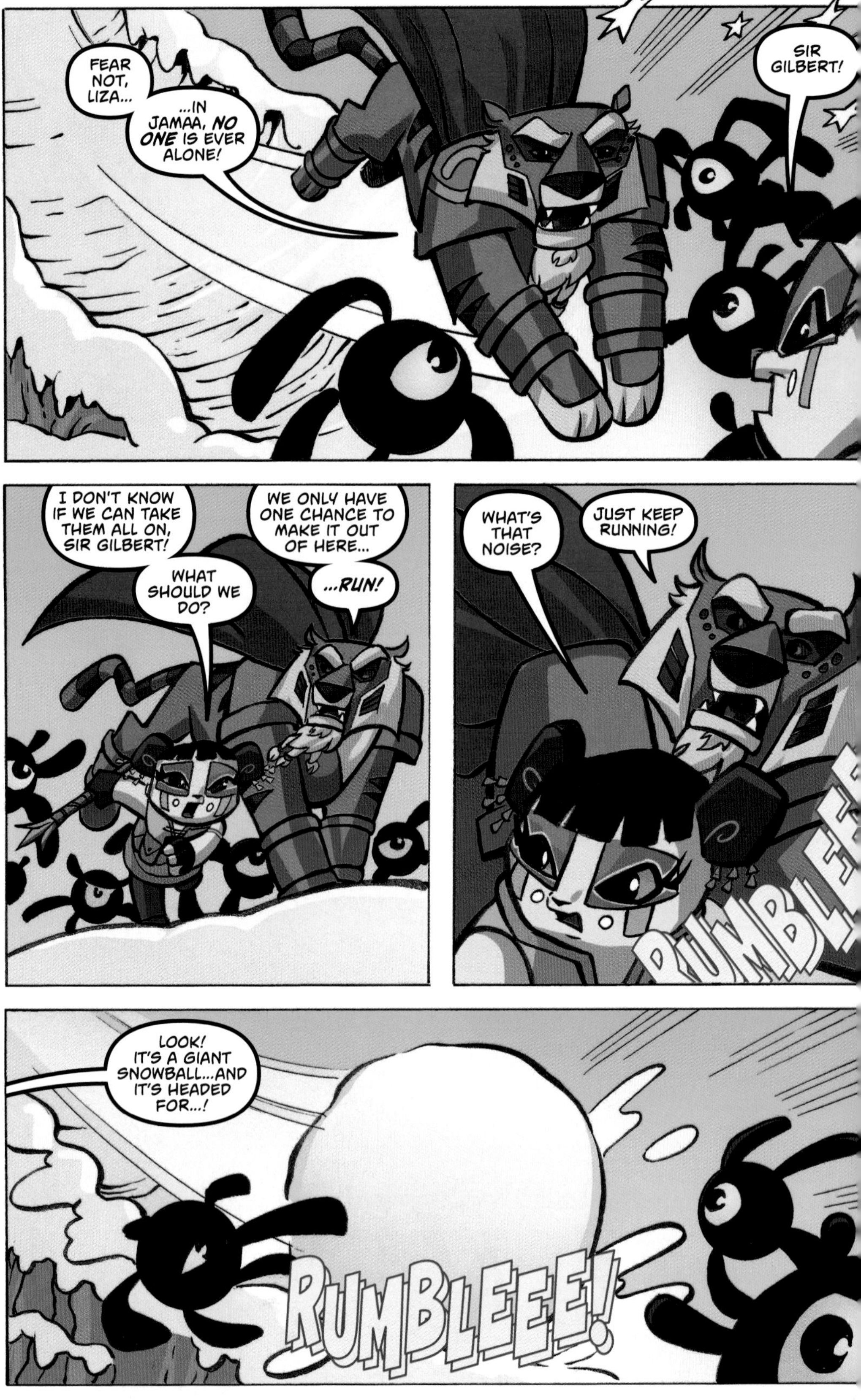
FEAR NOT, LIZA...
...IN JAMAA, NO ONE IS EVER ALONE!
SIR GILBERT!
I DON'T KNOW IF WE CAN TAKE THEM ALL ON, SIR GILBERT!
WHAT SHOULD WE DO?
WE ONLY HAVE ONE CHANCE TO MAKE IT OUT OF HERE...
...RUN!
WHAT'S THAT NOISE?
JUST KEEP RUNNING!
RUMBLEEE
LOOK! IT'S A GIANT SNOWBALL...AND IT'S HEADED FOR...!
RUMBLEEE!

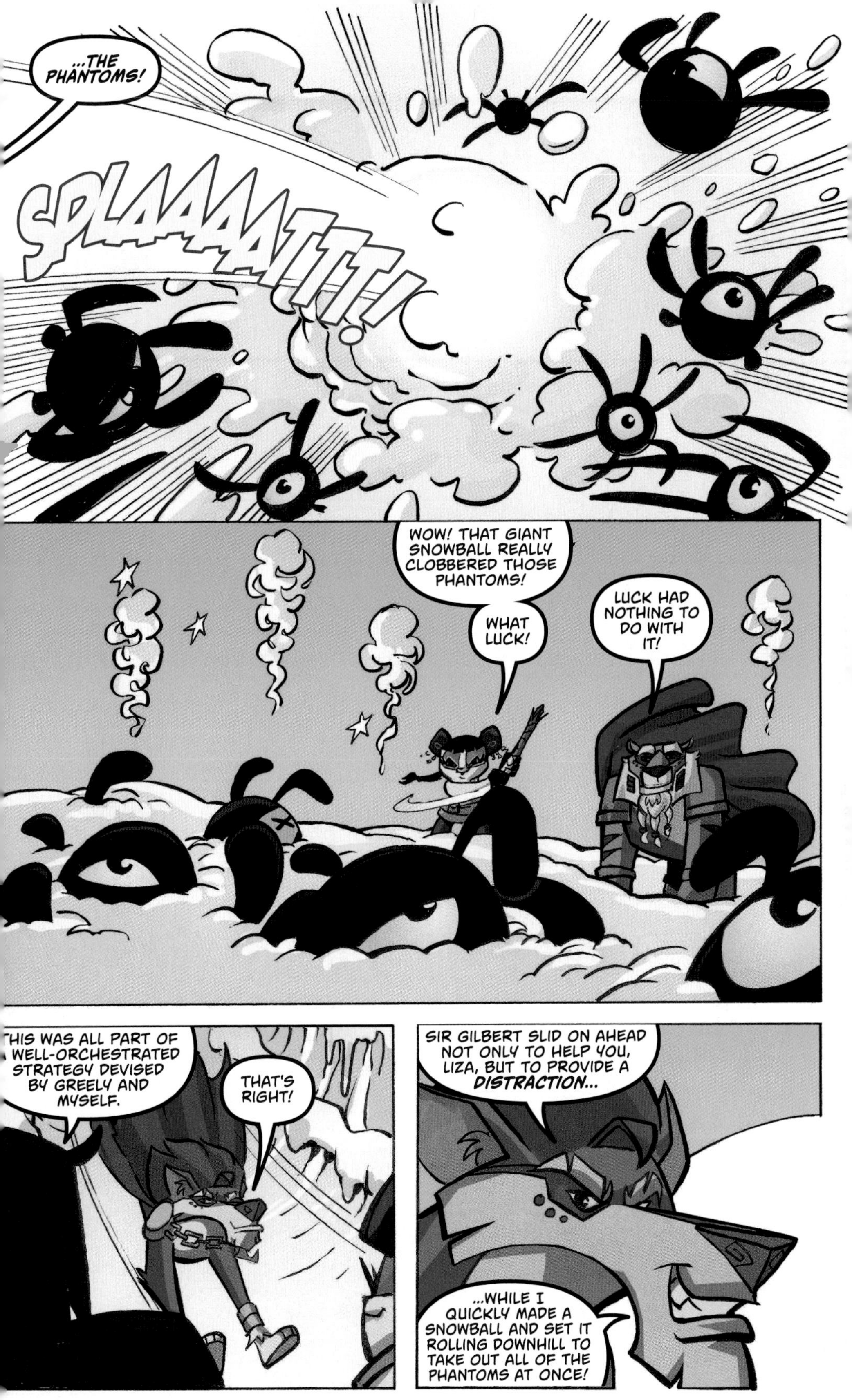

...THE PHANTOMS!
SPLAAAATTT!
WOW! THAT GIANT SNOWBALL REALLY CLOBBERED THOSE PHANTOMS!
WHAT LUCK!
LUCK HAD NOTHING TO DO WITH IT!
THIS WAS ALL PART OF A WELL-ORCHESTRATED STRATEGY DEVISED BY GREELY AND MYSELF.
THAT'S RIGHT!
SIR GILBERT SLID ON AHEAD NOT ONLY TO HELP YOU, LIZA, BUT TO PROVIDE A *DISTRACTION*...
...WHILE I QUICKLY MADE A SNOWBALL AND SET IT ROLLING DOWNHILL TO TAKE OUT ALL OF THE PHANTOMS AT ONCE!

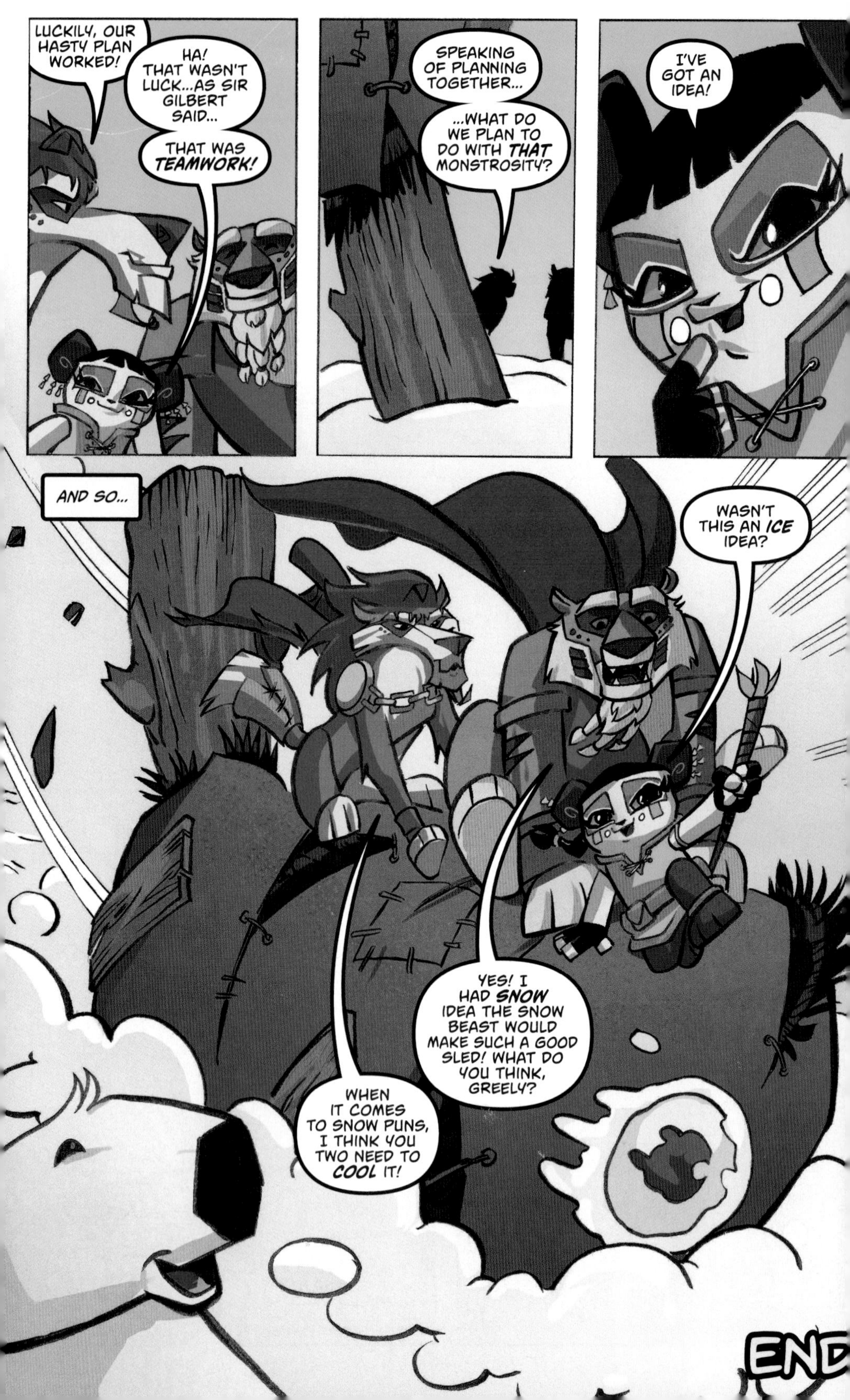
LUCKILY, OUR HASTY PLAN WORKED!
HA! THAT WASN'T LUCK...AS SIR GILBERT SAID...
THAT WAS *TEAMWORK!*
SPEAKING OF PLANNING TOGETHER...
...WHAT DO WE PLAN TO DO WITH *THAT* MONSTROSITY?
I'VE GOT AN IDEA!
AND SO...
WASN'T THIS AN *ICE* IDEA?
YES! I HAD *SNOW* IDEA THE SNOW BEAST WOULD MAKE SUCH A GOOD SLED! WHAT DO YOU THINK, GREELY?
WHEN IT COMES TO SNOW PUNS, I THINK YOU TWO NEED TO *COOL* IT!
END

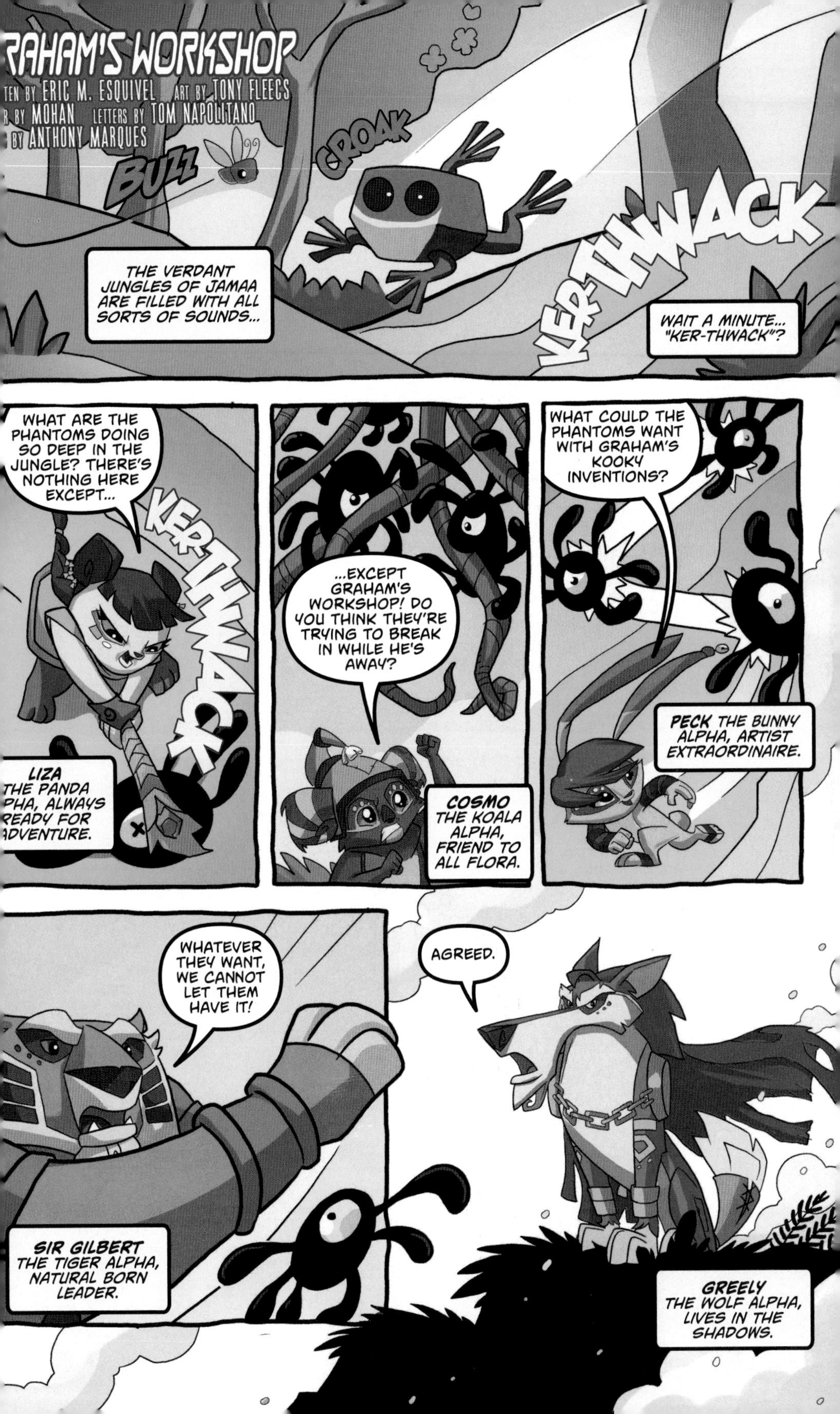
RAHAM'S WORKSHOP
TEN BY ERIC M. ESQUIVEL ART BY TONY FLEECS
R BY MOHAN LETTERS BY TOM NAPOLITANO
BY ANTHONY MARQUES
BUZZ
CROAK
THE VERDANT JUNGLES OF JAMAA ARE FILLED WITH ALL SORTS OF SOUNDS...
KER-THWACK
WAIT A MINUTE... "KER-THWACK"?
WHAT ARE THE PHANTOMS DOING SO DEEP IN THE JUNGLE? THERE'S NOTHING HERE EXCEPT...
KERTHWACK
LIZA THE PANDA PHA, ALWAYS READY FOR ADVENTURE.
...EXCEPT GRAHAM'S WORKSHOP! DO YOU THINK THEY'RE TRYING TO BREAK IN WHILE HE'S AWAY?
COSMO THE KOALA ALPHA, FRIEND TO ALL FLORA.
WHAT COULD THE PHANTOMS WANT WITH GRAHAM'S KOOKY INVENTIONS?
PECK THE BUNNY ALPHA, ARTIST EXTRAORDINAIRE.
WHATEVER THEY WANT, WE CANNOT LET THEM HAVE IT!
AGREED.
SIR GILBERT THE TIGER ALPHA, NATURAL BORN LEADER.
GREELY THE WOLF ALPHA, LIVES IN THE SHADOWS.

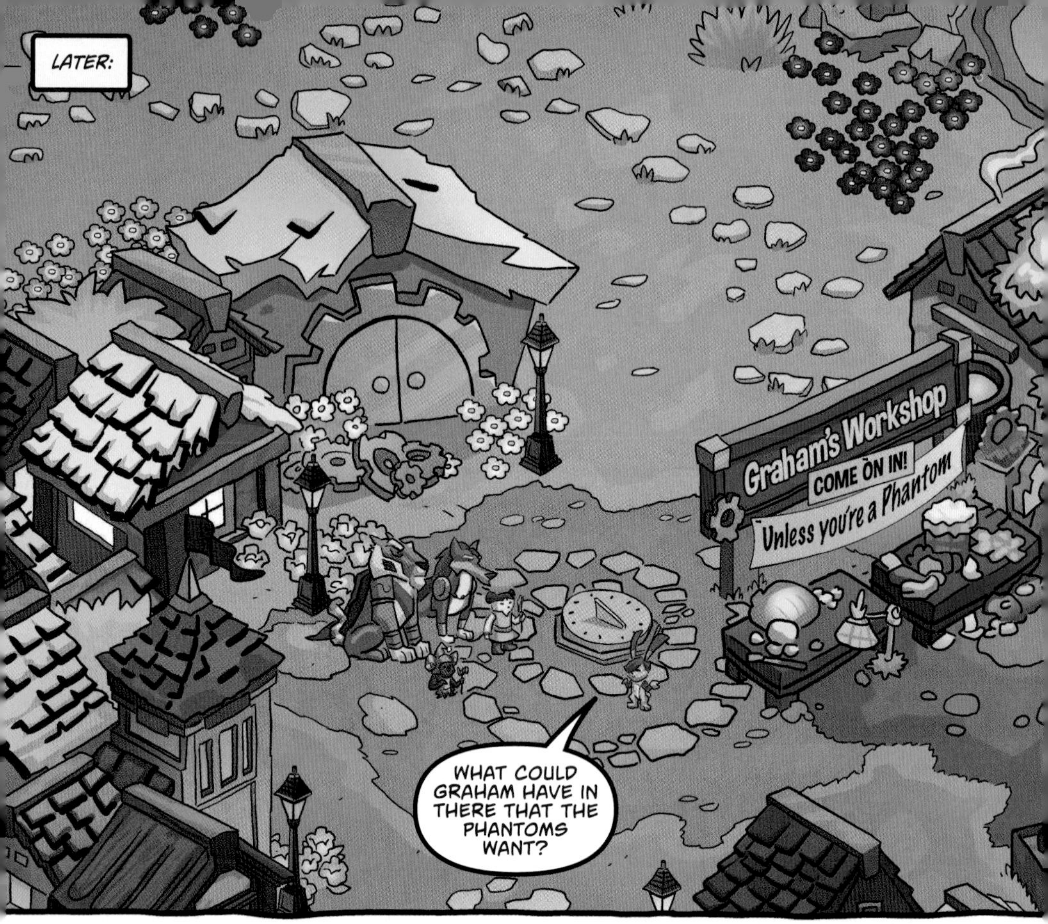
LATER:
Graham's Workshop
COME ON IN!
Unless you're a Phantom
WHAT COULD GRAHAM HAVE IN THERE THAT THE PHANTOMS WANT?

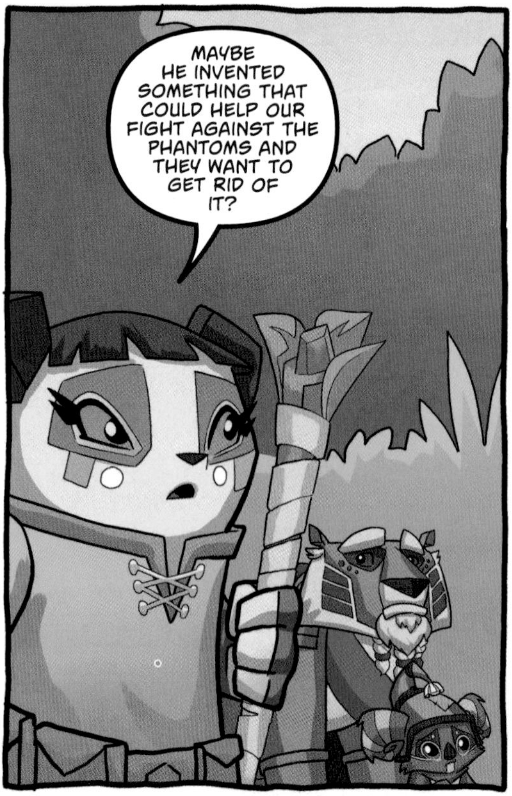
MAYBE HE INVENTED SOMETHING THAT COULD HELP OUR FIGHT AGAINST THE PHANTOMS AND THEY WANT TO GET RID OF IT?

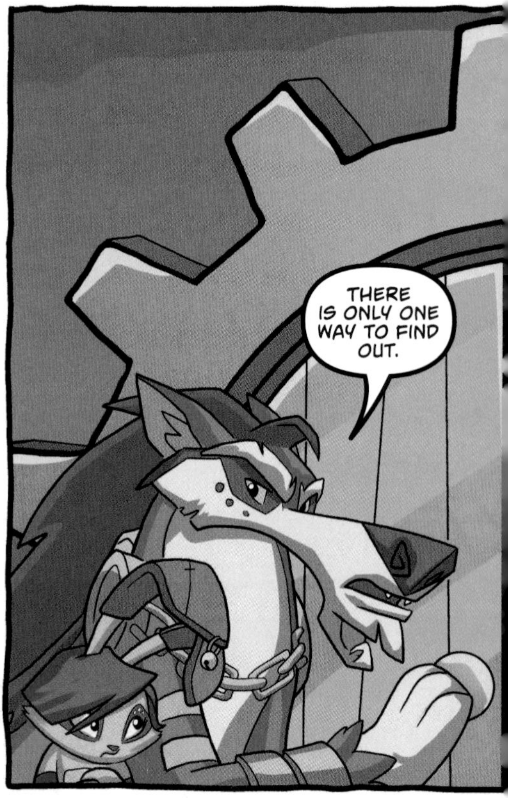
THERE IS ONLY ONE WAY TO FIND OUT.

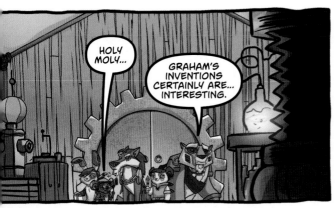

HOLY MOLY...

GRAHAM'S INVENTIONS CERTAINLY ARE... INTERESTING.

HEY! YOU GUYS SEE THAT?

WHAT *IS* THAT THING?

A BACK-SCRATCHER?

SOME KIND OF MODERN ART PIECE?

MAYBE A SPATULA?

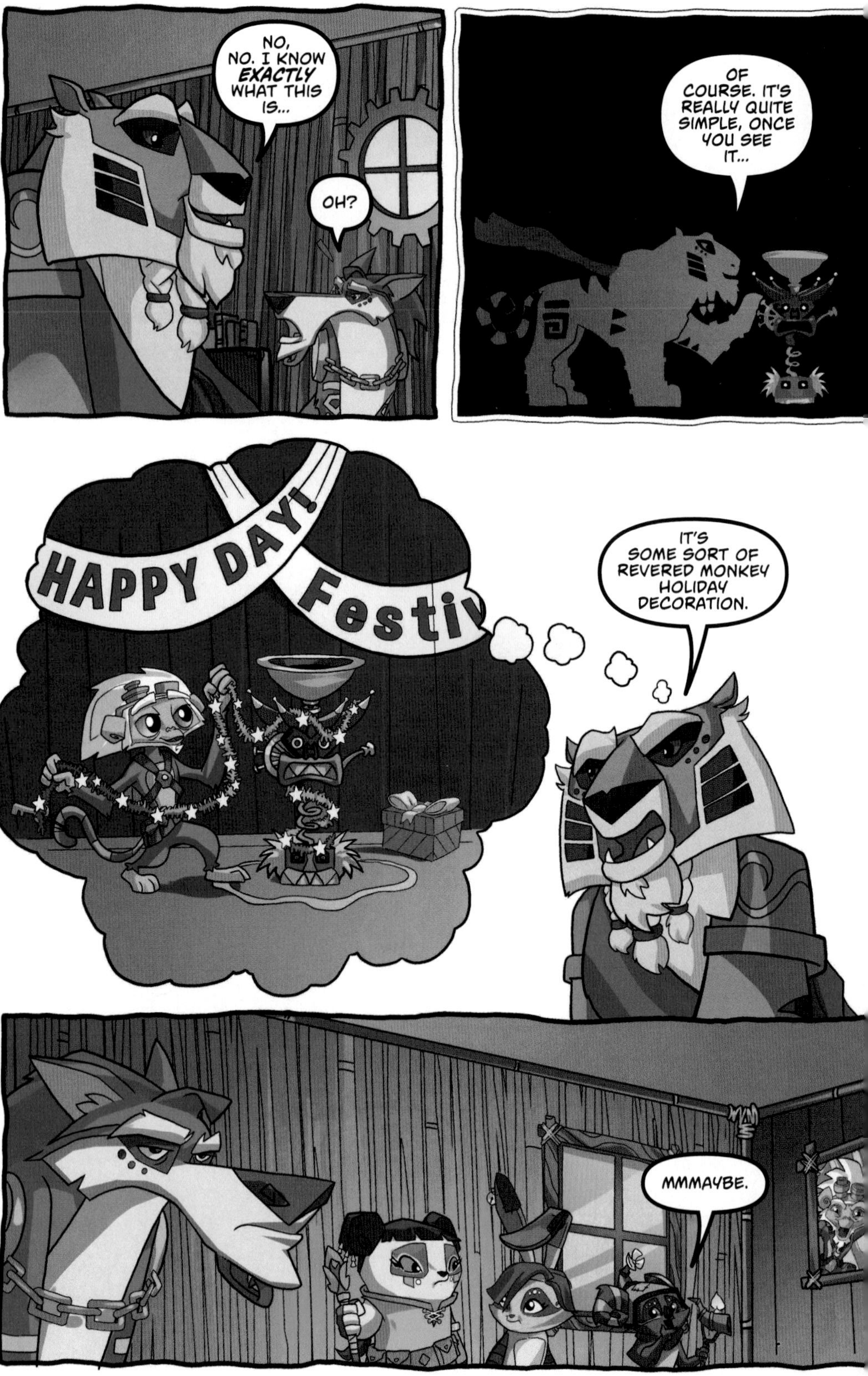
NO, NO. I KNOW *EXACTLY* WHAT THIS IS...
OH?
OF COURSE. IT'S REALLY QUITE SIMPLE, ONCE YOU SEE IT...
HAPPY DAY!
Festiv
IT'S SOME SORT OF REVERED MONKEY HOLIDAY DECORATION.
MMMAYBE.

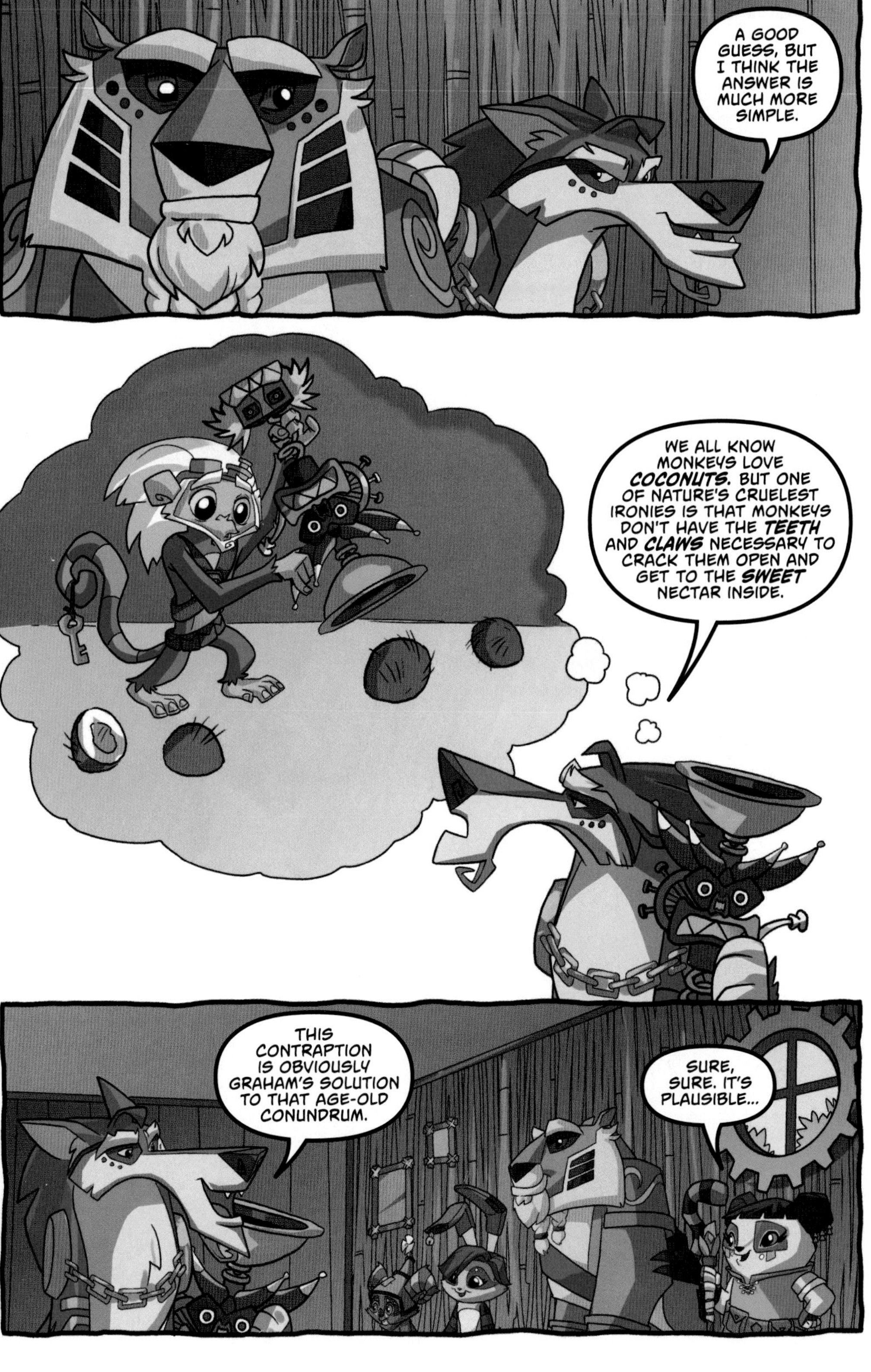
A GOOD GUESS, BUT I THINK THE ANSWER IS MUCH MORE SIMPLE.
WE ALL KNOW MONKEYS LOVE COCONUTS. BUT ONE OF NATURE'S CRUELEST IRONIES IS THAT MONKEYS DON'T HAVE THE TEETH AND CLAWS NECESSARY TO CRACK THEM OPEN AND GET TO THE SWEET NECTAR INSIDE.
THIS CONTRAPTION IS OBVIOUSLY GRAHAM'S SOLUTION TO THAT AGE-OLD CONUNDRUM.
SURE, SURE. IT'S PLAUSIBLE...

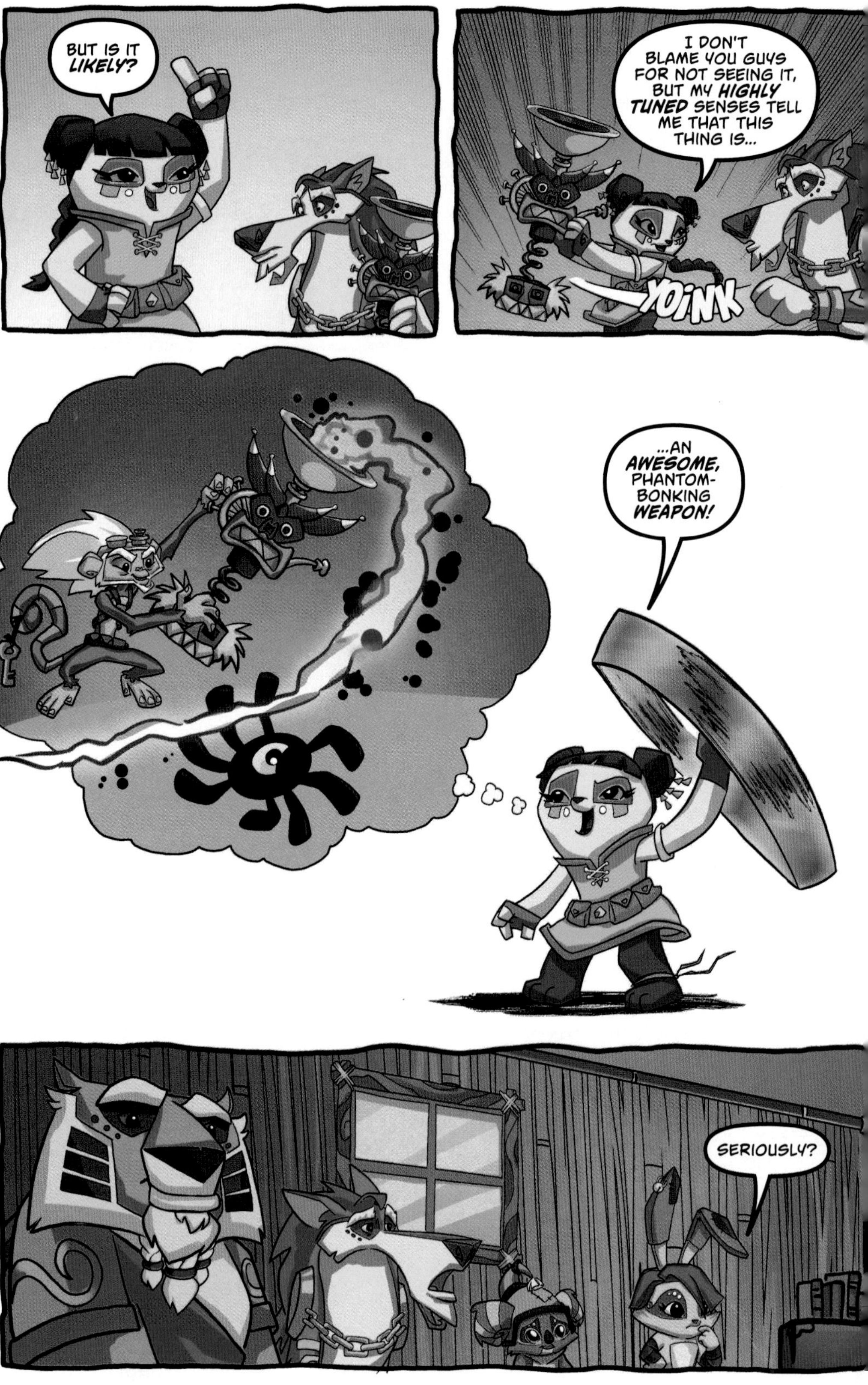

BUT IS IT LIKELY?
I DON'T BLAME YOU GUYS FOR NOT SEEING IT, BUT MY HIGHLY TUNED SENSES TELL ME THAT THIS THING IS...
YOINK
...AN AWESOME, PHANTOM-BONKING WEAPON!
SERIOUSLY?

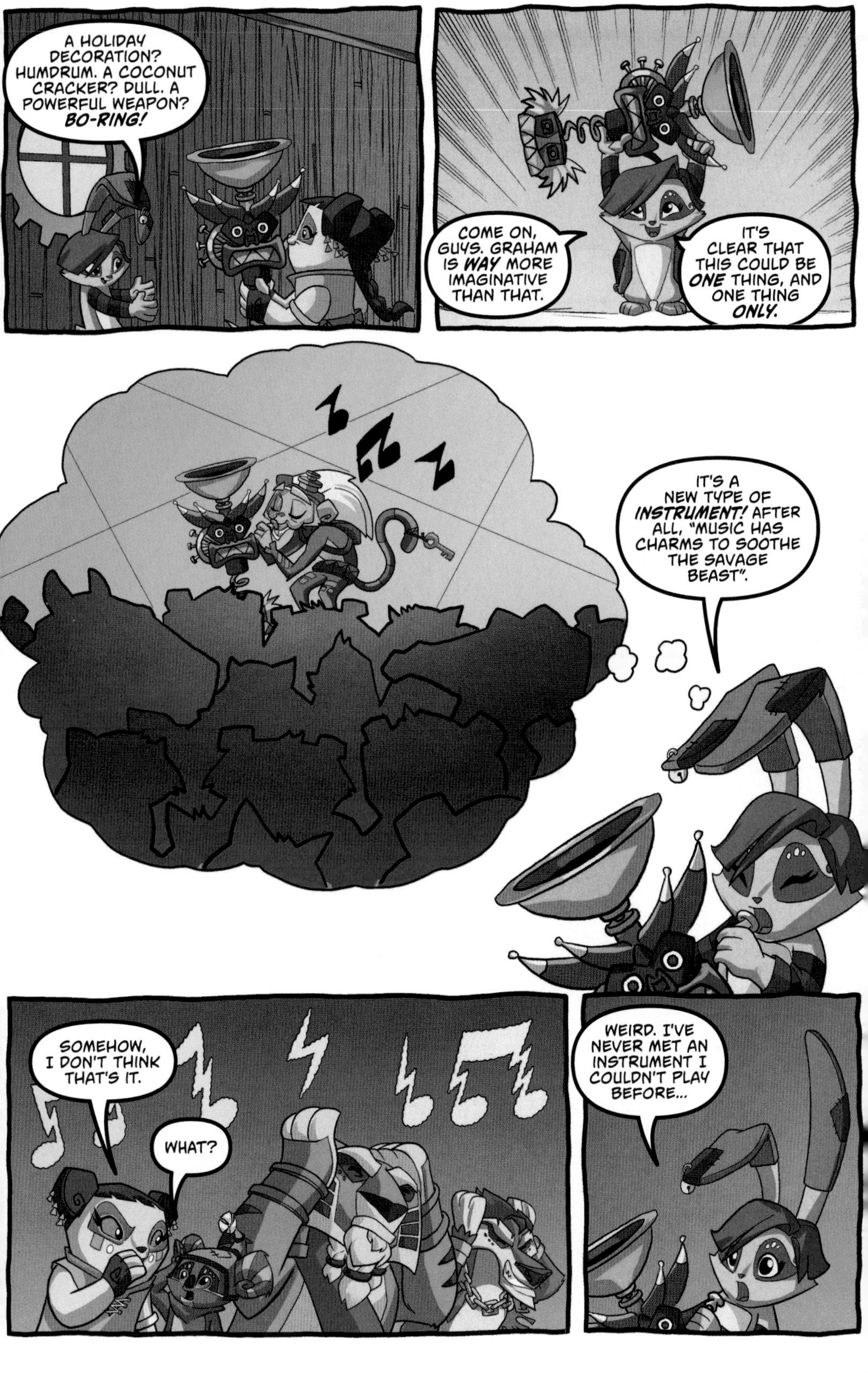
A HOLIDAY DECORATION? HUMDRUM. A COCONUT CRACKER? DULL. A POWERFUL WEAPON? BO-RING!
COME ON, GUYS. GRAHAM IS WAY MORE IMAGINATIVE THAN THAT.
IT'S CLEAR THAT THIS COULD BE ONE THING, AND ONE THING ONLY.
IT'S A NEW TYPE OF INSTRUMENT! AFTER ALL, "MUSIC HAS CHARMS TO SOOTHE THE SAVAGE BEAST".
SOMEHOW, I DON'T THINK THAT'S IT.
WHAT?
WEIRD. I'VE NEVER MET AN INSTRUMENT I COULDN'T PLAY BEFORE...

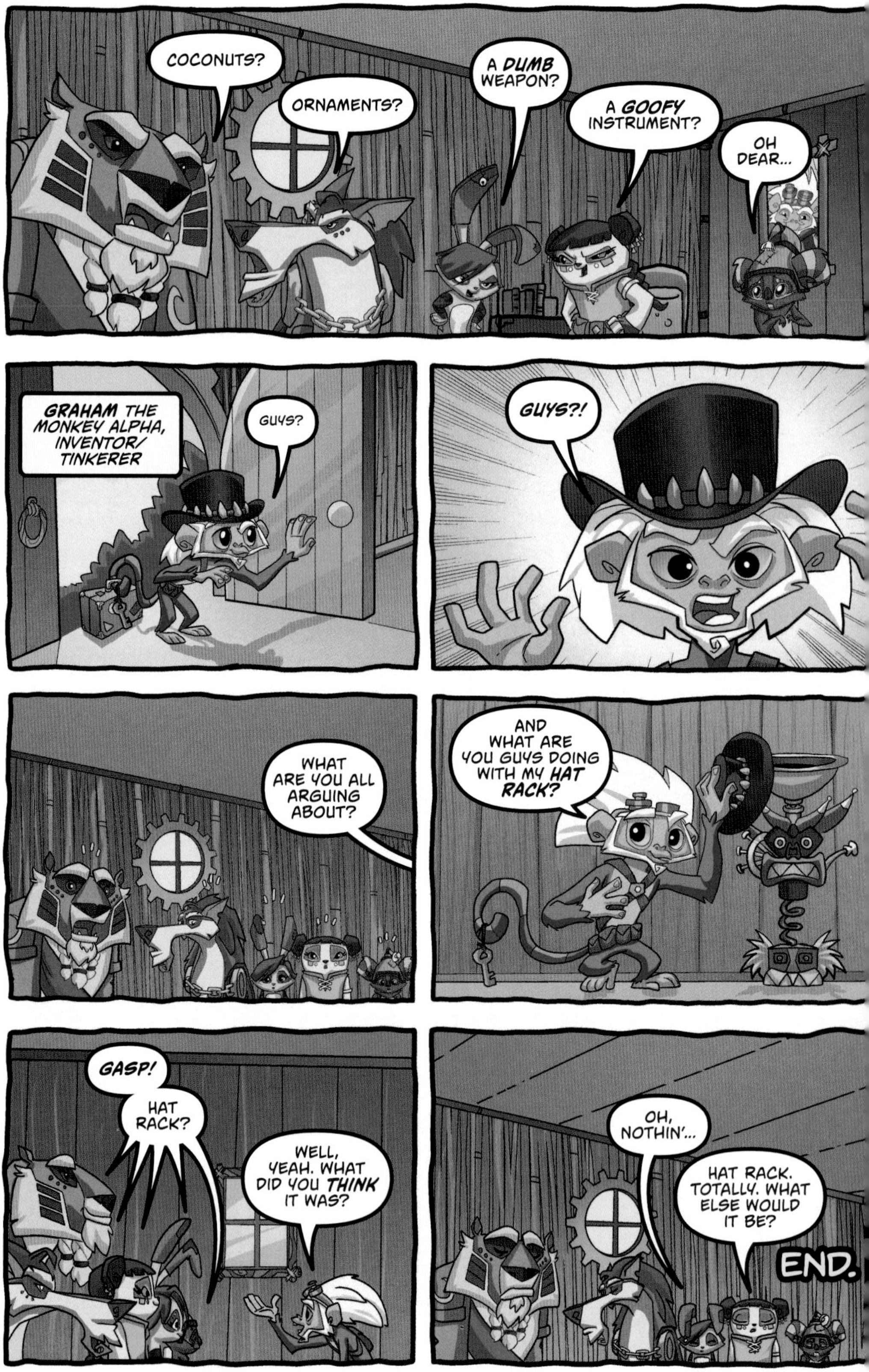
COCONUTS?
ORNAMENTS?
A DUMB WEAPON?
A GOOFY INSTRUMENT?
OH DEAR...
GRAHAM THE MONKEY ALPHA, INVENTOR/ TINKERER
GUYS?
GUYS?!
WHAT ARE YOU ALL ARGUING ABOUT?
AND WHAT ARE YOU GUYS DOING WITH MY HAT RACK?
GASP!
HAT RACK?
WELL, YEAH. WHAT DID YOU THINK IT WAS?
OH, NOTHIN'...
HAT RACK. TOTALLY. WHAT ELSE WOULD IT BE?
END.

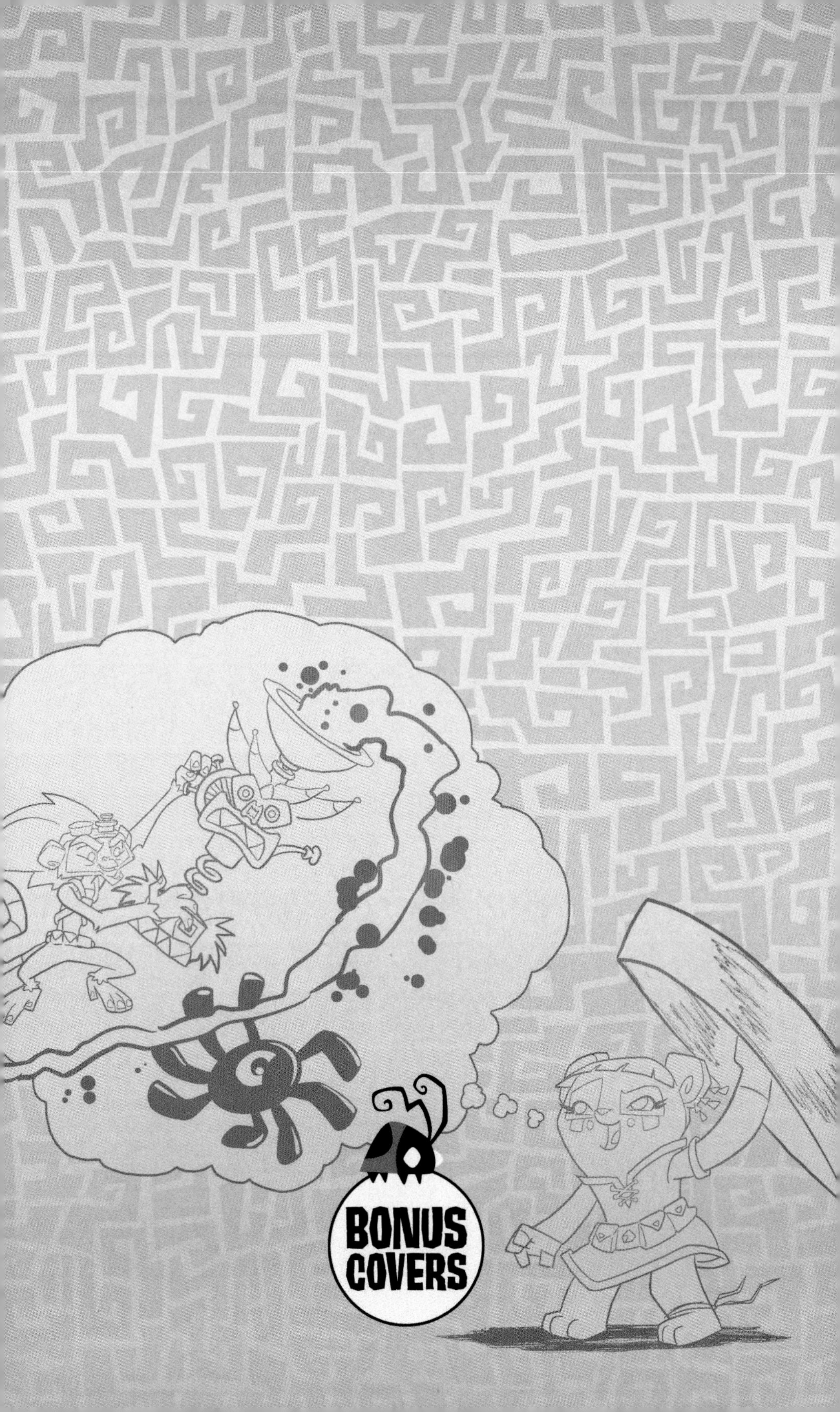
BONUS
COVERS

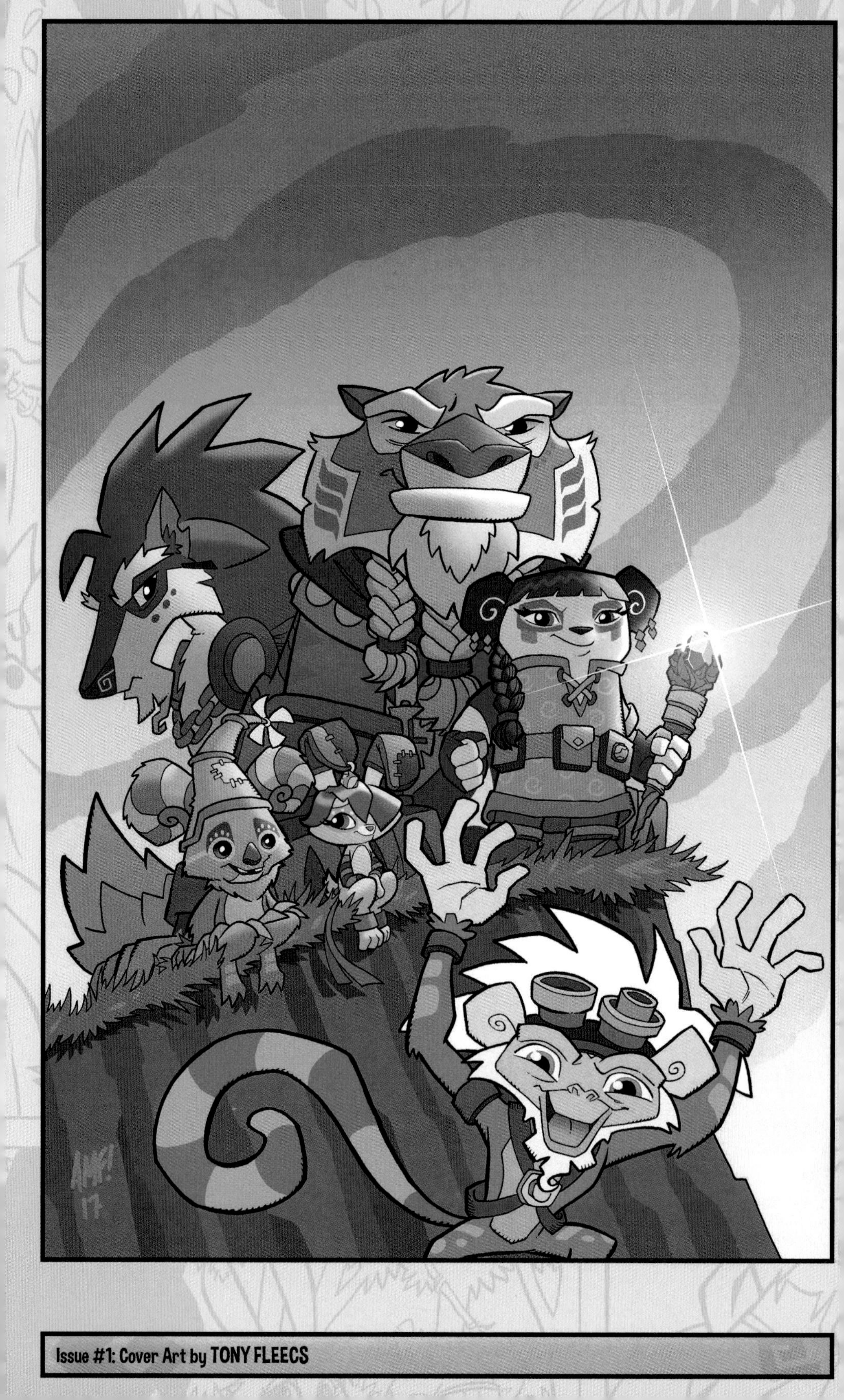

Issue #1: Cover Art by **TONY FLEECS**

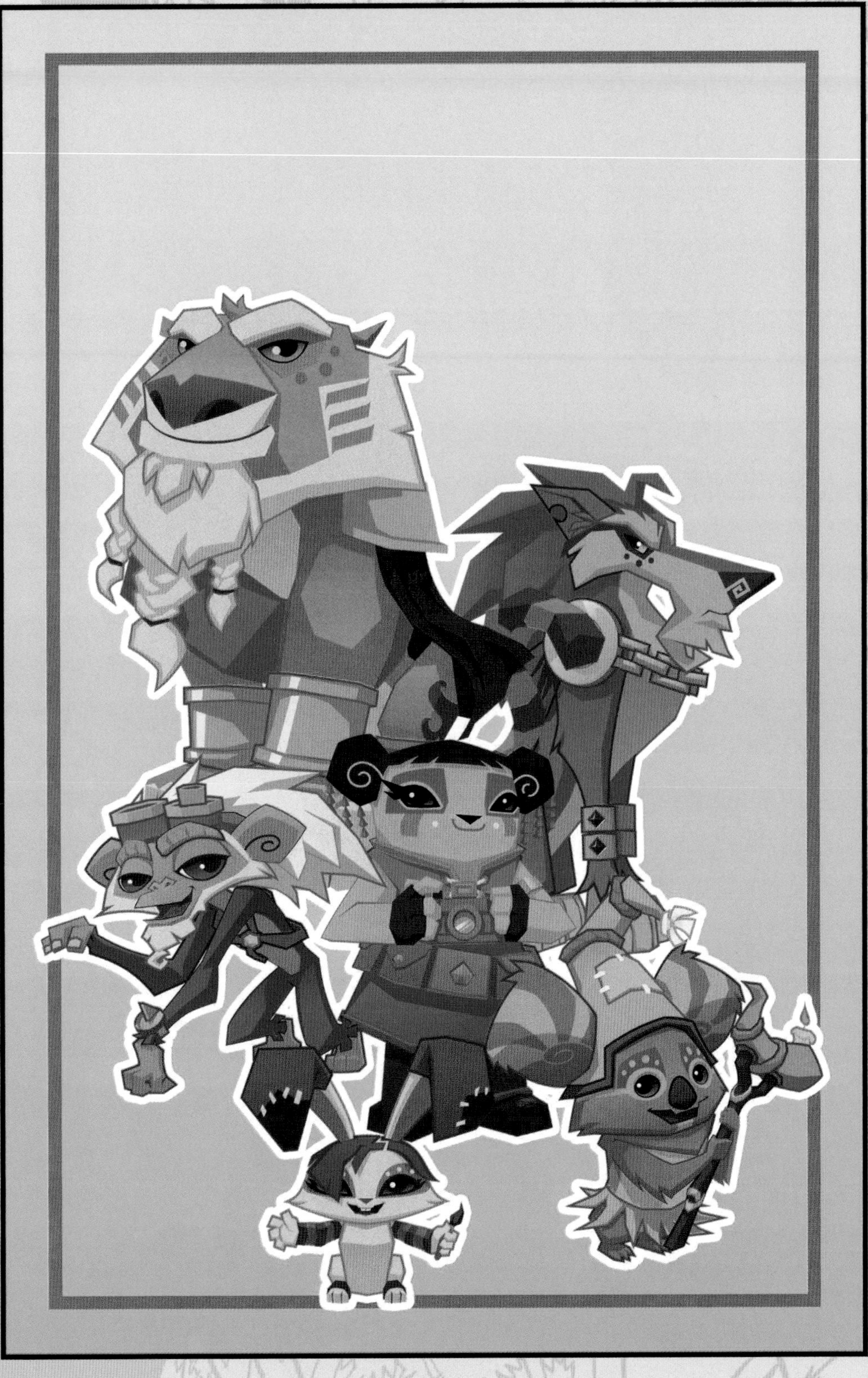

Issue #1: Gameplay Cover Art

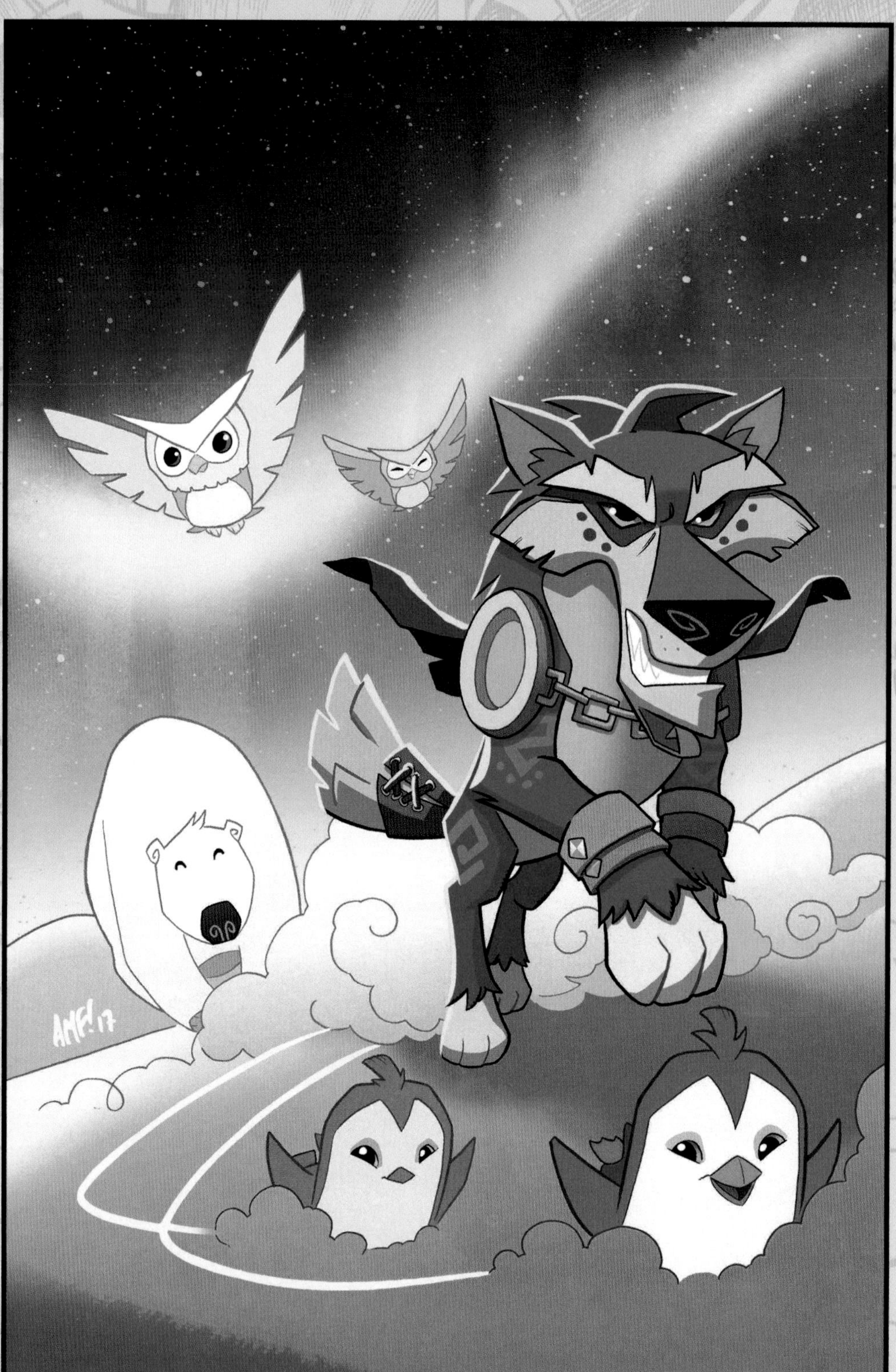

Issue #2: Cover Art by TONY FLEECS

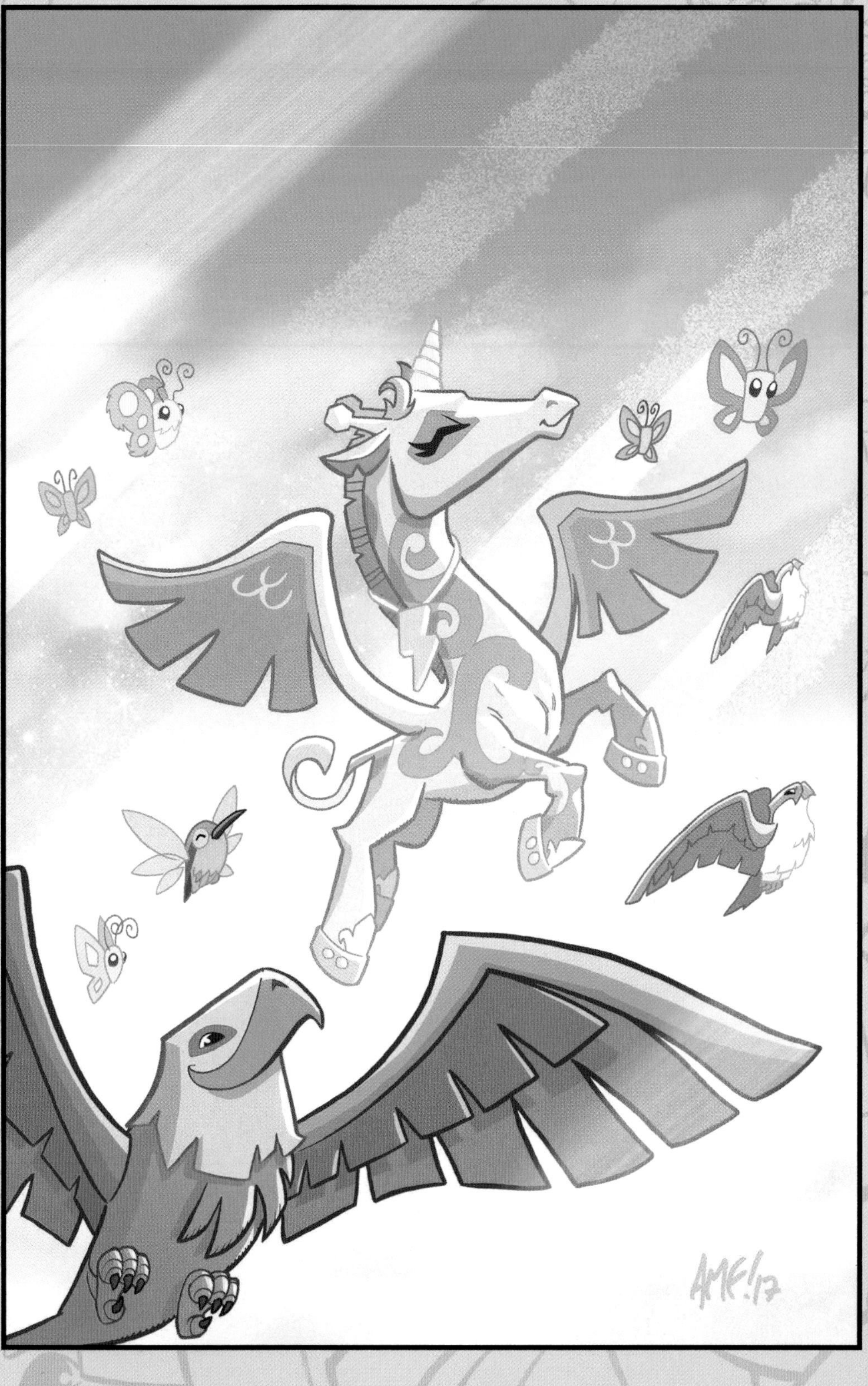
AME!17

Issue #3: Cover Art by **TONY FLEECS**

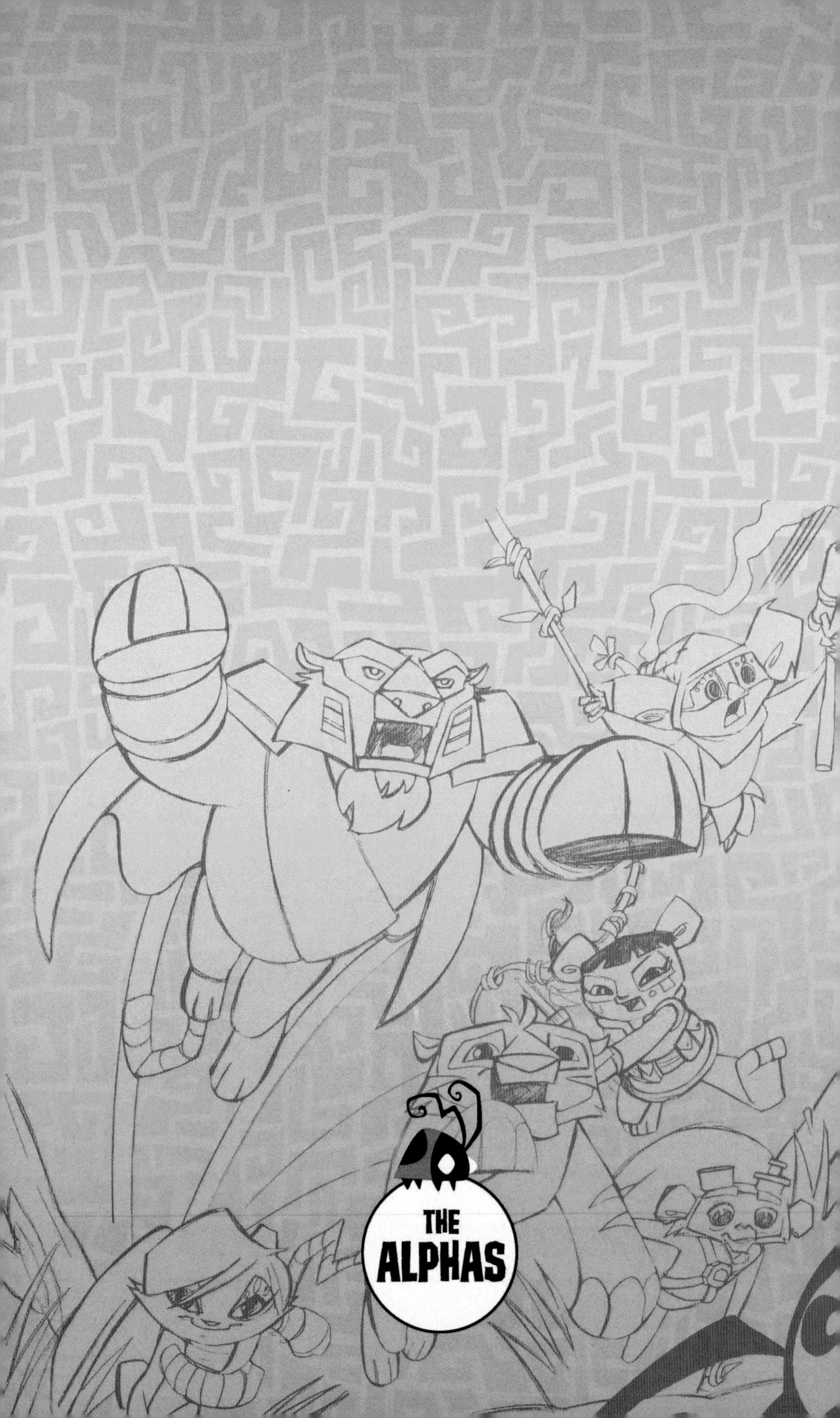
THE
ALPHAS

Sir Gilbert

TRAITS:

Skills- Strength, strategy, leadership

Personality- Regal, friendly, commanding, genuine

Likes- Justice, storytelling

Dislikes- Evil

Weakness- Stubborn

Goal- Stop the Phantoms once and for all

Inner Voice- "Everyone is counting on me. I cannot fail."

Liza

TRAITS:

Skills-	Intuition, diplomacy, adventurous spirit
Personality-	Reserved, focused, warm
Likes-	Exploring, reading, photography
Dislikes-	Inequality
Weakness-	Overly-compassionate
Goal-	Unite the animals of Jamaa
Inner Voice-	"I hope I can be there for everyone."

Greely

TRAITS:

Skills- Stealth, observation, knowledge

Personality- Mysterious, quiet, terse

Likes- Solitude

Dislikes- Parties

Weakness- Doesn't trust others

Goal- Learn everything possible about the dark Phantoms

Inner Voice- "The only one who will never let me down is me."

Peck!

TRAITS:

Skills-	Creativity, art, music
Personality-	Talented, energetic, happy
Likes-	All kinds of art
Dislikes-	Sitting still
Weakness-	Impulsive
Goal-	Make Jamaa as cheerful and peaceful as possible
Inner Voice-	"The world of Jamaa is such a beautiful and fascinating place!"

COSMO

TRAITS:

Skills- Knowledge, resourcefulness, ability to speak with plants

Personality- Clever, youthful, introverted

Likes- Plants, jokes

Dislikes- Confrontation

Weakness- Timid

Goal- Help keep Jamaa clean and beautiful

Inner Voice- "One day, I hope everyone will be able to get along."

GRAHAM

TRAITS:

Skills- Ingenuity, creativity, innovation

Personality- Intelligent, focused, jovial

Likes- Inventing, tinkering, puzzles

Dislikes- When things don't work

Weakness- A bit scatterbrained

Goal- Learn the "what", "how", and "why" of everything

Inner Voice- "The world is filled with fascination."